WALKING RAIN

A HOWARD MOON DEER MYSTERY

Books by Robert Westbrook

Howard Moon Deer Mysteries
Ghost Dancer
Warrior Circle
Red Moon
Ancient Enemy
Turquoise Lady
Blue Moon
Hungry Ghost
Walking Rain

Coming Soon!
Eagle Falls
A Howard Moon Deer Mystery

The Torch Singer *series*
An Overnight Sensation
An Almost Perfect Ending

Left-Handed Policeman *series*
The Left-Handed Policeman
Nostalgia Kills
Lady Left

Other Books
Intimate Lies:
F. Scott Fitzgerald and Sheilah Graham – Her Son's Story
Journey Behind the Iron Curtain
The Magic Garden of Stanley Sweetheart
Rich Kids

WALKING RAIN

A HOWARD MOON DEER MYSTERY

Robert Westbrook

SPEAKING VOLUMES, LLC
NAPLES, FLORIDA
2022

Walking Rain

Cover design by Hannah Linder

ISBN 978-1-64540-686-0

Once again, and always, for Gail

This is a work of imagination. There is no town in northern New Mexico called San Geronimo, nor a La Chaya reservation. I have changed the geography to suit my narrative needs, while at the same time doing my best to capture the true enchantment of the Southwest. Any similarity to actual events is coincidental.

Chapter One

Her name was Bao Zhao.

She didn't speak a word of English.

She came from a picture-book land of lush karst mountains that rose into the mist terraced with rice paddies that curved gracefully around the contours of the hills.

But for all its beauty, the people who lived there were very poor. When she was 15 years-old, there was a famine in the village and in order for the rest of the family to survive, her father sold her to a Russian trader, who was willing to pay $100 US dollars for a plain peasant girl who looked like she could be worked hard.

The Russian raped her before he sold her to a Thai ship captain, who raped her again.

She traveled to the New World by sea in a closed container, in a dark, crowded space with thirty-seven other migrants who were often seasick. The ship sailed seemingly forever across rough waters. Bao Zhao had never imagined a distance so far. At last, the ship docked in the port of Oakland, in the state of California, where huge steel arms lowered the container onto the back of a truck.

The ground was a relief after the turbulent ocean. But it was almost pitch black inside the steel container, with only a hole in front that let in a single beam of light.

The truck revved its mighty engine, like a monster coming to life. It changed gears, rumbled, and drove off into the heart of an unknown continent.

Twice a day, the back door of the container was lifted open into the blinding light and boxes of food and bottles of water were tossed inside before the door closed again. Both the food and water were inadequate for so many people, and there were no provisions for sanitation.

Two of those inside died on the journey, and their bodies were left among the living. The thirty-five who survived sat in silence, numb with resignation and sorrow.

After days of travel, the truck stopped and the captives were let out into a desert of red cliffs and huge vistas that went on as far as the eye could see. The wind had a bite to it and whistled a song of loneliness. Far to the north, there was a chain of mountains, their tops white with snow against the pale blue sky. Bao Zhao had never seen a land like this. It was more than foreign, it was a different planet, beyond her comprehension.

She was put into the back of a smaller truck and with seven others she was taken to a camp a few hours away. In the camp, she was forced to do hard labor in the fields, and at night she was shared by the guards, who passed her from bed to bed.

The weeks turned into months. The burning heat of the desert became freezing white cold. Then it was summer again. For Bao Zhao, it was endless. In her misery, she lost tract of time.

In the end, it wasn't either the work or the rape, not the heat nor the cold, not even the monotony. It was loneliness that drove her mad.

Her life was unendurable.

She ran away.

***

Bao Zhao ran away from the camp on a morning in mid-July, which was the hottest time of the year. She ran off into the desert with no idea where she was going. She didn't have a plan, she simply couldn't take another moment more.

The guards at the camp were lazy. They believed escape was impossible, so they weren't paying attention. Often the guards spent hours in the big white tent that they used as their command center, playing cards and watching television.

They would have missed Bao Zhao entirely except for an accident of nature. One of the guards had been drinking beer and he needed to pee. This meant walking across a barren patch of ground to the latrine. It was while walking that he spotted the figure running along the arroyo to where the valley became wider.

"Stop!" he cried.

He flung the rifle from his shoulder and took aim. The shot was loud enough to scare the birds from their nooks in the cliffs. The sound echoed up and down the valley.

But the figure ran off around a boulder and disappeared. By this time, half a dozen guards had appeared from the tent with their guns, but the Chinese woman had gotten away. When they got to where she had been last seen, she was nowhere in sight.

Bao Zhao felt a sting in her left thigh as she ran, but she didn't realize that she had been shot. She was strong and young, accustomed from an early age to hard labor, and she ran for several hours until the sun was high in the sky, burning hot.

The desert was a rocky, tortured land. There were hills, cactus, dry creek beds, brush that tore at her clothes. Once she saw a large snake with diamonds on its back. It slithered away quickly.

Gradually, she slowed to a jog and then a walk. The wound had continued to bleed and she was increasingly faint. It wasn't an unpleasant feeling. She hadn't brought water and her mouth was dry as the earth. In the distance she saw the snow capped mountains she had seen from the camp. They seemed closer now, green and cool. She turned her footsteps their way.

Bao Zhao was happy to be free. She hoped the men didn't find her and take her back. But as the hours passed, her steps faltered. She tripped into a rocky gully and fell onto a cactus, which pierced her arm with prickly stickers. She wasn't certain she had the energy to pick herself up and go on. The sun made a halo of blinding light around her.

After a rest, she found the will to rise to her feet. The desert around her seemed more and more unreal. Gusts of wind created dust devils that swirled her way and disappeared. There was nothing left to do in this dead land but die, yet she still staggered on, lurching from side to side.

She was dreaming on her feet, remembering the green wet rice terraces of Yunan, when a dust devil larger than the others rose up in the desert. It looked to Bao Zhao like a mighty dragon. He was blue. A blue dragon!

"Please, dragon!" she said through her cracked lips. "Save me!"

The dragon came toward her in a plume of dust. Bao Zhao staggered forth to meet the magical beast.

Her feet found something new. A road. A wide, hard-packed dirt road. The dragon sped her way with two glowing white eyes.

Bao Zhao fell to her knees and collapsed onto the ground.

The sun began spinning in the blue heavens above, making her so dizzy she toppled onto her side just as the beast came to a stop.

She looked up to see a man crouching above her studying her with concern. His face might have been Chinese. There was something almost familiar about it, like a cousin from a distant land. His eyes were kind.

"X'ie-x'ie!" she told him. *Thank-you!* This was the only Mandarin she knew. Her family had spoken a mountain dialect. She didn't know precisely why she was thanking the man, except he seemed a very magnanimous presence.

All she wanted now was rest.

She closed her eyes as a great wind lifted her and carried her away.

Chapter Two

Howard Moon Deer didn't see the woman until the last second.

The sun was in his eyes, low in the afternoon sky, and she appeared out of nowhere: a tiny figure in a shabby blue sweatsuit.

He had no idea where she had come from. She seemed almost to be floating on the wind from the desert onto the road. She was hardly more than a hallucination.

He jammed his foot on the brake and swerved hard to the left. He'd been going nearly sixty, which was too fast on a dirt road. He skidded sideways, fishtailed, and spun in a circle before he came to a stop.

"What the hell!" he cried.

It had been a woman. But had he hit her?

Howie fumbled with his seat belt and jumped out of his dusty Subaru. The woman was on the road lying on her side a dozen feet from his right wheel. She wasn't moving.

Howie knelt by her side and examined her. She was alive, at least. She looked up at him with an oddly hopeful expression in her eyes. But she didn't look well.

"Are you all right?" he asked, knowing she wasn't.

She was a small woman dressed in sweatpants, a stained yellow T-shirt, and canvas shoes without socks. Chinese was his first impression. Perhaps Cambodian. She was young but ageless. She had Asian eyes and a broad peasant face.

Howie didn't know if this was his fault. There were no obvious signs that he had hit her. But she didn't look well. Her lips were blistered, her eyes were red, she was burned by the sun.

"I have water!" he said, seeing that she was dehydrated. She didn't look as though she understood English. "Hold on!"

"X'ie-x'ie!" she said. She said it so softly, he wasn't sure afterwards if he had really heard it. As it happened, *thank-you* was the only Mandarin he remembered from a three-week trip to China fifteen years ago.

He jogged back to his car to get the water bottle he kept propped up in the holder between the two front seats.

He returned with the water, knelt by her side, and was about to bring the bottle to her lips when he saw that she was dead.

He sat back on his haunches and sighed. She was such a frail creature, she looked more like a dead bird than a human.

It was then, while he was looking at her, that he noticed that the left leg of her sweatpants was soaked with blood. The cheap synthetic material of the pant leg had been torn away to show her thigh underneath. Her skin had a round wound that looked like a bullet hole.

"You've been shot!" he said incredulously.

Which changed everything for the worse.

***

Howie sat on a rock by the side of the road and studied the dead woman with dismay and disbelief.

He had seen death before, but this had happened out of nowhere, on a very ordinary day, and the sudden absence of life was shocking. One moment there was a person, the next only a discarded skin.

She was hardly larger than a child. She couldn't have weighed more than eighty pounds. It was obvious that she'd had a hard life. Her hands were rough, there were bruises on her arms. She couldn't have been much older than twenty, yet everything about her was wizened and ageless. Her blue sweatpants were stretched and baggy, and there were several holes in the material. It looked like a wind could pick her up and blow her away.

6

Howie walked back to his car where he had his phone plugged into a charger and called 911. He didn't expect service out here in the desert, but miraculously the call went through. New Mexico wasn't a cell phone friendly state.

He explained the situation to the dispatch operator in the simplest terms: that a woman had staggered out from the desert onto a country road and had died. He had no idea who she was, or anything about her except for the fact that she appeared to be Asian. He couldn't even tell the operator exactly where he was.

The operator kept him on the phone for several minutes trying to pin down his location. At last she told him that she would be sending help as quickly as possible.

"Great!" he said as he shut down his phone. He couldn't help but feel a little sorry for himself. This was definitely the pits, to be stuck in what had to be the ugliest corner of New Mexico with a dead body. Among other things, his cat, Orange, was going to be seriously pissed when he wasn't there at his usual time to feed her.

But, of course, this was a selfish way of looking at the situation. Howie was alive. He wasn't lying dead on this shortcut from hell.

He nodded sorrowfully at the dead woman.

"Sorry," he told her.

***

He shouldn't have taken the shortcut. He should have stayed on the highway. He should have known that shortcuts generally turn out to be longcuts in the end.

But he'd been driving nearly nonstop for two days, and this particular shortcut had looked like it would save him more than forty miles of driving through an arid stretch of the Four Corners that he needed to cross in order to get home.

Howie was returning from Salt Lake City, a rushed trip in order to pick up a tepee at the house of his cousin Jake. The tepee was lashed to the crossbars atop his Outback. He had come in the opposite direction only yesterday, leaving San Geronimo at four in the morning.

The tepee had been in his family for over a hundred years. It was beautifully crafted and only slightly mildewed with time. It had belonged to Howie's great-grandfather, a Lakota of the old days, and through a number of generational twists it belonged now to Howie and several of his cousins, all of whom lived in suburbia or cities. None of them wanted a tepee in their backyard except, at this moment, Howie.

The tepee was for Howie's Scottish daughter, Georgina, who was coming to visit in two weeks' time. She had never been to America and Howie intended to give her an inkling of her native heritage.

He had been preparing for this visit for over a year, and now that it was two weeks away, he was nearly frantic with last minute worries. Starting last fall, he had built a small forest cabin with a bathroom, a flushing toilet and a shower. These were things, it seemed to Howie, that a teenage daughter from one of the world's major cities would require.

Howie had first met his daughter in Glasgow when she was fifteen, and he had been arranging this visit ever since. Now she was just turning seventeen and Howie was terrified. He could hardly sleep at night. He was determined to be the best father in the history of fatherhood. He was determined that every second of her visit would be terrific.

The story of Georgina's birth was long and complicated and sad. Her mother had been Howie's first serious girlfriend when he was nineteen. There had been several months of lust, mostly in the dunes of Cape Cod, from which Georgie had sprung, to be given up to adoption at an expensively discrete hospital for unwed girls in the Highlands. Eventually,

Howie knew he would need to tell Georgie the full story, but he hoped to put this off as long as possible.

July had been a stressful month. Along with getting ready for Georgie, he had been working full time at the detective agency he ran with Jack Wilder, his boss. Unfortunately, Jack had been ill for a month and was taking less and less a part of the business, which put the burden on Howie.

He was making money, at least. He had turned Wilder & Associate into a profitable business, mostly with a series of well-paying insurance cases that were shuttled his way by law firms. At the moment, he had three such cases going simultaneously. This was far more work than he wanted, but he needed the money to pay for his building spree. The cute like cabin in the forest alone cost more than $100,000.

Responsibilities weighed on him. Howie was coming up to the age of forty, and he wasn't sure he was liking life as a stressed-out adult. He was tired.

Which was why he had decided to take his chances on the short cut. On his large Rand McNally map, which Howie preferred to the digital map on his phone, the slightly dodgy looking squiggle through the desert looked like it would save him at least an hour of driving time. It appeared to be paved, it was going the right direction, and forty fewer miles would be welcome.

But the paved highway quickly turned to dirt and took him meandering through the high desert, up and down a vast, primal land of arroyos and mesas and dry creek beds. At four in the afternoon, when the sun had been at its hottest, he passed a sign that said:

ENTERING LA CHAYA RESERVATION
PLEASE OBEY TRIBAL LAWS

Howie wasn't entirely surprised to find himself on Indian land. Large sections of the Four Corners were reservations of one tribe or another, primarily Navajo and Apache. The La Chaya tribe was said to be an offshoot of the Mountain Utes, who were generally found farther north in Colorado, Howie believed. But he knew very little about them.

The sign was punctured with bullet holes, which wasn't promising. He realized later that this is where he should have turned around. But at this point, it would have cost Howie several hours of lost time to return to the highway, and being a busy man, he had decided to continue onward.

Now, sitting in his Outback with the engine off and the windows open, listening to the wind, he wished he could rewind time. The shortcut had led to the dead Chinese woman, and he was stuck waiting for officialdom to arrive. However this worked out, he saw a delay of several hours.

Through his windshield, he could see a range of high mountains in the distance a dozen miles away with dark clouds hiding their tops.

More dark clouds were floating in from the north, casting moving shadows on the land. The clouds had black streaks of rain falling from them, thousands of spindly spider legs that shifted in the wind, making the legs bend and sway so that it seemed as though they were walking. The air was too dry for the rain to reach the ground. People in the mountain West called this phenomenon walking rain, which was a common sight in the summer.

With the ominous sky, and the dead woman on the road, and the falling legs of rain, Howie had an odd sense of danger galloping his way. He was starting to wonder if maybe he should start his engine and get the hell away from here, when he saw a plume of dust coming his way from the south. Law enforcement, he imagined.

10

It was too late now to leave. He stepped out of his Subaru and was surprised to see another dust plume coming his way from the north, the direction from which he had just come. More law enforcement, he presumed.

Both sets of vehicles were converging on him. Howie had a tingly feeling of alarm.

***

It took almost five minutes for the plume of dust in the south to coalesce into two black SUVs that were hurrying his way. The front vehicle came to a stop a dozen feet from where the body of the woman lay on the road. Both vehicles had the words La Chaya Tribal Police on the side.

Two Indians in tan uniforms with guns on their belts came out of each vehicle, slamming their car doors behind them. They didn't look happy to see him.

The oldest cop, a large man in his forties, knelt by the body of the woman and checked the pulse on her neck, while the three younger cops stood back and watched.

"What'cha doing out here, boy?" the older cop asked, rising to his feet. He towered nearly a foot above Howie and he looked mean. "You're trespassing on tribal land. Didn't you see the sign?"

"I saw a sign that said I was entering reservation land, but there was nothing about trespassing."

"The gate was open?"

"What gate?" Howie asked. "Look, on the map, this looked like a good shortcut to San Geronimo. I was trying to save time, that's all."

The cop gave Howie a hard look. His face was as brutal as the surrounding land. He had an ugly scar on his left cheek that looked like a knife wound. His hair was strange, cut into a severe crewcut, flat on top, which made his face seem like a square.

"I'm Lakota," Howie said hoping to stir feelings of indigenous solidarity.

It didn't work. The cop snorted. "Did you kill this woman?"

"Of course not! I was just driving along and she stepped onto the road and collapsed. She looked like she'd been wandering in the desert a long time. I think she might be Chinese."

"Yeah? And what gave you that idea?"

Howie shrugged. "Well, take a look at her—tell me what you think."

"What I think is that you killed this woman, boy. And you came out here to dump the body. Is that what you did?"

"Of course not! Why would I want to kill her?"

"Search him," the hard-nose cop said to the three younger cops who were lounging near their vehicles. "Let's see who we're dealing with here."

Howie started to object, but two of the cops held him while the third went through his pockets and pulled out his wallet.

"His name's Howard Moon Deer," said the third cop, looking at his driver's license. He continued rifling through his credit cards and the odds and ends in Howie's wallet.

"For fuck's sake, he's a private eye, Chief!" he said when he found Howie's investigator's license.

"Is he?" said the Chief. "Now, that's interesting. What brings a private eye out this way, boy?"

"I'm not on a case. I went to Salt Lake City to pick up a tepee at my cousin's house and I'm on my way home, that's all."

"A tepee, huh?" the Chief said sarcastically. "You carry your home around with you?"

"It's lashed down on the roof of my car. Take a look if you want." Howie was starting to feel annoyed at the way he was being treated. "My daughter is coming for a visit and I'm putting the tepee up on my land for her. This has nothing to do with work."

Howie looked up into the Chief's eyes, which was a mistake. They were cold. He looked like a killer robot. His eyes bore down like drills. Howie felt a physical quiver of fear in his innards, which were quickly turning to jelly.

"I think you're telling some tall tales, boy," the cop said with calm menace. "I think you're telling me a donkey load of lies!"

"I'm telling the truth!" Though he was afraid, Howie believed in truth more than he believed in most things, and he wasn't going to be bullied about something so fundamental. "And incidentally, I'm not a boy. I'm 38 years-old and feeling very grown up actually!"

It felt good for a second, to stand up to the bully cop. But the victory was brief. Without warning, the tribal police chief gave Howie a hard punch in the stomach. Howie doubled over in pain, the breath knocked out of him.

"That's what I do with people like you," he said. "I think you killed this woman, didn't you? 'Fess up now, Moon Deer—it'll go easier on you. You killed her and then you thought you'd find some wide-open spaces to dump the body."

Howie was barely able to stand, much less speak. The pain in his stomach radiated up and down his body.

"Chrissake!" he managed. "If I killed her, why the hell would I call 911?"

"You called 911?"

"Of course. Didn't you . . ."

Howie stopped. He had assumed the tribal police had come in answer to his 911 call. But now he realized the two events were unconnected.

Which meant . . .

"Hey, Chief, we got company," said the cop who had been looking at the tepee.

Howie looked up and saw the plume of dust that he had seen earlier coming from the north was now almost upon them.

"Fuck!" said the Chief in a meditative tone.

"Should I let him go?" asked one of the cops who had been holding Howie by the arms.

"Not yet." The Chief wound back his right arm and struck with lightning speed, giving Howie another hard punch in the stomach.

"That's to remind you not to come trespassing this way again," he said. "Next time I see you, boy, you'll regret it."

Howie already regretted it. He lay on the ground in misery as a white van without any markings on it arrived at the scene. From ground level, straining his neck, he saw a government license plate on the front bumper.

"Well, well, Inspector!" he heard the Chief say.

"What do we have here?" asked a voice that was new.

"I was just about to get you on the radio."

"Were you?"

Howie was getting up onto his hands and knees when, from his vantage point, he saw a pair of cowboy boots walking his way. They were fancy boots, good leather with a patchwork of stampings and different colors.

Nausea roiled upward from Howie's stomach. He put his head down and threw up.

The fancy boots wisely backed away.

Chapter Three

"That guy in the cowboy boots saved my ass from the tribal cops, but I never found out much about him," Howie said to Jack late the following morning. "The cop who slugged me called him Inspector. That's all I know."

Jack smiled dreamily from his hospital bed. He'd had a triple bypass three days ago and he still seemed in a mist.

"It was odd," Howie said pointedly, trying to get his interest. "The Inspector, whoever he was—whatever he was an inspector *of*—he appeared totally in charge of the situation. He had two guys to back him up, but he was definitely the cock of the walk."

"FBI," said Jack. "FBI has jurisdiction on Indian land. At least when a felony has occurred."

"Right, Jack. I know that. Well, it was tense there for a few minutes, the guys from the van and the tribal cops giving each other the hairy eyeball. I thought it was going to be Gunfight at OK Corral. But then the chief dude from the tribal cops, the big guy who punched me, got a phone call. He stepped away so I couldn't hear what he was saying, but when he joined us again, he made nice to the guy in the cowboy boots. He said he had no idea who the dead woman was, and he was glad to let the Feds take over, no problem. Then he and his crew got in their cop cars and skedaddled."

"He called them Feds?"

"Yep. As I said, three guys plus Cowboy Boots. They were very neutral types, all four of them. Mid-thirties, neat hair, all of them dressed in slacks and light nylon shells."

"Definitely FBI," said Jack. "Though maybe Justice . . . or Interior. They have a law enforcement arm, too, you know. How long did they hold you?"

"About an hour. Cowboy Boots took me into the back seat of the van and he asked me to describe everything that happened. I had to repeat it several times. I told him why I was making the trip, about the tepee I'm putting up for Georgie . . ."

"Howie, doubtlessly he was fascinated. What did you say about the dead woman?"

"I told him everything, Jack! What do I have to hide? I told him how I decided on that shortcut, how I was driving along with the sun in my eyes when, wham-bang—I see this woman in my peripheral vision and I jammed on my brakes to avoid her."

"You're sure you didn't hit her?"

"I'm 90 percent sure, Jack. But they didn't allow me near the body again, and they didn't tell me a thing."

Jack shook his head. "Well, something's going on there. But fortunately, it's not our business. All's well, that ends well. They let you go!"

"Of course, it didn't end well for the Chinese woman," Howie mentioned.

"Oh, well!" said Jack vaguely. "Life, death, eternity . . . the whole banana!"

"That's the philosophical view, is it?"

"That's the only view an old man can have who's just gone through a triple bypass," Jack replied. "You're still in your frivolous youth, Howie. When you get to my age, you'll look at things with a wider perspective."

Jack was sitting up in bed in a private room at San Geronimo Mercy Hospital, looking very regal in his wrap-around dark glasses. He wore his white hospital robe like a toga. He was hooked up to a monitor that beeped occasionally and showed a graph of his heartbeat. There was a bottle on a hook by his bed dripping glucose into his arm.

Jack had undergone the heart surgery to repair a blocked valve. It had been a serious procedure but he was recovering well. Now that it was over, he was full of cheer, almost a new man. Howie had never seen him so grouch free.

"So, you're feeling okay, Jack?" Howie asked cautiously.

"Howie, I feel like I've gone through the wringer. But what the hell."

"That's it? *What the hell*?"

"Exactly." Jack smiled serenely.

"So, do you want to hear how things are going at the office?" Howie prodded, wondering if he could bring Jack down to Earth.

Jack smiled good-naturedly, like a parent humoring a child. But he wasn't really listening. "You know, Howie, the world is so beautiful!" he said unexpectedly. "And so very sad!"

***

Howie had been left in charge at the agency for the past month, ever since Jack had become ill. He had an assistant to help him, Buzzy Hurston, and also Ruth, the agency secretary. Still, it was a lot of work to run a busy private investigations business while simultaneously getting ready for his daughter to arrive. Howie didn't mind, but he often found himself grouchy, impatient, and tired. It was a middle-aged state of mind that the younger Howie had vowed would never happen to him.

After the shortcut from hell, he had arrived home late Friday night. Late enough so that Orange gave him grief. In fact, she had plenty of kibble left in her bowl and it wouldn't be bad for her to lose weight. However, for Howie to be meowed at, in such a tone, was one more aggravation.

He hadn't gotten much sleep Friday night. On Saturday morning, his phone woke him at 6:30 because his closest neighbors, Ocean and Sage, were coming over at 8 and he needed to spend at least an hour before they arrived responding to email.

Howie had hired Ocean and Sage to set up the tepee that was currently dumped off at the end of his driveway by the trail to his eco-complex, as he was beginning to call it. With the cabin he had just finished, and now the tepee that he planned to set up overlooking his stream, he was starting to feel like a man of property.

It was embarrassing for Howie that two young white hippies knew how to set up a tepee, when he didn't. Fortunately, he had more money than time at the moment and this was a way to give Ocean and Sage some much needed cash.

Ocean and Sage were a sweet young couple from Tennessee, very idealistic. Ocean was 22 or so, tall and gangly with a beard and long brownish hair that was tied to the back of his head in a kind of Japanese bun. Sage was short, blonde, and plump. A plump blonde fairy, as Howie thought of her. She had just turned twenty.

Howie liked them. The couple had come to New Mexico from Tennessee full of good sentiments, intending to live in harmony with the land. It was a noble goal, but in their innocence, they hadn't considered the hard winters and harsh realities of the Southwest. New Mexico was beautiful, but it could be a tough place to survive. The farming failed after the first two years and they would have starved except for the sale—Howie suspected—of several illegal pot plants.

Ocean and Sage didn't believe in "the money economy," as they liked to say, but Howie had convinced them to take $30 an hour for their help. Starting last fall, they had helped build the cabin, the new bathroom, and the plywood platform on the bank of a fast-moving mountain stream where the tepee would stand.

Howie hoped that his Scottish daughter would like sleeping in a tepee by a mountain stream, contemplating the Lakota side of her ancestry. But if not, she would have the cabin. As a father, he was ready for anything, he thought.

Saturday morning, Howie spent an hour with Ocean and Sage discussing the tepee and where it should face. Ocean was a devotee of Feng Shui and he wanted to place the door facing a propitious direction, but in this case Howie was firm. Feng Shui or not, he wanted the door to face out onto the stream.

*****

When these matters were settled, he drove into town for his visit with Jack at the hospital, and afterwards he made his way downtown through heavy traffic to the office in order to check in with Buzzy and Ruth. As was often the case, he was running late.

The Wilder & Associate detective agency occupied a one-story adobe building in the historic district of San Geronimo. The building was over two hundred years old and it was an attractive heirloom of Old New Mexico before statehood. Visitors were impressed with the authentic mud and straw walls, the kiva fireplace, and the heavy natural wood, the vigas and a herringbone pattern of latillas overhead.

Jack, with Emma's help, had furnished the office with beautiful old wood cabinets, chairs, and a desk large enough to serve a banquet from. Unfortunately, the building was falling down around them in slow motion, one problem after another, a money trap that took endless time and effort to keep in good repair.

Howie parked in the alley behind the building and came into the office through the rear screen door. Buzzy was seated at Jack's desk, in

Jack's rocking chair, bent over his cell phone. His nose was barely an inch from the screen.

"Up, Buzzy! Go sit at your own desk, please," Howie said in his severest adult voice. "I've got a zillion things to do and I don't have time for slouchy teenagers on cell phones!"

Howie knew he was being unfair. Buzzy was simply the target of Howie's general stress and anxiety. Buzzy looked up from his screen and shook his head.

"Slouchy teenager, huh? You'd better get used to it with your daughter coming."

"My daughter," said Howie, "doesn't slouch. She's going to Cambridge next year. She a serious girl."

"Seriously? A serious girl? And she's seventeen?"

"Yes, Buzzy. Now, up and at 'em!"

Buzzy stood and moved to the client chair while Howie sank into Jack's big wooden rocker. He had been using Jack's office for the past month while Jack was away, giving Buzzy his own small cubicle at the front of the building facing Calle Dos Flores.

Buzzy Hurston was nineteen but he still looked like an underweight, gangly kid. He was brilliant, but difficult. Howie had volunteered to be Buzzy's Big Brother back when he was in the Fifth Grade and had been recently suspended from school for selling pot to his classmates.

He hadn't been an easy kid to mentor, and during the first year Howie had nearly given up. But when Buzzy was in the 6th grade, Howie gave him a used Mac laptop, and it changed everything. Buzzy took to computers like a duck to water, and within a year he had reprogrammed the entire agency, making big improvements—some of which were legal, others not. Simply put, Buzzy was a genius when it came to the cyber world. Navigating the real world, however, was another matter.

Because of his unusual computer skills, Howie was able to get Buzzy a full scholarship to Stanford. This would have made for a happy ending, except Buzzy screwed up. After one year in California, he got himself kicked out of Stanford for hacking into BART, Bay Area Rapid Transit. He managed to shut down the entire system for four hours, stopping all the trains that passed through the Transbay Tube from Oakland to San Francisco. Buzzy did this as a class exercise, a demonstration of how easy it was to hack American infrastructure. But BART wasn't amused, and neither was Stanford.

At loose ends, Buzzy had returned to New Mexico where Jack hired him to help out at the agency, primarily as a driver. It was a temporary arrangement, but Howie was glad for Buzzy's help when Jack became ill.

"So, how's Jack?" Buzzy asked, lounging in the client chair. Somehow, no matter what chair he was in, he managed to wiggle himself into bizarre positions.

"He's oddly cheerful," Howie answered. "I'm worried about him, frankly."

"You think cheerfulness is bad?"

"With Jack, cheerfulness is worrisome. Now, I've got something for you today. I want you to go up to the Peak and talk to the lift supervisor. His name is Johnny Santistevan. In the summer, he runs the tourist chairlift that takes people up the front side of the mountain. It turns out he actually saw the accident last winter—the drunk dude who fell out of the chair. I need you to find Johnny and get a statement from him. Okay? Don't get distracted, please. I want this case wrapped up today. You can take my Subaru if you like, but I'll skin you alive if you don't get it back to me by four o'clock. Are we on the same page?"

"We are, man. The same page," Buzzy said. "I promise."

The Case of the Drunk Who Fell From the Chairlift was their biggest insurance job at the moment. The incident happened last season at San Geronimo Peak. Halfway up the mountain, the drunk had fallen from the chair thirty feet into snow that was soft, fortunately. He was suing the ski area for a hundred million dollars, thinking he'd won the jackpot, getting himself hurt at an expensive ski resort. The Peak had hired a team of lawyers to defend themselves and had hired Wilder & Associate to investigate the circumstances of the accident.

Happily, Howie had the goods on the drunk. He had traced the man's movements backward to lunch earlier that afternoon at one of the village bars, where the future victim of the chairlift mishap had downed four margaritas and played a game of throwing popcorn into the air and catching the kernels in his mouth. To sew up the case, all he needed now were a few signed witness statements. Which Buzzy, hopefully, was about to get.

Howie had more instructions for Buzzy, but there was a knock on the office door and Ruth poked her head inside. She had knocked at least, though she hadn't waited for an answer.

"Yes?" said Howie, trying to hide his impatience. Ruth was a gray-haired terror, a retired New York City public high school teacher accustomed to keeping order with unruly teenagers. She usually treated Howie as though he were the worst student in the class.

"There's someone out there who wants to speak with you." Ruth had a Manhattan accent, with a strong hint of Brooklyn. "She says it's urgent. According to her card, her name is Lydia Cordell-Smith. She's with an organization that calls itself WWAT. Two W's. Don't ask me what it stands for. Will you see her?"

For Howie, the name Lydia Cordell-Smith summoned an image of a person he'd frankly rather not see. "Does she have an appointment?"

"Oh, come on, Moon Deer! When does anybody need an appointment around here?"

"It helps," Howie said defensively. "In any case, I'm busy—"

"Before you make up your mind, you need to hear this. She has two large thugs with her. They look strong and sort of blank-eyed. They're definitely muscle."

"And they're all in the reception area?"

"No, the woman came inside by herself. The thugs are outside guarding the front door."

Howie could only shake his head. "A woman with bodyguards! . . . well, what the hell, you'd better send her in."

Chapter Four

Lydia Cordell-Smith was a surprise. She came into the office with a small dog on a leash, a puggy little thing with black lips, pink tongue, and small black eyes.

The dog looked at Howie and began yapping fiercely.

"There, there, Flossie," said the woman. "Don't bark at the nice man . . . thank you for seeing me without an appointment, Dr. Moon Deer. I hope you don't mind Flossie. She's my emotional support dog."

Howie was taken aback. He wasn't sure what had taken him aback the most: the yappy dog, the woman, or the fact that she had addressed him as Dr. Moon Deer.

It was true. Quite incredibly, he was now officially Dr. Howard Moon Deer. Six months ago, after many years of malingering, he had finally been awarded his PhD in cultural anthropology from Princeton. He didn't advertise the fact, however, and nobody (except Claire, jokingly) had ever called him Dr. Moon Deer. A doctor, as far as Howie was concerned, was somebody who put a stethoscope to your chest and made you say ah.

As for emotional support dogs, he had mixed feelings. In most cases, it seemed to him a form of cheating, a way for people to bring their pets into restaurants and markets where dogs would not normally be allowed. But he didn't know about Lydia Cordell-Smith. She looked fragile. She looked like she could use any emotional support she could find.

"Please have a seat, Mrs. Cordell-Smith," he said gently, indicating the client chair. "And please, just call me Howie. I only got my doctorate recently and it wouldn't help my image if it got out. We're supposed to be tough guys."

She laughed, which made her look suddenly younger.

Lydia Cordell-Smith was very pretty in a chaste, severe sort of way. Nun-like, Howie would have said. She was only a decade or so older than he was, but the conservative clothes she wore made her appear older than that. She was dressed in a brown skirt that went down nearly to her ankles and a cream-colored blouse with a Peter Pan collar. Her light brown hair was pulled back in a tight bun. Her skin was as pale and smooth as porcelain. She would need to watch herself in the New Mexico sun.

Flossie growled.

"Hush, Flossie!" Lydia Cordell-Smith told her support dog. "I don't know what's got into her! Usually, she's so good with new people!"

"Probably she smells my cat," he replied. "So, what brings you to the office of a private detective?" he prodded.

"I'm the current secretary of WWAT," she said. "You know our work, I hope?"

Howie was mystified. "WWAT," he repeated. What is WWAT?"

"W-W-A-T. Washington Women Against Trafficking."

"I see," said Howie. In fact, he was starting to see too well. It was that shortcut again, come back to haunt him. *Why in God's name didn't I stay on the main road?*

"So, you're all Washington women," he pressed. "Is that the state?"

"No, the District of Columbia," she said with a self-deprecating laugh. "We're the invisible women who are married to important people in the government. Basically, we met at functions where all we were supposed to do was keep our mouths shut and smile. But a few of us were rebellious, and we started to talk to one another about the big issues in the world, and what we could do about them."

"From behind the scenes, is that what you're saying?" Howie asked.

"Well, it was that way at first. But now we've come out strongly as an organization in our own right. Washington Women Against Trafficking. We've raised millions of dollars for the cause."

"Which is human trafficking around the world?" he said cautiously. "Or only in America."

"Everywhere, of course! It's a global problem, as I'm sure you know. But it seemed best to start in our own backyard. And the Southwest, I'm afraid, is a very active theater for trafficking as well as illegal migration. The majority of victims are girls and young women who are coerced into sexual slavery, but boys and men are often victims as well. The narratives span from young women forced into unwanted marriages, to children captured in guerrilla raids forced to become child soldiers. It's a multi-billion-dollar industry with huge profits. Most of the victims come from impoverished, war-torn countries. Sometimes they're sold by their parents to unscrupulous dealers, often they're tricked by promises of jobs and marriages. Generally, the victims are brought from poor countries to wealthy nations, but this isn't always the case. In Southeast Asia, for instance, boys are often trafficked to work in the domestic fishing industries, which is particularly hard, dangerous work. If they object, they are simply thrown overboard."

"That's terrible!"

"Well, it is!" Lydia Cordell-Smith was getting worked up. A pink flush had come to her pale cheeks. "And the United States isn't immune! Each year, an estimated 14,500 to 17,500 foreign nationals are brought to America by traffickers. And the problem doesn't stop there. The Department of Justice estimates that 200,000 American children are at risk each year of being trafficked into the sex industry."

Howie shook his head. It was awful to hear of such things, though it wasn't entirely news. Meanwhile, Howie had a pretty good idea why Lydia Cordell-Smith had come to see him.

"It's the woman I came across yesterday, isn't it? The Chinese woman I found in the desert?"

"Yes!" she said passionately. For a second, she looked like she was going to leap on Howie. "I want to know all about what happened! I want to hear everything!"

Howie gave her the short version. He had told the story a few times by now and was able to reduce it to its salient points. He frankly disliked telling a story again and again.

"And she just stepped out in front of your car and died . . . in the middle of nowhere!" Lydia said at the end, nodding to herself in quiet astonishment.

"That's all I know about her," Howie admitted. "That and the one word she said in Chinese. *X'ie-x'ie.*"

"Thank you! But why should she say thank-you?"

"I was getting her water, though I'm not sure she knew that. She didn't seem to understand English. Of course, she was at the end of her rope, in an extreme state. She'd been wandering in the desert probably for hours. And she'd been shot in the thigh. If she'd had medical care, I'm guessing she would have survived. But she bled to death."

Lydia Cordell-Smith was silent as she allowed herself to imagine the scene. She closed her eyes for a moment. She shook her head.

"We want to hire you, Howie, to find out who that woman was. We want to know where she came from, how she died, and who is responsible. We want to enlist you in our crusade against modern slavery!"

Howie sighed. This was a noble cause, to be sure. A crusade, even. But he was much too busy right now to get involved in any cause however noble it might be.

"Lydia, I'm flattered to be asked. But, you see, my daughter is about to come for a visit and I'm terribly—"

"Busy, yes, I know that. I've been told that your agency is very successful and you turn down many requests for work. But this is more than a job, Howie. Slavery is a terrible problem and we must work together to stamp it out!"

Howie sighed yet again. He was sympathetic; he didn't like human trafficking either. But he didn't have time for this. Even his afternoon was full. He needed to get back to his land to see how the construction of the tepee was coming along.

Lydia was watching him closely.

"I think I mentioned," she said, "that WWAT has been able to raise quite a bit of money to aid our work. So, we are in a position to be able to offer you a rather substantial retainer. To be honest, we've been keeping our eye on you for some time, even before this poor woman you found in the desert. You seemed exactly what we were looking for. Somebody with a native knowledge of the Southwest—"

"Lydia, I grew up in South Dakota."

"Forty thousand dollars," she said. "If you agree to take this case, we will give you a forty-thousand-dollar retainer, which will be considered non-refundable, disregardless of how much time or little time you spend on the case."

This stopped Howie cold. $40,000 wasn't the largest retainer Wilder & Associate had ever received, but it was close. It would certainly go a long way into paying for the improvements he had made on his land.

"And of course, we'll pay your expenses, too," she added.

The offer was tempting but Howie shook his head. "I'm sorry but I can't, Lydia. My daughter is coming for a visit from Scotland, and I need to take the time off to be with her. It's my one chance in a lifetime to be a parent. And in any case, you don't want a small-town private detective for something of this size—what you need here is the government, the Department of Justice. Human trafficking is a problem with a global reach. I simply don't have either the experience or the resources to take on something of this magnitude."

Lydia sat quietly for a moment, considering what to say. "Well, you see, Howie, the Justice Department is already involved in this struggle, though they haven't been very successful. Human trafficking manages to carry on beneath the radar and there hasn't been much that Washington has been able to do. So, what we're looking for locally—here in New Mexico—is someone who can come and go without attracting attention. Someone who will fit in. You're the perfect candidate."

Howie wasn't sure he liked what she was saying. "Because I'm an Indian?"

"Exactly. I know that sounds rather blunt. But you found this woman on an Indian reservation and that's where you would need to go to document her story. People would be more willing to talk to you than they would to an outsider."

Howie kept shaking his head. "Lydia, I've always been an outsider, especially here in New Mexico where the local tribes aren't particularly friendly to the Lakota Sioux. By the way, how do you know about this Chinese woman? This only happened yesterday."

Lydia Cordell-Smith looked uncomfortable. She fidgeted in the client chair. The pink blush in her cheeks became more pronounced.

"Well, you see, as it happens, I have quite a few connections to law enforcement. My husband . . . well, he was the Deputy CIA director in the Obama administration. He's in the private sector now, of course, running the family bank, but he still has a number of good friends in government who have been very helpful to us Washington Women. We are determined to stamp out this terrible evil!"

"Of course," Howie said. "But you still haven't told me how you heard about the Chinese woman."

"So, I'll be honest with you," she said. "The Attorney General is my brother-in-law."

Howie gave her a dead-pan look. "The current Attorney General? In Washington?"

"That's right. And we have a standing request for all law enforcement encounters with trafficking to be reported to us immediately. In this case, I was actually in Santa Fe, so it was quite straight forward. There's a small team of U.S. Marshals working out of Santa Fe who were kind enough to inform me of your encounter yesterday on the La Chaya reservation."

Howie wasn't sure he liked U.S. Marshals talking about him.

"Look, Lydia—the woman I found in the desert, there's really no evidence that she *was* trafficked. Sure, she was Chinese—or at least, I think so—but you'd be surprised how many Chinese Americans live in this part of the world. Even small New Mexico towns have Chinese restaurants, with extended families that work them. And then there's the Los Alamos Lab, which employs quite a number of Asian scientists."

"Howie, all we want you to do is find out what you can about her. Who she was, where she came from, what she was doing out there in the desert. Please," she said. "Won't you consider my offer? You found this poor woman, after all. Aren't you curious about her?"

He was curious, as a matter of fact. Very curious. Though he didn't have time for curiosity. He wanted to tell her no, but the way she was looking at him—as though he was her last hope—made that hard.

"I tell you what, let me think about it overnight," he told her. "Of course, I'll need to talk it over with my boss, Jack Wilder."

That's what I'll do! I'll say no and blame it on Jack!

"And you'll phone me tomorrow with your decision?"

He promised that he would.

Chapter Five

Howie loved the long summer twilights on his land, the deepening light on the forest and meadows. He startled a deer as he walked up the trail to his house from the road. Butterflies floated among the wildflowers. There were other bugs, too, that weren't so pleasant—no-see-ums looking for blood. When Claire was here, they ate her up alive, but they tended to leave Howie alone. He wasn't as tasty.

It was after 7 o'clock before Howie had been able to leave the office. Ocean and Sage had finished setting up the tepee and had gone home. The tepee made an impressive sight rising up on the far bank of the mountain stream with colored ribbons flying from the top poles. Howie crossed the stream on the narrow foot bridge and took a moment to give the tepee a closer look. It sat on a plywood platform that was thirty-five feet square. This was a modern touch, but except for that, the tepee was entirely traditional, like something you might find in Montana a hundred and fifty years ago.

Would his daughter like it? Howie didn't know. Georgie was a city girl. She had spent her life in Glasgow, with only occasional trips into the Scottish hinterlands. He worried that the wilds of northern New Mexico might be overwhelming. She might hate living in the woods. She might hate him.

He knew he was worrying too much, but he had missed the first crucial years of his daughter's life, and this visit seemed his last chance to forge a bond between them, before she might be gone from his life forever.

And now he had an additional problem: Lydia Cordell-Smith, who was offering a $40,000 retainer to investigate human trafficking in New Mexico. Not only was the money good, it was the most interesting case that had come his way in a while. He wanted to take the case, of course he did. But he couldn't, not with Georgie arriving in less than two weeks. Once Georgie arrived, he needed to devote his time entirely to her. He couldn't be running around the country after human traffickers...

Howie returned across the foot bridge to the clearing on the far side where his home stood. Georgie might find his eco-pod even more odd than the tepee. It had come as a kit, designed by two young avant-garde German architects. Claire liked to say that it looked like a large metallic egg supported by four chicken legs.

There was a satellite dish on top, solar panels, and antennas, for the pod contained a number of sophisticated electronic devices. Howie had added a few improvements of his own, including a cat door that he'd had cut from the metal shell that had a small airlock attached. There was a second outer door so that Orange could come and go in the winter without letting in cold air. There were also additional solar panels on a meadow two hundred feet from the pod and a pump house that brought filtered water from the stream. Howie enjoyed his off-the-grid existence in the woods, but the simple life wasn't cheap. Which was why he needed to keep making money, money, money.

So, what was he going to do about Lydia Cordell-Smith? He needed to make a decision.

Howie went inside, he fed Orange her can of Alaskan salmon—she wasn't cheap either—then he sat down at his computer nook to find out what he could about his prospective client. Fortunately, Lydia had a fairly large digital footprint. Howie hated that term, digital footprint, which always made him think of a dinosaur leaving tracks in a marsh. Lydia appeared to be what she claimed, the secretary general of WWAT, Washington Women Against Trafficking, as well as the wife of an important political insider. In Howie's opinion, WWAT was a terrible acronym, but no one had asked his advice.

Lydia's husband was David Forsyth III, from a long line of Philadelphia bankers, Harvard educated, Yale Law School, on the board of numerous charitable organizations, 24 years older than his wife (according to their Wikipedia birth dates). To add to his luster, he had been the Deputy Attorney General in the Obama administration. Cordell-Smith was Lydia's maiden name, and she too came from old money and power—her father had been the president of Swarthmore College. Together they seemed to be quite the moneyed, aristocratic do-gooder couple.

Do-gooders!

Well, why not? Howie thought. Rich people doing charities turned him off somehow. But why not try to make the world a better place? Lydia and her husband appeared to have their hearts in the right place.

Howie mulled this over for some time. $40,000, his daughter's visit, the chance to give closure to the death of an unfortunate woman . . .

"You know what, Orange?" he said to his cat. "I'm going to give Lydia exactly one week of my time. I can do that and still be ready for Georgie when she flies into Denver!"

It would be a very limited investigation. He would offer to find out the identity of the woman who had died. He could do that in a week, he believed. If it turned out that she had been trafficked, he would let the appropriate government agencies take over. Human trafficking was a global problem, after all. It was a matter for governments to solve, not a small-town private investigator.

Meanwhile, he had to be fair—he would not accept Lydia Cordell-Smith's generous offer of $40,000. He would only accept his usual agency fee of $200 an hour plus expenses. Well, okay, he would add a surcharge, upping the fee to $250 an hour. After all, it was a rush job and he was short on time.

Howie felt better once he had made this decision.

But with only one week, there was no time to lose.

***

Howie began immediately with a phone call to the celebrated Navajo artist, VS Moreland—Victor, to his friends—to ask if he could stop by tonight. He needed to know more about the La Chaya tribe, and if anyone could fill him in, it was Victor.

"Of course, my dear!" said the artist, once he was located inside his mansion. He always called Howie "my dear." There was a great deal of noise on his end, cavernous sounds of music and laughter, a party going on.

"You have guests," Howie said. "But if you could fit me in for just a few minutes—"

"Of course, and you must come immediately! It's one of those sad evenings with the usual crowd and I'm feeling morose. Why have you been staying away?"

VS Moreland was an outrageous local figure, the most famous living artist in San Geronimo. He was often in the news, these days not so much for his art but for getting ejected from restaurants and bars for bad behavior. Howie liked Victor. It was difficult not to. But he almost always found ways to turn down invitations.

"I'll be there in twenty minutes," Howie promised, avoiding the question of why he had been staying away.

Victor had grown up on the Newcomb Chapter of the Navajo tribe in an impoverished part of the reservation 35 miles south of Shiprock, but he ran away to California when he was sixteen. As a young, handsome, gay Indian full of talent and charisma, bohemian San Francisco opened its doors to him. He studied at the San Francisco Art Institute and later lived in Italy for nearly ten years as his fame grew. Rome. *La Dolce*

34

Vita. Eventually, he settled in San Geronimo where he instantly became king of the local art scene.

Howie knew Victor because one of his paintings was stolen a few years ago—an expensive painting, worth over $100,000—and he had hired the Wilder & Associate Agency to get it back. Howie found the painting quickly enough—it had been taken by an unscrupulous Arizona collector—and Victor decided that Howie was his dear boy. They were both outsiders—a wealthy Navajo artist and an overeducated Lakota PI, and Victor decided they should stick together.

Victor's house was a modern adobe palace on multiple levels sur-rounded by a high wall on the north edge of town. The gate was open and Howie drove on through to the parking area where he found a dozen cars that ranged from fancy BMWs to ancient pickup trucks. Whatever else Victor might be, he wasn't a snob. You could expect to find the high and the low at his gatherings, the town's shakers as well as street artists who had never sold a thing.

The party was around the back of the house on the large verandah by the pool, which was lit up from beneath the water with colored lights. Twenty or so guests milled about the verandah under Japanese lanterns, everybody with drinks in their hands. The noise level was overwhelm-ing. Two huge speakers in front of the pool changing room blasted out hypnotic techno music that went on and on with neither beginning nor end.

Howie heard a scream as someone fell backward fully dressed into the pool. This was greeted by peals of laughter. The artists who came to Moreland's parties seemed determined to live up to some Gatsby-esque image they had of themselves.

"There you are!" cried a voice, coming up behind him. "How's my lamb chop?"

Howie managed to hide his embarrassment. "Victor," he said, turning around.

"You've been avoiding me, you bad boy! And now I only see you when you want something!"

"I've been seriously busy, Victor. You see, my daughter's coming—"

"You don't have a daughter! Come, come!"

"I do, actually. I didn't know about her until two years ago. She came, well—from a relationship I had when I was in college."

This was a simplification of a complex love affair and Howie hoped Victor would leave it alone. But he didn't.

"And you didn't know about her until two years? Ooh! This sounds like soap opera!"

"Well, it had a sad ending, I'm afraid. Look, Victor, do you think we could go someplace quiet to talk?"

VS Moreland had a square, Navajo face with long black hair that was held in place with a red headband. Howie suspected his black hair was dyed. The headband had an Egyptian-looking eyeball painted on the front. He was dressed in loose white yoga pants and a collarless white shirt that had gold embroidery. There was a large turquoise pendant on a silver chain dangling from his neck and more turquoise jewelry on his fingers.

He nodded solemnly. "Are you hot on the heels of a fiendish killer?" he asked dramatically.

Howie played his part. You had to be theatrical around Victor if you were going to get anywhere. "Exactly," Howie told him.

"And you want my expertise on Diné matters? You'd better follow me, my dear boy. Somewhere private where we can be alone."

***

"Actually, Victor, it's not the Navajo I've come to ask about," Howie said from a velvety red armchair in Victor's book-lined library. "It's your neighbors, the La Chaya. I had a sort of incident there last Sunday that I'm curious about."

"The La Chaya? You're serious? *Them*?"

"You sound scornful."

"You bet I am! First of all, I'm not even sure how those people became a federally registered Indian tribe, showing up in the Four Corners just a few years ago. They said—they proved, it seems—that they were the rightful tribal owners of an obscure piece of Ute land that nobody else really wanted. Which is probably how they got away with it."

"When did this happen?"

"Oh, Moon Deer, *don't* ask for dates! Time goes by so quickly I can't stand it!"

"Give me an approximation at least,"

"All right, all right, for you I'll try. Let's call it thirty years. Thirty years ago, these Indians showed up saying they were the La Chaya tribe and they claimed they had an historical right to a useless stretch of land none of us had ever even thought about. I went fishing there once when I was a kid, because there's a nice little stretch of river in one of their valleys, but there was nothing else there."

"So, you don't think the La Chaya tribe is for real?"

"*Real*? Moon Deer, reality is up for grabs, and I'd say they grabbed it. But what do I know? I've been gone from that part of the country for twenty . . . well, okay, forty years. But I do have an old friend who's still there, and I bet he could tell you a thing or two. He's Diné, a serious dude. Would you like an introduction?"

Howie said he would. Beneath the glitter and outrageous behavior, Victor Moreland was an intelligent man. He had invented a theatrical persona for himself, but he was no fool, and an introduction into the

Native American tribes of the Four Corners would be helpful. The Diné, as the Navajo called themselves, were a world of their own, one where outsiders like himself would have a hard time getting in.

"He lives in Shiprock. I'm sure you've heard of him. We were kids together. He's Sun Walker, the famous flute player. I know he can tell you a lot more about the La Chaya tribe than I can. Here, I'll write a note for you to give him. Be sure to give him my regards."

Howie waited while Victor sat at his desk and wrote a short note. When he was finished, he turned the paper over and drew a map to Walker's cabin, explaining that there were no street addresses in this part of the reservation, and he wasn't sure if there was any phone service out there either.

"Of course, I haven't seen him for several years, not since he came to San Geronimo to give a concert, so he may have moved since then. But I doubt it. Time stands still on the rez and nothing ever changes. Which is why I got the hell out of there. Now, how about a drink?" he offered.

"No, I have to get going, but thanks."

"Look, when your daughter arrives, we'll throw her a party," Victor said as he walked Howie from the library. "We'll do a real bash for her, don't you think? A coming out party!"

Howie laughed. "Thanks, Victor, that's very kind but not really necessary."

"It'll be my pleasure! What fun we'll have introducing your Scottish lass to all the interesting people in this town."

Howie thought about this as he drove home. It was nice of Victor to offer to throw a party for his daughter, though he wasn't sure what she would think of a flamboyantly gay Navajo artist or the "interesting" people in town.

Howie loved Native American flute music and Sun Walker was one of the masters. His playing was as pure and mysterious as the wind.

Walker was a legend among those who knew Indian music and Howie looked forward to meeting him.

He set his watch, his iPhone, and an old-fashioned alarm clock for 5:30 Sunday morning. Howie relied on three separate devices to make sure he didn't oversleep. He had the alarms set at five-minute intervals— his wrist watch for 5:30, the iPad five minutes later, and the alarm clock five minutes later still.

Howie wasn't a morning person, but it was going to be a busy day tomorrow and he needed to get an early start.

Chapter Six

There were days when getting up at 5:30 wasn't early enough. Days when no matter how fast you moved, you were always running late.

Howie's first stop on Sunday, after picking up a breakfast burrito at Maria's food cart, was Jack and Emma's. Jack had been released from the hospital on Saturday night, and Howie needed to check in on him and make sure he was on board for "the Chinese Case," as he was referring to it in the file he had begun.

The Wilder house was a pretty, two-story Territorial style house on the edge of town that had been built in 1905. Emma had inherited the house from a distant aunt when they were still living in California, and they moved here after Jack lost his eyesight in a hostage situation gone wrong. It had taken Emma years and a good deal of money to restore the home from its dilapidated state, but she had kept at it and done a wonderful job. Every time Howie walked in the door, he felt as though he was going through a time warp back to an older world.

"It's like a museum," Jack sometimes said, not in an entirely flattering manner.

Howie liked Emma Wilder. She was a hearty, no-nonsense, well-educated, gray-haired woman in her mid-70s who most often could be found in jeans and flannel shirts. She met Howie at the door, saying she had taken the day off from household chores to look after Jack on his first day home. Starting tomorrow there would be a day nurse to be with him while she was at her job at the library.

"And how is he?" Howie asked.

"I'm not sure," Emma admitted. "He doesn't seem himself."

"Well, he's gone through a lot, Emma. A triple bypass. I'd call that a transitional life event."

Emma laughed. "Yeah, but don't go feeling sorry for him, Howie. The doctor said he came through the operation with flying colors. Everything went smoothly, he's fine. Actually, he's out back on the patio right now in his big garden chair. He said he wanted to listen to the birds singing. He didn't want to be in bed."

Listen to the birds singing? Jack? This was more serious than Howie had imagined. Howie followed Emma through the house to the backyard, where Jack was stretched out in the shade of a cottonwood tree on a deck chair that was twice the usual size. He was propped up on pillows with a piece of Guatemalan material covering the bulge of his stomach. Beneath the material, he wore a purple bathrobe. His dark glasses were pointed upward at the bough of the tree where a bird was chirping. Howie wasn't sure if he was deep in thought or asleep. The pad beneath him, dark blue, was five inches thick, as good as a mattress.

"Hey, Jack," he said uncertainly. "So, they let you come home?"

"They did," Jack replied.

"And you're feeling okay?"

Jack turned his dark glasses in Howie's direction. He was the only person Howie knew who could make the lenses of dark glasses appear scornful.

"What do you think, Howie?"

"Well, I don't know, Jack. That's why I'm asking."

"I'm taking in the sounds and scents of summer, Howie. New Mexico in July under the shade of a big leafy tree. I'm inhaling the breeze, every molecule . . . and do you know why?"

"Jack—"

"— because every moment is precious, Howie! Every moment could be your last!"

"Jack, you're not going to die! You're going to be okay. That's what your doctor says."

41

Howie sat down on the edge of Jack's huge deck chair so that he could press this point home more earnestly.

"For God's sake!" Jack cried. "You're sitting on my foot!"

Howie sprang back to his feet. In fact, he hadn't actually sat on Jack's foot. He had sat on the Guatemalan material which in turn had pressed Jack's foot with a small downward pressure. It was only a small mishap.

"Sorry," Howie said. He took a wrought iron garden chair and pulled it closer across redwood decking. Unfortunately, the bottom of the chair made a screeching sound as he pulled it.

"Howie! For chrissake, what do you want? You're spoiling my perfect morning!"

"You don't seem especially tranquil, Jack," Howie told him. "Now, calm down. I just stopped by to discuss a client who wants to hire us. It's a big job and I'm inclining to take it, though with some serious limitations. But before I get back to her, I want your opinion on it."

"Howie, what does my opinion matter? I'm going to be checking out any day now. Wilder & Associate is your baby now, so you decide. You can cross my damn name off the shingle!"

Howie sighed. "We don't have a shingle, Jack. We have a small, discreet sign in the front window."

"Yeah, yeah, yeah," said Jack.

"Okay, I've already told you what happened on Friday. I was taking a shortcut through the Four Corners when this Chinese woman stepped out from the desert and dropped dead on the road. You remember me telling you about this, I hope?"

"Howie, I'm blind, my heart's shot to hell, but my memory's just fine."

"Just checking, Jack. Anyway, yesterday afternoon a woman from a group that calls itself Washington Women Against Trafficking came to the office wanting to hire us to investigate who that woman was, where she came from, and if she was trafficked. These women have plenty of money to throw around. They're rich do-gooders from back East. Cultivated types. Lydia Cordell-Smith—that's the woman who came to the office—offered me a $40,000 retainer if I'd take the case . . . Jack, are you listening?"

"Sure, I am, Howie."

He didn't look like it. His head was tilted back and he appeared to be concentrating on a magpie that was making a fuss in one of the upper branches of the cottonwood.

"What did I just say, Jack?" Howie challenged.

"Rich do-gooders from back East. There are worse kinds of clients, Howie."

"I told her I needed to ask you. But here's the problem. Georgie is arriving in less than two weeks, and once she's here, I'm giving her every second of my attention. So, what I'm thinking, I'll offer the Cordell-Smith woman one week of my time to identify the Chinese woman and see if there's any reason to believe she was trafficked. After that, the Feds can take over, whatever. But I'll be out of it. Meanwhile, I'm not going to accept her $40,000 retainer. I'm going to charge her a bit more than our usual rate since this is a rush job, but that's it."

"Howie, why is that magpie making all that noise?"

"There's a grey cat that just climbed over the fence into your back-yard. Magpies have strong feelings about cats."

"That's the neighbor's cat," Jack said. "Jezebel. She sits on my lap sometimes. I like her."

Howie sighed. "Great!" he said. "Cats and birds are lovely. But right now, I'm hoping to get your opinion about taking on this case."

Jack waved his left hand dismissively. "For chrissake, it's your deci-sion. Take it, Howie—if it makes you happy."

"Jack, human trafficking doesn't make me happy!"

"Then don't take it. Life's too short for unhappy things. You'll understand that one day when your time's running out."

"That's your new philosophy, is it? Be happy?"

"Exactly," said Jack. "Now, leave me alone! All this nonsense is making me tired so I'm going to catch some sleep."

***

Howie left the Wilder home with concern. *Is he losing it*, he asked himself as he walked past Emma's rosebushes through the white wicker gate to his car? *Or has he found some mystic serenity with the approach of death*?

What did Howie know? Frankly, he could use some mystic serenity himself.

It hadn't been a satisfying conversation with Jack. Not where the business was concerned. Howie was particularly miffed that Jack hadn't even really listened as he had presented the Chinese Case, Wilder & Associate against international human trafficking. Which left it up to him whether to accept even a limited version of the job Lydia Cordell-Smith had offered.

No, he decided, changing his mind from what he had decided last night. He drove back to the office through the tourist clogged streets of downtown San Geronimo, reminding himself that though this was a noble cause, he truly, honestly, *really* didn't have time for it.

I've got to clear space in my head for Georgie's visit!

In fact, he was ready for Georgie now. With the tepee up, he had done everything. He even had a bed made up for her in the cabin with new sheets and big fluffy towels in the shower room. All there was to do now was sit and worry.

Was he prepared for fatherhood? Howie didn't know. He was like a soldier on a troop carrier about to land in Normandy. The future was unclear and he was nervous.

The office was closed on Sunday, but Howie found a bill that Ruth had left on his desk which brought him to his senses. The bill was for $18,236.23, which represented the second half of a payment to install a flush toilet in the otherwise woodsy cabin he had built on his land. Howie himself had made do with a composting toilet for years, but he'd been afraid that this might be too much of a transition for a teenage girl from Glasgow.

But another $18,236.23! Howie despaired at the figure. In his calculations, he had forgotten that this payment was due. The company that had done the septic tank and the water system had been first rate—Green EcoSystems of San Geronimo, a group of New Agey young "eco-engineers," as they called themselves. They had been excited by "the challenge," as they saw it, of Howie's situation, that he was off in the woods with only a year round stream for his water source. But they hadn't been cheap.

Howie settled himself at Jack's desk—*his* desk, apparently, now that Jack had lost interest in the business.

He told himself that it would be better for him to be gainfully occupied for the next week rather than sitting around worrying about fatherhood.

He called Lydia Cordell-Smith to accept her case.

***

"One week only, I told her, not another day more," Howie said to Claire, the love of his life, two hours later. "I made it clear why I had to quit at that point, and suggested she hire someone else to take over if she

45

wanted. As long as she understood that I could only give it limited time, I'd try to find out who the Chinese woman was, and what she was doing in that empty stretch of desert."

"I bet she wants you anyway!"

"Well, yes, she does. I was the person who found that poor woman, after all. I was there. She agreed to give me a retainer of ten grand. I couldn't accept her forty thousand, though I was tempted. You see, I got this bill today—"

"Howie, hold on a second, I need to close my dressing room door so I can hear better . . ."

In Howie's world, it was just before five in the afternoon. He was at home with his phone to his ear while packing supplies for his trip to Shiprock while talking to Claire on WhatsApp. Claire, on the other end, was backstage in her dressing room at the Royal Concert Hall in Edinburgh, Scotland, where it was nearly eleven at night. She had just finished performing the Shostakovich Cello Concerto in G Major.

When Howie had first met Claire, she was playing her cello for tips in the San Geronimo town plaza with her two young children after fleeing a bad marriage in Iowa. Now she was famous, playing with the great orchestras of the world. It had created some problems between them, her newfound fame and fortune, but they had managed somehow with only a few hiccoughs.

It was particularly useful now that Claire had been based for the past year in Edinburgh where she was a soloist with the Royal Chamber Orchestra. Glasgow, where Georgie lived, was only two hours away by train and Claire had visited Georgie and her adoptive parents several times. She had been very helpful organizing Georgie's upcoming trip, taking on the role of surrogate parent. Claire had lost her own children in an extremely unfair court battle with her ex-husband, who had become an evangelical Christian, and who had convinced the Iowa judge who was also an evangelical that he was a more fit parent than his gadabout musician wife. Unfortunately, the kids had sided with their conservative father, believing that "the artistic life" their mother was leading was immoral.

Claire, of course, had been deeply hurt, and Howie believed this was at least part of the reason she had made the effort to befriend Georgie. It was a way for her to be a sort of parent to Howie's daughter after being denied the parenthood of her own children. Meanwhile, Claire was a celebrity in Scotland, with her name on posters in both Glasgow and Edinburgh, and frankly Howie doubted that Ray and Carol, Georgie's adoptive parents, would have allowed her to go to far off America if it hadn't been for her involvement. She had convinced them that Howie was a responsible person who would get Georgie back to them safe and sound in time to attend Cambridge University, where she had been accepted. She'd been accepted by Oxford, too. Georgie was a smart girl.

Howie had been hearing a good deal of background noise from her end of the conversation, voices and laughter, but the noise faded as she closed her dressing room door.

"Here I am again," she told him. "So, you're getting paid well for this job?"

"Yes, and the money will be helpful. I just got an invoice for $18,000—it's for the flush toilet I've installed. You'll like it, Claire, the next time you're here. Real plumbing. You just pull the handle—"

"Yes, Howie, I'm familiar with toilets that flush. They have them in Scotland. But honestly, I didn't mind your composting toilet. I like living simply."

"Simple is one thing," Howie told her. "Crude is another. I've had to do some serious updating for Georgie's visit. Wait 'til you see the cabin I built! I even made a swimming hole by damming up the stream and doing a bit of dredging. It's only five feet deep, but you can swim laps . . .

well, short laps, maybe ten feet in each direction, but I'm hoping she'll like it."

"Howie, Georgie is going to like *you*. That's the main thing to remember. You've got to relax and stop worrying. She's a nice young woman and I'm sure the visit will go just fine."

Howie sighed. Claire knew Georgie better than he did. He had done video chats with her, but he had only met her in person once.

"Does she have her passport in order?"

"She does, Howie, she does."

"And you're still going to be able to take her to the airport in Glasgow?"

"I am. Now, stop worrying, Howie! I'm taking two days off just so I can be with her if the flight is delayed."

"And she knows I'll be meeting her plane in Denver? She'll have to go through passport control on her own, but I'll be waiting for her just outside of customs."

"Darling, we've been over this a dozen times. She knows you'll be there."

"I know, I know. I should relax!" he admitted. "I'm just afraid I'll run out of things to do with her."

"Howie, you need to listen to this. Georgie isn't fifteen years old anymore. You won't need to entertain her every second. She's seventeen."

"Well, that's only two years more than when I met her."

"Howie, for a girl that age, between fifteen and seventeen there's a lifetime. And you need to prepare yourself."

Howie hadn't considered this. "Really?"

"Yes, really. She's lost weight, she got rid of those gawky glasses she used to wear. She has contact lenses now, she wears makeup, skintight jeans. And guess what? She likes boys."

Howie couldn't speak for a moment.

"Boys? . . . she *is* going to Cambridge next year, I hope?"

"Yes, of course. She's a very bright girl. But she's also a teenager. What you need to do most of all, Howie, is be yourself, and listen to her. Really *listen!*"

Howie was sitting in his computer nook. *Be myself. Listen to her!* he wrote on the pad he kept by his laptop. He underlined this three times so he wouldn't forget.

The voices and laughter on Claire's end grew abruptly louder and he heard somebody with a Scottish accent calling her name.

"Claire, darling, we're all waiting for you!"

"I'll be right there, Bertie," she called to the invisible person.

"Is there some sort of party going on?" Howie asked. "Who's Bertie?"

"It's just a small reception backstage," she told him. "For the guest conductor. Bertie's the concert master. I'll have to go in a minute. They're popping champagne."

"I'm sure you've earned it. How did the Shostakovich go?"

"Pretty good. I'm not sure about the tempo, though. I think we played it too fast."

"So, who is this guest conductor?"

Claire paused. "Well, it was Sir Richard . . . now don't start worrying, Howie! It's totally over between us! Nothing is going to happen!"

Howie felt like somebody had punched him in the gut. One of the difficulties that came with Claire's sudden fame were the wealthy, talented, sophisticated men she encountered on the high end of the classical music circuit. Claire had had a brief affair with Sir Richard Watson-Fowles, a famous maestro twice her age who had seduced her while they were working on the Dvorak cello concerto. This was a few years ago, but it still hurt.

49

"Howie, talk to me. That was a big mistake, but it's never going to happen again."

"I know, Claire, I know. So is Sir Richard there with you now popping champagne?"

"He's backstage with the rest of the orchestra. But please don't worry. He has a new girl in tow, a Korean violinist who's nineteen years old. He's barely said hello to me outside of rehearsals. He's such a ridiculous egomaniac, I'm sure he doesn't even remember that we had that little . . . well, fling."

Howie sighed. Sir Richard Watson-Fowles was a flamboyant figure who liked to toss his hair around a great deal while conducting an orchestra. Women loved him.

"Howie?"

"It's okay, Claire. I trust you, of course I do. I just wish I wasn't four thousand miles away!"

"I'm going to be home next month, darling. So, you just need to relax and forget about Richard. And for God's sake, stop worrying about Georgie! Okay? I love you, Howie."

He disconnected, leaving Claire to enjoy her champagne reception backstage at the Royal Edinburgh Concert Hall with the charismatic, oversexed maestro.

"What, me worry?" Howie said to Orange.

It was a small matter, but she had never called him darling before. It was the sort of uppity endearment she had always made fun of.

Was fame and fortune getting to her, the high life of a rising star? Were smarmy sophisticated guys sniffing around her door?

Of course, he was worried!

Howie finished gathering up his sleeping bag and tent and one-burner stove, not certain what he was going to need in the Four Corners.

Just before he left home, he opened the small safe he had installed in his computer nook and took out his 9mm Glock.

Howie didn't like guns. He believed people should solve their differences in a calm, civilized manner. But in a dangerous world—horny old men trying to steal your girlfriend, women dropping dead in front of your car!—the wise private eye went prepared.

Chapter Seven

Jack Wilder woke late Monday morning in his downstairs bedroom with a sense that something was wrong. A cool breeze drifted in through the crack of his open window. In the distance, he heard a growl of thunder. He felt rather than saw the darkness of the day. He smelled the moisture. In New Mexico, even in July, when clouds obscured the sun, the temperature plunged.

Katya jumped up on the bed from the floor and nuzzled against his side. When Jack had been paired with Katya at the New Mexico School for the Blind, he had been told he shouldn't treat her like a pet. Guide dogs were highly trained work animals. Jack had done his best for a few months to maintain a professional distance. But it didn't last. Over the years, she had become a beloved, cuddly member of his family.

"How's my girl?" he asked, petting the furry patch between her ears. Katya was a German shepherd, a police dog, as they were once called. Which in his case was appropriate.

But what was wrong? It took him a moment to pin it down. It was something Howie had said when he came by yesterday. At the time Jack hadn't entirely been paying attention. He had been floating in a post-op haze. But he wasn't floating now. Gravity pulled. He felt pain in his chest where they had torn him open, and pain in the crook of his right arm where a needle had been stuck into him for more days than he could remember.

What had Howie been saying? It came back slowly: they had a new client, a woman from an organization that concerned itself with human trafficking.

Jack sat up in bed with a frown. In his experience, there were various levels of evil, ranging from mere narcissism to Satanic madness, cutting up bodies with chain saws. As a cop he had seen it all, and human traffickers were some of the worst. Howie's skill was research and Jack wasn't sure he was up for this kind of job.

"Nancy, get me Howie," he told his computer.

"Phone or text?"

"Just get him! Please," he added because you need to stay on the good side of your computer.

"He doesn't answer, Jack. Would you like to leave a voice mail?"

"Yes, I would. *Call me, Howie!*" Jack bellowed to the microphone in the ceiling of the bedroom.

"That should get his attention," Nancy said. "But you shouldn't let yourself become stressed, Jack. Remember what the doctor said."

"Fuck the doctor!"

"Would you like me to get you some nice morning music, Jack? Perhaps a little Mozart?"

"No!" he growled.

Nancy had such a pleasant voice it was easy to forget she wasn't real. She was a specially adapted Mac with Kurzweil software for the blind that Buzzy had goosed with all sorts of added features. Generally, Jack adored Nancy. She was his link to the world, his constant companion. But he wasn't in the mood for her now.

Jack took a deep breath to calm himself, which wasn't easy when you were the sort of person who believed the world would fall apart without your constant vigilance.

As Jack lay fretting, there came a knock on his door.

"Yeah?" he said unhappily.

It was Debbie, the day nurse Emma had hired to watch over him while she was at work.

"How are we feeling?" she asked.

"*We* are fine! Thank you very much."

Jack hadn't made up his mind yet about Debbie. She sounded young. She sounded clueless. But what did Jack know? Emma was always telling him that he needed to keep an open mind. ("I *have* an open mind!" Jack always replied. "Sure, you do," was Emma's usual refrain.)

"There's a guy in the sitting room who would like to see you," said Debbie.

"A guy?" he repeated caustically "Well, tell the *guy* to beat it. If he was a doll I might be interested. But a guy—forget it!"

The joke, such as it was, was clearly lost on Debbie. She would never have heard of *Guys and Dolls*. She wouldn't even know who Frank Sinatra was.

"His card says he's Inspector Elliot Borello from the U.S Marshal's office in Washington, D.C. But don't worry, Mr. Wilder. I'll tell him to get lost."

"Hold on!" said Jack, raising an imperious hand. The rank of inspector meant that this was a senior investigator on a special assignment, not your average knucklehead.

"Tell him I'll be out in a moment. We'll keep him waiting while I get out of my damn pajamas!"

"Would you like me help you pick out some clothes, Mr. Wilder?

"*No!*" he shouted, loudly enough to blast her from the room.

***

Jack came into the living room dressed in a zippered cream-colored sweat jacket with matching pants that had an expanding elastic waistband, XXXL. With his dark glasses and beard, he looked like a cross between a terrorist and Santa Claus.

Katya followed Jack into the room and stretched out on a Navajo rug near the fireplace from where she could give Inspector Borello a good looking over. Jack didn't need her help as he moved about the house. As long as there were no obstacles, he knew his way.

Jack listened as Inspector Borello rose to his feet from where he had been sitting in Emma's rocking chair. By the active motion of the chair as it was relieved of its weight, Jack sensed a large man.

"Thanks for seeing me, Commander," the man said affably. "Nice dog," he added, giving Katya a nod.

"She *can* be nice," Jack agreed. "But you have to be careful around her. She'll tear people apart if she senses the least bit of danger to me."

"I'll remember that," said the Inspector.

"Have a seat. I'd offer you a drink, but I suppose you're on duty. I'm not drinking myself because I just got home from the hospital yesterday."

"I heard that. You're recovering okay?"

Jack settled himself in his La-Z-Boy recliner. "I'm doing fine. That's what they tell me anyway."

"Well, we have to do what they tell us. Which is why I'm here, as a matter of fact. My boss has instructed me to pay a visit, Commander."

"Not Commander, just Jack," said Jack. He liked to hear his old rank from San Francisco and he was flattered that the U.S. Marshal bothered to use it. But it was only a memory from long ago.

As a blind person, Jack listened intently to people's voices. Usually he could picture a good deal about a person from the timbre of their voice, as well as the words they said and how they said them. But Inspector Borello spoke almost entirely without inflection, with a mid-America accent that was neutral to the point of invisibility. His voice gave nothing away. Jack couldn't even tell if he was young or old. This was a difficult skill to master, the art of being hard to remember, hard to describe.

Jack smiled harmlessly, which was his own camouflage.

"How about a cup of coffee, Inspector? Maybe a cheese chile croissant? My wife picked up some at a new bakery in town. They're pretty good, if you like pastry that has a snap to it."

"Thanks, Jack. I like things that have a snap to them. But if I don't hurry, I'm going to be late for an appointment in Santa Fe."

Jack shrugged. "Then let's get right to it. Why are you here, Inspector?"

"As I said, it's my boss. He thought it would be a good idea if we had a talk."

"Your boss?"

"The AG. He knows your reputation so he knows you'll understand what I'm about to ask you. The other day your associate, a Mr. Moon Deer, unwittingly got involved in an operation we're running here in New Mexico. It's something that's at a delicate turning point. Something we've invested a good deal of money and time into. So right now we need you and your associate to keep your distance."

Jack understood where this was going. He had never liked to be warned off and he didn't like it now. But he kept his affable smile.

"Ah-ha! Howie's shortcut from hell! I get it, Inspector. He was driving home from Utah and thought he'd save himself a few miles. I gather he stumbled upon a dead woman who appears to be a victim of human trafficking."

"Possibly," said the Inspector. "Unfortunately, there's a good deal of trafficking in this part of the country. Slavery's one of the constants of history, Jack. Why lift a heavy rock if you can find somebody else to do it for you? The Native Americans kept slaves, too, you know—captives from other tribes. The Spanish did it too, of course. They enslaved Indians."

"And let's not forget gentlemen tobacco farmers in Alabama," said Jack. "So, who was the woman Howie found?"

Inspector Borello laughed. "Well, you see, this is why I'm here. To tell you this is something you don't need to know. Now, I can imagine why you're curious. It's to your credit that you'd care about some poor woman who died in the desert. But you were a cop, so I know you'll understand what I'm going to tell you. We're in the middle of a big case and we don't want outsiders bumbling in, spooking the suspects. Arrests are coming, but we need more time."

"I do understand," Jack said sympathetically. "I've been in the same position many times. The only problem is we have a client. An organization that wants to know about this lady in the desert. We've accepted their money. We've signed a contract." Jack was ad libbing. He hoped this was true about the contract, but he didn't know. "So, it would be difficult for us to turn around now and tell them no. But please, don't worry—we won't get in your way. And anything we find, we'll turn it over to you right away."

The Inspector chuckled. "As it happens, I know your client well. Lydia Cordell-Smith. I've had a few dealings with her. She's a quack, you know. A well-educated, well-meaning quack who represents a foundation of well-meaning, well-educated rich people who want to feel good about themselves. Good for them! We welcome the idealism of the privileged few. Why not? But this is a job for the U.S. Justice Department not a bunch of amateurs."

"I'm not an amateur, Inspector."

"I'm aware of that, Commander Wilder. But this isn't your turf, this isn't your war, and these aren't people you want to mess with."

"Why don't you tell me about these people."

"Leave it be. And please tell your associate to do the same. You'll only get hurt if you pursue this."

Jack threw up his hands. "Hey, I dealt with traffickers back in California and I believe you. These are bad guys through and through.

Robert Westbrook

Nevertheless, as I've mentioned, we have a client, we've accepted her money, and when you're a private detective you do what you've promised. This is capitalism, after all—money in the bank for us. So, we're going to keep on keeping on, I'm afraid."

Inspector Borello was silent for a moment. "You're determined to find out about that dead girl, are you?"

"Yep," said Jack. "We are."

"Well, okay, let's talk about what's public knowledge. Have you been following things in Hong Kong?"

"A bit," said Jack. "Young people in Hong Kong have been protesting for democracy, and the government in Beijing has been clamping down."

"Right. And as you can imagine, Hong Kong money—which there's a lot of—has been migrating out of the country to safer havens. People have been migrating as well. Those who can get to the West with their money intact are doing so before Beijing makes it impossible. And this goes for the crime families as well. The Triads, the Tongs. They're looking for greener pastures."

"I see," said Jack. "And some of this Hong Kong money has been finding its way to New Mexico?"

"I'm not giving details, Jack, but use your imagination. Let's say there are possibilities in the great open spaces of New Mexico that Chinese crime families find appealing. You can hide a lot of stuff in a state like this. Especially if you have the help of an obscure Indian tribe that's not entirely on the up and up."

Jack nodded. He tried to remember the name of the tribe that Howie had mentioned. It came to him after a moment. "The La Chaya tribe, right? Well, well!"

"And that's all you need to know," said the Inspector. "Trafficking, a Hong Kong Triad, the Justice Department getting a case together. We

58

have resources, we have the guns, so let us do our job. That's what I'm asking."

"And a very reasonable request it is," Jack agreed. "Except for that contract I mentioned. And the fact that Howie has already set off."

"Set off? Where is Moon Deer now?"

"Well, I'd tell you if I knew, but I don't. You see, I'm not taking much part in the business right now. My health. I saw Howie briefly yesterday, but I haven't heard from him since. He's saying I should just rest."

"You could try phoning."

"Yes, I could. But you know how it is here in New Mexico. Not much cell coverage. I tried to get him just an hour ago, but I had no luck, I'm afraid."

"That's too bad," said Inspector Borello.

"Yes, it is," Jack agreed. "If you'd come to see me yesterday, perhaps I could have been some help. But now the contract's signed, Howie is off somewhere, I'm stuck at home recuperating from surgery—there's not much I can do. However, in his own stumbling way Howie's actually pretty good at what he does, Inspector. So, I tell you what I'll do. If he gets to the bottom of this trafficking situation before you, I'll certainly keep you up to date."

Inspector Borello stood up. Jack could feel his presence nearby, a darkness in the room.

"That's generous of you, Jack," he said finally. "All right, we'll see how this plays. Meanwhile, you'd better tell Moon Deer to watch his step. And hope he's not in over his head. These Hong Kong guys play for keeps."

***

59

When Inspector Borello was gone, Jack remained in his La-Z-Boy for a long time, lost in thought.

"Try Howie again," he said to Nancy at last. Though he was in the living room, Nancy had an ear in every room of the house, except Emma's bedroom and the upstairs bathroom.

"He's still not answering," Nancy told him. "No voicemail either. It's been turned off."

Jack frowned. "Turned off . . . christ, Howie, what the hell have you done now?"

"Are you okay, Jack?" asked Debbie the day nurse, coming into the room.

It was the wrong time to disturb him. "I'm fine, Debbie," he said patiently. I just want to sit here a moment by myself."

"I could make you a sandwich—"

"Thank you, no. Thank you very much, Debbie. I just want to sit here and think! If you don't mind!"

There was no mistaking the tone. Debbie was about to vanish quickly when Jack stopped her.

"What was he wearing on his feet?" he asked.

"I'm sorry?"

"On his feet, Debbie. What kind of shoes was he wearing?"

"Well, boots, I guess."

"Boots, okay. What kind of boots?"

"Boot boots," she answered.

Jack nodded. "Yes, I get that. But what kind of boots? Hiking boots? Motorcycle boots? What?"

"Well, they were cowboy boots."

"Ah! Cowboy boots! Were they plain cowboy boots, would you say? Or fancy cowboy boots?"

"Fancy. Real good leather."

Jack smiled pleasantly. "Thank you very much, Debbie. You may go," he said decisively.

When he was alone, he sank back exhausted into the contours of the La-Z-Boy chair. He never used to get tired so easily and he didn't like it. It kept you from getting things done.

He was worried about Howie, why he wasn't answering his phone. And now there was Inspector Elliot Borello to worry about as well. This was clearly the government man in the white van who had saved Howie from a bad beating. His presence made Jack feel boxed in. He took the U.S. Marshals seriously. They weren't people you wanted to mess with.

It wasn't a good situation and he felt it was his own fault. He should have been paying attention. He had been in a dreamy mush when Howie had told him earlier about the case, asking his advice, and now it seemed too late. His options were as limited as his physical predicament, to be a blind old man laid up at home.

Jack hated feeling helpless.

However, as he sat and stewed, a few ideas came to mind. Not ideas, really, but a starting point. In fact, there were several things he might do. He *wasn't* helpless.

"Nancy, wake up! Get me Buzzy," he ordered.

"He's up in the mountains, Jack, on San Geronimo Peak. Here he is..."

"Buzzy, it's Jack," said Jack, taking over. "I need you right away. Down here. I'm at the house."

"Well, sure. But Howie asked me to finish up this insurance case," Buzzy said. "I'm just about to finally talk to the lift operator who saw the drunk guy fall out of the chair. The liftie I needed to see wasn't here yesterday when I came up—"

"Screw the drunk guy. This is more important. Get down here right away."

"I'm—"

"*Now!*" said Jack.

Once Nancy had disconnected, he gave her a new command. "Get me Santo Ruben!"

Chapter Eight

Lieutenant Santo Ruben, the head of the State Police substation in San Geronimo, was Jack's friend of many years. It was his day off and Jack reached him at home working in his backyard with a weed wacker, taming the meadow behind his house.

Jack got to the point right away.

"Hey, Santo, why don't you put down that weed wacker for a minute and take a break. I have some questions for you. I'm trying to get information about illegal aliens in New Mexico."

Santo's laugh had a slight malicious edge. "Little green men in flying saucers? I thought you were done with that."

Jack sighed. Several years ago, Howie had gotten the agency involved in a case he did his best to forget, a UFO scam. "Very funny, Santo. But right now I'm more interested in the human kind of aliens, the sort who arrive here without papers."

"Well, sure, we have them here, just like everywhere. These are people who have been traumatized by poverty and violence and are willing to pay every cent they have to get to America. A small number of them end up in San Geronimo, but to be honest I do my best to leave them alone. I figure they've had enough sorrow in their lives. And besides, the majority of them are honest, hardworking folks who are thrilled to be in America and don't cause any trouble. Every now and then, ICE leans on me to take a greater interest in rounding them up, but I have my ways of stalling them."

"I'm sure you do. Look, here's the deal. On Sunday, Howie was driving back from Utah when he came across a Chinese woman wandering in the desert not too far from Shiprock. She died before she could tell him anything and we're trying to find out if she was trafficked."

"Hold on, Jack—you're supposed to be resting! You don't want to get involved in something like this, not now. Does Emma know you're taking on new cases?"

"No, this is Howie's case, not mine. I'm just making a few phone calls for him. I'm taking it easy, Santo, I promise."

"Howie has the client?"

"It's his entirely. An organization from back east that wants to put an end to human trafficking. I'm trying to get some background information for Howie and to be honest, I'm not quite sure where to start. I'm hoping you can point me in the right direction. I'm especially interested in the Chinese angle, and if the situation Howie encountered is connected with organized crime in Hong Kong."

"Hong Kong Triads? That's a big leap, isn't it?"

"Probably. But this woman spoke a single word in Chinese before she died and she didn't appear to know any English. So, I'm wondering how she got here."

"*If* she was an undocumented alien, you mean. Which again is a leap. There's a considerable Asian population in New Mexico, you know, who are here legally."

"I know that, and if this woman turns out to be a legal immigrant, that's fine and dandy. I'm simply examining the possibilities."

Jack was reluctant to mention his visit this morning from the U.S Marshal's office, fearing it might make Santo clam up. "So, imagine for a moment that this woman was trafficked from China," he continued. "How would she get here? And who organizes something like this?"

"Well, that's a big question and I'm not much of an expert. I've heard of undocumented Asians being brought across the border from Mexico, but from what I understand, that's rare. Mostly, they would be transported by ship to the West Coast and then be trucked to the Southwest. I don't suppose the travel arrangements are very pleasant. As I say, this isn't at all my field, but I do know somebody who might be able to help you."

"That's exactly what I'm looking for!"

"Her name is Christine Chang. She's an investigative reporter at *The Albuquerque Journal*, a young Chinese-American woman who contacted me a couple of months ago asking about this same issue. She wanted to know if I had any knowledge of Asian sex workers who had been trafficked into New Mexico. It was an interesting question, but I had to tell her I didn't know of a single case, not up in my part of the state, anyway. She bought me lunch and I liked her, but I couldn't help with the story and I never heard from her again."

"Christine Chang," Jack repeated for the benefit of Nancy who was listening in. "Thanks, Santo."

"Sure, Jack. But go easy, my friend. You need to remember that you're recovering from some serious surgery. You should be in bed listening to peaceful music. Brahms, maybe. Lullabies."

"I'm feeling terrifically peaceful, Santo," Jack assured him.

The moment Jack disconnected with Santo, he raised his voice to the microphone in the living room ceiling.

"Nancy, get me Christine Chang at *The Albuquerque Journal!*"

***

After hanging up with Santo, Jack phoned Christine Chang at the *Albuquerque Journal*, using the extension number which Nancy had been able to find for him. She answered almost immediately.

"Chris," she said distractedly, a busy young woman who was most likely doing three things at once.

Jack put on his most pleasant voice for her, a kindly older man. "Hel-lo, Ms. Chang, my name is Jack Wilder. Lieutenant Santo Ruben of the

State Police gave me your name and suggested I contact you. I run a private investigation agency up here in San Geronimo and there's a case I'm working on that I believe will interest you."

"I know who you are, Mr. Wilder. I covered the Senator Stanton murder for the *Journal*."

"Oh, good, that will save us the need of a lengthy introduction. Now, I gather you had lunch with Lieutenant Ruben a few months ago. You told him you were doing a story about trafficked Asian sex workers in New Mexico and you were hoping he could help you—is that right?"

Her voice was suddenly cautious, but he had her attention. "Well, yes. But I'm afraid he wasn't able to tell me much, and after a few weeks of getting nowhere I decided to drop the story."

"You're no longer investigating trafficked women in New Mexico?"

"No, I'm not. It was just one of those ideas you get that fizzle out. I kept coming up blank so I moved on to other things."

Jack absorbed this. "You're saying you don't believe there *are* trafficked Asian women in the Southwest?"

"No, I'm not saying that at all. It's just that I couldn't come up with anything solid and with the time restraints at the *Journal*, I needed to turn my attention to a story that would lead to more tangible results."

"Well, perhaps I can give you more tangible results. My partner was driving on a back road in the Four Corners on Sunday and a young Chinese woman stepped out in front of his car from the desert and collapsed and died. She'd been shot. We're thinking she was a trafficked woman who had escaped somehow from whoever was holding her."

"The Four Corners?" she asked hesitantly. "This was on the Navajo reservation?"

"No, it was on La Chaya land. They're a much smaller tribe nearby."

"I see," she said. Though Jack wasn't at all sure what she saw. "Your partner . . . that's Howard Moon Deer?"

"Do you know him?"

"I know of him from the article about the Stanton case. Well, look, I gotta go, I have a deadline to meet on a story I'm writing about the balloon fiesta. Like I said, I dropped my idea to write about trafficking but maybe you'll find somebody else to help you. That's what you're looking for, isn't it? Information?"

"It is. Modern slavery is an important issue, Ms. Chang. I'm sorry you lost interest in it."

"It's not that. It's . . ." She was flustered. "It's . . . look, I really have to go. I'm sorry, but I can't help you."

She hung up, leaving Jack somewhat baffled. He would have thought any ambitious young journalist would be eager to write about human trafficking. It was the sort of story that could make a career.

He tried to analyze something he had heard in her voice that worried him. It was a young voice, without depth or timbre. A very pleasant voice, really. He pictured an attractive young woman. But she sounded frightened.

As he sat thinking his phone rang again, this time with a frog croak that indicated an unknown number. Buzzy had programmed his phone with a variety of rings.

"Is that another damn robocall?" he asked Nancy.

"It's from Albuquerque, Jack. That's all I know."

"Answer it!"

He wasn't entirely surprised to find it was Christine Chang calling back from a different phone.

"Sorry for the intrigue," she said quickly. "I couldn't talk from the office. Look, why don't you meet me in one hour at the Cottonwood Mall in Albuquerque. I'll be in the food court near the carousel."

"It'll take me two and a half hours to get there from San Geronimo."

"Okay, but please hurry! And make sure nobody is following you!"

She hung up abruptly leaving Jack intrigued and worried, but not quite so baffled as before. His first impression had been the right one: she was frightened.

Chapter Nine

Buzzy picked up Jack and Katya half an hour later. They were waiting impatiently for him in the living room, dressed and ready to go. Katya was in her harness.

"You took your time!" Jack complained.

Buzzy wasn't sure whether to tell Jack that his shirt was buttoned up the wrong way. Generally, Emma laid out Jack's clothes for him with an eye to colors that didn't clash. But Emma was at the library and Jack had been in a hurry, grabbing the first clothes he could find by touch in his closet: a long-sleeved green checkered shirt that, in Buzzy's eye, made him look like a rural hick, and a pair of old khaki pants that had obviously been used at some point for gardening. There were dirt stains on the knees. He looked like a crazy person from a homeless shelter.

"Are you sure this is a good idea, Jack? I thought you were supposed to be resting at home."

"Just drive, Buzzy."

"You know, your shirt isn't buttoned right."

"What? Oh, thanks," Jack muttered, running his hands over the buttons. "You could have told me this before!"

Fortunately, Buzzy was used to eccentricity. He had grown up in a commune in the desert west of town that had been started by a mad anarchist professor who had been fired from Harvard. There had been about twenty-five adults, all of them with strong opinions, and a dozen half-wild children. It was paradise, almost, living simply, sharing everything, going back to the land, back to the garden. But, in Buzzy's view, a paradise lost.

They were cruising south on I-25 at 80 mph. Buzzy was glad Jack couldn't see the speedometer.

"So, Jack, are you going to tell me why we're rushing down to Albuquerque?"

"We're going to meet a journalist."

"This is about the dead Chinese woman?"

"Maybe, Buzzy. Maybe. I don't know yet. Now keep quiet so I can think!"

Buzzy found Albuquerque an ugly city, a dull city, a flat brown sprawl in the desert. L.A. was an ugly city too, but L.A. had zap. Albuquerque had no zap.

Buzzy maneuvered his way off the freeway onto Coors Boulevard and drove west to the Cottonwood Mall. It was 94 degrees outside according to the car thermometer, and the city seemed paralyzed in the heat. Cars floated by with their windows closed, everybody in their bubble of air-conditioning.

"Hey, look, Jack, we could pop into Dillard's and get you a change of clothes."

"Damnit, Buzzy—we're not here to go shopping!"

"Just saying, Jack. Sartorially speaking, your appearance could use an uplift."

"Buzzy, it's not my ambition to be a fashion model!"

"Well, that's excellent, then. You've achieved your non ambition with flying colors."

Buzzy parked in a field of concrete that was larger than many northern New Mexico towns. They crossed the parking lot with the sun beating down, no mercy for shoppers. They entered the complex through a double-door near Dillard's, with Jack in the middle, Katya in her harness on his right, and Buzzy on the left guiding Jack lightly with one hand on his arm.

Shopping malls had seen their glory days come and go, and this mall was no exception. Inside the cavernous, air-conditioned city, the outside world disappeared. Here there was only shopping, money waiting to be spent, goods to be consumed. But the throngs of teenagers who once used malls as meeting grounds with their friends were gone. The shoppers who remained roamed the lonely arteries in silence, almost furtively, like survivors of an apocalypse. Some were not shoppers at all, but old folks who had come out in sweatsuits for their daily exercise up and down the air-conditioned halls.

Buzzy guided Jack through a long artery with stores on both sides, some of which were empty, their windows plastered with newspaper. They made their way toward the food court.

"Do you see an Asian woman anywhere?"

"I do, Jack. There's a Chinese babe by herself near the kiddie carousel. Which isn't running, by the way, probably because there aren't any kiddies. Her back is to us."

"Lead us there. And for chrissake, don't call her a babe!"

Christine Chang stood as they approached. She was an attractive woman in her mid-twenties dressed in office clothes, black pants, a frilly white blouse, and a subdued but colorful scarf. She had a black leather laptop bag over one shoulder. Buzzy tagged her immediately as Not My Type. She appeared much too conventional for him. He couldn't imagine the two of them together fighting for anarchy.

"Jack Wilder?" she queried. "What a lovely dog!" Katya wagged her tail at the compliment. "Thanks for agreeing to meet me! I must have seemed kind of mysterious on the phone."

"Mysteries are what we're here to solve," said Jack chivalrously. He was old-fashioned when it came to young women. "This is my assistant, Buzzy Hurston."

Jack found a chair by the table and managed to feel out its contours in order to sit down. He didn't like being in unfamiliar places where he needed help. The interior of the shopping mall felt cavernous to him, a

71

huge unknown space in which he had no moorings. He fought his rising agoraphobia by concentrating on getting the interview under way.

"So, you write for the *Journal*?"

"I do. I was the editor of *The Daily Californian* when I was at Berkeley. That's the student paper. But this is my first real newspaper job. I've been in Albuquerque three years now and I'm working hard to do a good job."

"I bet you are! So, you're from the Bay Area?"

"San Francisco."

"Is that so? I grew up in North Beach. Buzzy's spent time in the Bay Area, too. He just got kicked out of Stanford."

"Jack!"

"So, Berkeley," Jack continued. "A great university. I went to San Francisco State myself. What part of the city did you grow up in?"

"The Avenues," she said. "My dad owns a Chinese restaurant on Geary close to the ocean. The foggy part of the city. We all had to work there as kids. But I wanted to be a writer."

"Hey, I know Chinese restaurants in that area!" Buzzy said. "What's its name?"

"The Emerald Buddha," she said modestly.

"The Emerald Buddha! I've eaten there!"

"Buzzy—"

"No, it's a great place, Jack. The best duck in the city! And it's huge!"

"But you wanted to be a writer," Jack pressed, hoping to shut Buzzy up.

"I did!" she told him. "I couldn't wait to get away from the grease and grime and stress of restaurant work. So, after college, I got the job with the *Journal*. To be honest, it wasn't the first paper I applied to, but the *New York Times* and the *Washington Post* weren't hiring. Not me, anyway."

"And how old are you now?"

"I'm twenty-four."

"Okay, let's talk about this article on human trafficking that you decided not to write. What happened? Did you just lose interest?"

"Ha!" came her unhappy laugh. "I didn't lose interest, I can tell you that!"

Jack scowled. "You were warned off?"

"I . . . well, put it this way. I became aware that what I was doing was dangerous."

"And who made you aware of this, Ms. Chang?"

"That's a story, I'm afraid. It's not me I'm frightened for, it's my family. You need to understand, I've had personal contact with trafficked girls. That's why I wanted to write this story in the first place. I know what it's like. I've seen it. The misery, the cruelty of being bought and sold . . ."

Her words trailed off. Jack found her voice clear and true and impossibly young. As far as he was concerned, she could keep on talking until the cows came home. But she seemed reluctant to continue.

"I can see this is a difficult subject for you, Christine. But please go on."

"Is it safe to talk here?"

Safe from whom? Jack wondered. "A food court in a large shopping mall should be reasonably secure. Did you tell anybody that you were coming here?"

"No, at work I said I was going to a dental appointment."

"And nobody followed you here?"

"I don't think so."

"Buzzy, what do you think? Is there anybody paying particular attention to us?"

"Doesn't look like it, Jack. This part of the court is almost empty. There's a mother with a baby in a stroller a few tables away, but that's it."

Jack smiled encouragingly. "I think we're okay," he told Christine. "Keep your voice down, but please continue. You say you've seen human trafficking?"

"In San Francisco, yes. In restaurants. . . in my dad's restaurant, actually. When I was twelve, I started working as a bus girl and I got to know one of them, a girl who was a few years older than me who was kept in the back doing a lot of the dirty work no one else wanted to do, cleaning fish and stuff. She was very quiet but there was something attractive about her that made me curious. She didn't speak a word of English and not much Mandarin either, but we were able to talk a bit when I came in and out of the kitchen carrying dishes. I found out she was from Yunan and she was homesick for her parents. But when I asked how she got to California she just shook her head and wouldn't say."

"She didn't tell you her story?"

"I thought she was just being shy. I didn't realize the danger she was in. Finally, I asked my dad about her, but he wouldn't tell me either. He only said that she was 'an unfortunate'—that's the phrase he used, an unfortunate—and he had put her in the kitchen as a favor to someone. A few days after that, she simply disappeared and when I asked the chef about her he wouldn't say. He said I should mind my own business. I never saw her again, I never found out what happened to her, but I never forgot her. Which was why I was writing the article, doing it on my own time. I wanted to expose this evil of modern slavery . . . and sure, I was hoping, careerwise, that it would get me out of Albuquerque and to New York."

Jack smiled at her candor. "And then what happened?"

"I got a phone call from my younger sister in San Francisco and she told me to stop. She said if I didn't stop they would kill our dad."

"*They* would kill your dad? Who is *they*?"

Christine sighed. "The guys from the society," she said. "Who else?"

Jack nodded. At one time, he had known a good deal about the Chinese Tongs in San Francisco, though it was a closed, secretive world. "Which one?"

"The Red Gecko Tong."

"I know the name," he said.

In San Francisco, back in his day, there had been three main Chinese criminal organizations, all with ties to Hong Kong: the Blood Feather Triad, the Red Gecko Tong, and the Mountain Cloud Boys. Triads were said to be larger societies while Tongs more like street gangs, though the terms were increasingly used interchangeably. Jack was aware that new gangs had most likely come and gone since his time in California.

"You know about the societies?" she asked. Christine seemed to prefer that word: societies. It had less sting in it.

"I was a cop in San Francisco, Christine. So yes, I knew as much as a non-Chinese cop might know, which wasn't much. What's your connection with these people?"

"My connection? I grew up in a Chinese neighborhood, and the kids I knew, my friends, came from families whose parents were running things. My Dad had to deal with the gangs in order to keep his restaurant going. I saw them in the restaurant all the time. Their meals were always free. My younger sister, Audrey, has an old friend in the gangs. Somebody approached her and gave her a warning. She's the one who phoned and told me I had to stop writing my article."

"How did anyone find out about you writing the article?"

"I was stupid! I went to a friend for information, a boy I knew in high school. He was really nice back then, we'd been close, so I thought it would be safe to ask him a few questions. But I was wrong. I asked him about New Mexico, the Four Corners, and if there was any funny Chinese interest going on there. He was friendly but evasive. Actually, he laughed at the idea that the gangs might have been interested in a nothing state like New Mexico. And then a day later, I got the phone call from Audrey telling me I had to stop."

"Okay, but back up a moment, Christine. Why were you suspicious about Tong activity in the Four Corners?"

Christine didn't answer immediately.

"How did you know to be so specific?" Jack pressed.

"I heard rumors, that's all. That there was some big operation happening in the Four Corners with big Hong Kong money coming into the state. But when I tried to pin it down, I didn't get anywhere. That's why I was interested when you said on the phone that Moon Deer had found a dead Chinese woman in the desert there. But I can't go any farther with this, Mr. Wilder. I hope you understand. I'd like to, but I can't. They'll kill my father if I do. These people do what they say."

"They're ruthless," Jack agreed. "I've seen the bodies in some of their turf wars. But tell me about these rumors you heard about something in the Four Corners. Who told you what?"

Again, there was silence.

"Christine, please," Jack said quietly. "I can keep your name out of it. I have a client, a group in Washington, D.C., that has hired my agency to find out the identity of that Chinese woman and what happened to her. This doesn't have to concern you at all. It's my case, and whatever happens, it'll be me who'll take the flack because I'm the one pursuing it. But I need all the help I can get. So please, where do these rumors come from?"

"Okay, but I'm not going to give you a name," she said reluctantly. "I have a friend who works as a bartender in an upscale Chinese restaurant. She said a Chinese guy came in a few weeks ago and he got really drunk at the bar. He tried to pick her up, came on to her, telling her how much money he was making up at the Four Corners, on an Indian reservation. And how if she was nice to him, he'd spend some of it on her."

"You're not going to tell me this bartender's name?"

"I'm not. Absolutely no."

"Okay. Now, listen to me. You've come this far. I know you want to stop this modern slavery. You can't do it because of your father, I understand that. And yet, you wanted to meet me. You're not willing to let it go."

"But I'm conflicted, Mr. Wilder. It's dangerous for me, for my father, my sister—for you, too, if you start nosing around."

Jack nodded. "Sure. But it's even more dangerous just to let things like this keep happening. That woman my partner found in the desert didn't die of thirst, she died of a bullet wound. If good people don't speak up when they see something bad happening, then the badness goes on. Sometimes you have to speak up. You have to take a chance."

She turned a little red. "I know that! I *have* spoken up! At least, I've tried!"

"Yes, I can see that. And I don't blame you a bit for being intimidated. Tell me about your sister Audrey. She's younger, is that right?"

"She's twenty-two."

"And she's dating the son of someone high up in a Tong?"

"Yes. But she's not like those people. She's a good person, very innocent, really. And she tells me things. Deliberately. I think she wants me to write about what she overhears."

"Does she work in the family restaurant?"

"Five nights a week. She's the night manager, Tuesday through Saturdays. My father likes one of the family handling the money. On week days, she's enrolled at the San Francisco Art Institute. She wants to be an artist."

"Well, that's wonderful. I used to know the Art Institute well. And you became a journalist, your sister wants to be an artist—your parents must have done something right. You both seem like very sound, smart young women."

"Thank you!"

"Now, I'd like to ask one more thing of you, Christine. I'd like you to talk to Audrey and convince her to have a phone conversation with me. Will you do that?"

"I can't, Mr. Wilder! It's just too dangerous for everyone in the family!"

Jack didn't say anything for a time. "I see," he said finally. "Well, I understand. Thank you for meeting me here, you've given me a few things to think about. I'll let you know if I ever have a story to give you that might get you to New York. Meanwhile, I'll have Buzzy send you my contact information, if you think of anything you'd like to let me know."

Buzzy told him afterward that Christine shook her head silently several times, waging an inner war. But at last she sighed and said yes, she would stay in touch.

Buzzy watched her go, disappearing around the corner into the artery where Kaye's Jewelry met the Gap. Though she wasn't his type, he had begun to like her. He wondered if their paths would ever converge again . . .

"Wake up," Jack told him. "This is no time for dreaming, Buzzy. We have a lot to do tonight."

"Oh, yeah? What are we doing tonight?"

Jack grinned like a naughty kid.

"We're catching a flight to San Francisco, of course. Let's find a place where you can get online and make reservations."

"Jack, Emma isn't going to like this."

"It's okay, Buzzy. I'll deal with Emma. Now let's get moving. California here we come!"

***

At the Albuquerque Sunport, before they went through security, Jack had to use the bathroom. He'd been putting this off as long as possible because public bathrooms in places like airports were a problem for a blind man. Not even Katya could help him here. He needed a human, Buzzy, to guide him down a long corridor and get him into a cubicle with the door shut.

Buzzy waited near the sinks with Katya, holding onto her harness, while Jack had some privacy.

Once he was alone, he sighed from his very core. This was a challenge for Jack—not the bathroom mechanics, particularly, but the humiliation and helplessness.

Fortunately, Buzzy was good in situations like this, unfazed by anything. Growing up on a post-apocalyptic commune in the desert, he had seen far worse things than an old man in a public bathroom. When Jack was finished, he washed his hands, took back Katya's harness, and Buzzy guided him through the exit into the corridor.

"There's a bench, Jack," Buzzy said, watching him closely. "It's for guys who are waiting for their girlfriends to come out of the Ladies Room. Maybe you'd like to sit there and rest."

"Yes," Jack admitted. "Where—"

"I got you," Buzzy said taking Jack's arm. "Sit . . . here."

Jack was relieved to be safely ensconced on the bench. He had to admit to himself that he was exhausted.

"Give me a few minutes, Buzzy. I just want to sit here a while."

"I can wait."

"No, I need to make a phone call. Go to one of those computer nooks that Howie always uses when he flies and get us a reservation for a motel in San Francisco, for tonight and tomorrow."

"Two nights?"

"Hopefully we won't need the second night. But yes, make the reservation just in case. Try the Manor Motel on Lombard. I used to know the manager there. It's a good cheap place, $36 a night."

Buzzy had to control his laughter. "Jack, have you been to San Francisco recently?"

"Try them," Jack insisted. "The Manor on Lombard. If they're full, see if you can get something else in that neighborhood. I believe there's a Howard Johnson on Van Ness. Use your judgement."

"Who's Howard Johnson?"

"Buzzy, *go!*"

Once he was alone, Jack took a breath and tried to relax his shoulders. He wished he felt better. He remembered a line from a book, that most of the world's work was done by people who didn't feel entirely well. That was him, all right, the unwell. You couldn't let that stop you, though.

Jack had turned off his phone for his conversation with Christine Chang, but now he turned it on again and listened to his voicemail.

Emma had phoned three times, and her messages were increasingly angry.

"Jack, Debbie phoned me at the library. Did you really go off somewhere with Buzzy? Tell me it's not true. Wherever you are, go home and get back into bed!"

That was message number one.

Message two: "Jack, I'm serious, this is ridiculous—running off like some teenager sneaking out the window. It's not fair to me, not knowing if you're dead or alive. So, call, Jack. If you're going to die on me, at least do me the favor of calling first!"

The third voicemail . . . he didn't even want to think about it.

She was right, of course, as Emma always was. He should be home in bed. That would be one way to die, from boredom!

He pressed his speed dial to phone Emma.

"Jack!" she exploded. "Where the hell are you?"

"I'm all right, Emma. You need to calm down."

"Calm down? WHERE ARE YOU?"

"I'm in Albuquerque. Buzzy drove me. Now, you need to relax, dear. I'm fine. I rode in the car for three hours, which basically was like being in bed. And then I had a very calm conversation with a nice young woman, a journalist. It's been more relaxing, honestly, than if I were home feeling frustrated."

"You're in Albuquerque? Is Buzzy driving you home now?"

"Well, not quite yet," he admitted. "I just have one more thing to do. We won't be home until tomorrow."

Emma was quiet for a moment. "Where are you going to spend the night?"

"In a motel," he answered truthfully.

"Jack, why do you do these things?" she asked plaintively.

He sighed. "I don't know, Emma," he admitted. "I hate feeling helpless, that's part of it. But somehow I know if I don't keep going, that's when I'm going to die. And if I die, I guess I want to die in the saddle."

Emma's laugh wasn't merry.

"You're a cowboy now?"

"Emma, I'm a doer. You should know that about me by now. I don't like to give up."

She sighed. "Jesus, Jack! Just get home, okay? Do you have your medicine with you?"

"I do. So don't worry. I've got my pills to take with dinner. And the ones with breakfast. Pill, pills, Emma—I'm tired of them!"

"And you promise to be home tomorrow?"

"I promise. My word of honor," Jack told her. "Though it might be late," he added.

Very late, Jack was thinking. Though if he made it home to San Geronimo by midnight tomorrow, he would technically be in the limits of his promise.

He was confident he could manage that.

Chapter Ten

Howie crashed his phone on the pavement outside a 7/11 in Shiprock, New Mexico, where he had stopped to fill his gas tank and buy ice.

Sadly, it was a literal crash, not just a virtual one.

After filling his tank, he had gone inside the convenience store to buy a seven-pound bag of ice and three impulse items he knew the stronger part of him should resist: a hot dog slathered with mustard, a medium sized orange soda, and a bag of potato chips.

He was tired from a long drive and he was hungry. *I deserve junk food!* whispered a five-year-old version of himself.

The clerk had asked if he wanted a bag, but Howie said he could manage.

And he was fine. He had his groceries under control. But then, as he was thinking of taking a giant bite of the hot dog, his phone rang with an incoming call from Jack. The ring tone was the special one he had set for Jack, the opening bars of Beethoven's Ode to Joy.

Howie consolidated the hot dog, the potato chips, and the orange soda in his left hand, with the bag of ice tucked under his left arm. This left his right hand free to reach into the front pocket of his jeans for his phone. He was raising the phone to his ear when he became aware that the hot dog was slipping slowly from its bun.

Howie made a grab for the hot dog, but now the potato chips were slipping from his fingers as well. In the middle of trying to save his junk food, his expensive iPhone, the latest model, flew from his hand.

"Damn!" cried Howie, as he did a little dance to catch his phone. It was a juggling act. He caught the phone with a soccer kick as it fell toward his knee. This sent the device sailing once again upward, giving Howie a moment of hope.

All his efforts failed as gravity took its course. The ice, the hot dog, the potato chips, and the soda went flying as he made a final effort to pluck the phone from the air before it shattered on the pavement.

All the while, he kept hearing Jack's tiny voice on the speaker: "Howie? Is that you? Are you there?"

He almost caught the phone. It was close. But he couldn't quite get a grip.

The phone hit the pavement with a smack and lay in desolation on the ground beside the hot dog, the soda, chips, and the ice.

It was funny, he supposed. You had to see the humor in life's slapstick moments. But Howie didn't laugh.

His phone was his umbilical cord to the world and without it he felt lost. Naked, almost. Powerless. Vulnerable. He would need to buy a new phone tomorrow, probably in Farmington, the closest large town.

"Damn!" he said again, wondering what Jack had called about.

Whatever it was, Howie was temporarily on his own. He would have to wait to find out until tomorrow.

***

Shiprock was a sprawling town of nine thousand people on the Navajo reservation, located among the classic monumental shapes of Southwest Indian land, the oddly shaped mesas with steep vertical sides that rose hundreds of feet from the desert. Shiprock itself—the rock not the town—was a high desert pillar on which you could imagine a mad saint meditating, refusing to eat until the secrets of the universe were revealed to him. The Navajo considered this a holy place.

Howie had camping gear in the car, complete with a Coleman stove and an ice chest full of food. But it was late and he decided to spend the night in a motel—a small complex of wooden cabins on the edge of town that was run by an East Indian family.

By morning, Howie had come to a decision about his phone. Buying a new iPhone, he realized, would be a major project, not cheap, something that needed time and effort and research. It was like a marriage, to find the right phone and the right plan. The chemistry had to be there. You wanted to fall in love with your new phone on sight. It had to be the right color. You wanted everything to go smoothly, everything to work. You didn't want frustrations.

Most of all, though Howie hated to admit it, when it came to phones, he could use Buzzy's help. Meanwhile, he couldn't allow this mishap to take time and energy from the investigation that he was here to pursue.

The immediate answer was to buy a temporary burner, a cheapo dumb phone so he could make basic phone calls to Jack and Ruth and Buzzy at the office. Unfortunately, this proved to be more difficult than he thought. There was a General Dollar store near his motel, but after wandering around lost in the store for ten minutes, he was told they didn't sell phones. Howie tried a second store, a supermarket, but the person who sold phones at the front counter couldn't be found. She was on a break, apparently, and after waiting ten minutes, Howie gave up.

Hell with it! Howie said to himself. Sitting in his car outside the supermarket, Howie examined the map that Victor Moreland had given him to get to the home of Sun Walker, the native flute master who he hoped would be able to give him a better idea of the La Chaya tribe. Victor had told him the cabin was "about fifteen miles" outside of Shiprock. Which wasn't far.

Howie decided he would simply do without a phone for the morning. He would finish his business here, pay a visit to the flute master, see what information he could gather, and then drive to Farmington where there would be a Walmart and phones galore.

***

Victor's map was beautifully drawn. It even had a cherub with puffy cheeks in the top corner blowing what Victor described as "the fucking endless Navajo wind"—a wind that was forever there, whistling among the mesas, through the small towns, outside the windows of your car, an overwhelming presence.

The map led Howie out of town, past strip malls and empty lots onto a crumbling two-lane highway that had weeds growing up between the asphalt cracks. The pavement turned to dirt after several miles and continued deep into the open desert as far as the eye could see.

The land was monumental and strange, with vertical cliffs that rose hundreds of feet from the desert floor to the flat mesa tops overhead. It was the classic Indian land of old Hollywood movies, a wild sculpture garden of impossible shapes that covered many miles. Personally, Howie liked a bit of green forest and water. But he recognized the beauty of this harsh landscape where the Navajo lived. The Diné inhabited a magical world.

The road kept going into a narrowing V-shaped valley that was bordered by steep cliffs composed of different layers of red and orange and beige. Howie had passed a hogan soon after the road changed from asphalt to dirt, but that was the last sign of human habitation. He stopped to check his map several times to make sure he wasn't lost. It was hard to imagine anyone living out here in this huge emptiness.

The road began climbing from the desert floor, and, after several miles, Howie came around a curve and was surprised to see a small body of water that was nestled up against the side of a mesa. A pond, really, but it had a ring of green vegetation around it. At the far shore stood a small but attractive cabin built of dark wood with a deck coming out in front.

Howie parked by a white Chevy pickup truck that was at least twenty years old and a dusty motorcycle, a Harley Davidson with raised handlebars. The front door of the cabin was open but there was no sign of Sun Walker.

"Hello!" he called, standing uncertainly in the doorway. But there was no answer.

"Hello, Mr. Walker!" he called again. "Sun?"

From where Howie stood, he could see that the interior of the cabin consisted of a single rustic room. There was a kitchen nook, a narrow bed against the far wall, an old leather couch, several overstuffed armchairs, and a number of Navajo rugs, both on the floor and the walls. There was a close, musty old man's smell in the air. The smell seemed permanently saturated into the furniture.

Several wooden flutes of different sizes were hanging in a corner. Each of the flutes was decorated with dangling leather thongs, feathers and beads. On the floor were several hand drums and an expensive looking guitar propped up on a metal stand.

"Hello, Mr. Walker? I'm Howard Moon Deer," Howie called. "Victor Moreland gave me a map to your house . . . hello?"

There was still no answer and Howie wasn't sure what to do. He remained in the open doorway and didn't want to walk inside until he was invited. You had to be careful walking into a stranger's home in a place where everybody had a gun.

The flute player didn't show himself and eventually there was nothing for Howie to do but turn and leave. He was just stepping onto the outside deck when, in his peripheral vision, he sensed something—someone—rushing at him.

Howie saw his attacker for only an instant. It was a huge young Indian man with long black hair and broad shoulders. He was bare-chested. There was a rifle in his hand that he was holding by the barrel, like a club. The expression on his face was fierce and remorseless.

"AAIIEEEE!" the Indian cried, raising the rifle butt as he charged.

"Wait!" cried Howie, raising his hands to defend himself.

The rifle butt swung down hard on his left shoulder. Howie staggered backward through the door into the cabin, off balance.

The Indian was on him in an instant, kneeling on his stomach. Howie felt a large knife pressing against his throat.

"Whoa!" Howie managed. It came out more like a gurgle than a word.

"Who are you?" the Indian demanded.

"For chrissake, get off me! I'm Howard Moon Deer. I'm trying to find Sun Walker. Victor Moreland sent me."

Howie felt the knife move away from his throat, but the Indian kept him pinned to the floor.

"What do you want with Sun?"

"I want to ask him a few questions, that's all. Victor thought he could help me with something."

"Victor Moreland?"

"Right, the artist. Is this your idea of Diné hospitality, knocking people silly who show up at your door?"

"Depends on who it is who shows up. What kind of Indian are you, anyway?"

"Lakota," answered Howie. "Where's Sun?"

The young man didn't answer for a moment.

"He's dead," he said quietly, moving off Howie's chest.

Howie sat up. "I'm sorry to hear that," Howie told him. "Sun Walker was a great flute player. Now, who are you?"

"I'm Rain," said the Navajo. "Rain Walker. Sun was my father. What did you want with him?"

Howie wasn't sure how much he wanted to say. "I'm hoping to get some information about the La Chaya reservation. Like I said, Victor thought he might be able to help me."

"So, you're what? Some kind of busybody?"

"No, I'm not. But I think there's something wrong going on over there. I was driving across La Chaya land last weekend when a young Chinese woman stepped out in front of my car and died. She'd been shot. I'm trying to find out about her. I want to know who she was and why she was killed."

The Navajo gave Howie a hard look.

"You're a cop?"

"Do I look like a cop?"

"Not like any cop I've ever seen," Rain admitted. "What are you then? . . . no, no, don't tell me! I got it! You're a do-gooder anthropologist, come to study your native brethren! God, I fucking *hate* people like you!"

Howie smiled reluctantly. "I'm a private investigator with an agency in San Geronimo."

"Sure," said Rain. "A Lakota private eye."

"Well, I am," said Howie.

Rain paused and seemed to change his mind about Howie. After a moment, he offered him a hand up from the floor.

"I was about to make tea," he said. "Would you like English Breakfast or Lemon Zinger? That's all I got."

"Lemon Zinger will be fine," said Howie.

***

Howie had a better chance to study Rain Walker as they sat across from each other at a rough wooden table inside the cabin with mugs of tea.

Rain was 19 years old, he found out later, which was close to Howie's initial guess. He was remarkably handsome with strong features, a wide forehead, broad shoulders, and piercing brown eyes. His long black hair was parted in the middle and fell loose down his back and shoulders. He looked like an Indian from the cover of a romance novel, the sort with a bare chest and a blonde girl trembling in his arms. From head to toe, he was every inch the bodice-ripping noble savage. Which made him—from Howie's point of view—just slightly ridiculous.

"Do you always attack people first and ask questions later?" Howie asked.

"I've got reasons to be cautious," the boy answered, giving Howie one of his deep looks. With a shake of his head, he tossed his long hair free of his eyes. That was a gesture Howie came to see often with Rain. Sometimes he used his hand to swipe away his hair. It seemed like an affectation. Personally, Howie would have bought himself a rubber band to tie his hair back, but Rain obviously enjoyed tossing it around.

The boy leaned closer across the table, the steam from his mug rising into his face. Along with his good looks, he seemed to take himself quite seriously. He was prone to pronouncements.

"This is a dangerous place you've come to, Moon Deer," he said dramatically, lowering his voice. "There are people here you don't want paying you a visit. Nobody just stops by casually. There are country roads out here you want to stay away from."

Howie believed him. He'd had a sense driving here from Shiprock that he had entered a no-man's land where you could disappear without a trace.

"You said your father died. When did this happen?"

"Why do you care?"

"I was a fan. I was looking forward to meeting him."

"Okay, then, he was killed three months ago. I tried to warn him. I said, you're asking too many questions, you're getting into stuff you should stay away from. But he didn't listen."

"What stuff did he need to stay away from?"

"The fuckers killed him!"

"What fuckers?" Howie asked. He wasn't sure if Rain was deliberately not answering his questions, or whether he was simply unfocussed.

Rain took a moment to wipe the curtain of hair from his eyes. He gave Howie a sullen look.

"How did your father die?" Howie pressed.

"They threw him off a cliff, not a hundred yards from here."

"Who is they?"

"Look, I don't know specifically who did it," Rain admitted. "But I know where they came from. They were La Chaya. They were sent by the new people who have taken over there. They were worried that my dad was looking into their secrets."

"Why did your father care about the La Chaya tribe? I thought people out here minded their own business."

"My dad was born La Chaya. He still has relatives there. These are his people."

"But I always thought Sun Walker was Diné. That's how he was billed on his CD covers. A Navajo flute player."

"He left La Chaya when he was a kid. His mother married into the Diné, so he grew up Navajo. That's the culture he identified with most of his life. And it looked good on the cover of an album. Navajo. Nobody would have cared about a La Chaya flute player. But when he got old, he got interested in finding out more about his roots."

"So, tell me—what is going on at the La Chaya reservation?"

"First, you've got to know about the new people. About six years ago, a bunch of really bad Indians took over the tribal government. It wasn't hard for them to do. Most of the people there are sheep herders who live pretty far apart from one another. They weren't any match for the wolves when they showed up."

Howie took a sip of tea. Native tribes in North America were frequently the victims of crooks and scammers. The casino business, especially.

"What did the police say about your father's death? There was an investigation, I presume."

"Not much of one. Two FBI guys came by and sniffed around for a few days, but that was it. They don't really care when an Indian is killed. As far as they're concerned, we don't count."

"What was their conclusion?"

"Their *conclusion*? They made *that* before they even got here! They decided it was an accident. They said my father fell."

"Was there any evidence to suggest it *wasn't* an accident?"

"Look, Moon Deer, my dad lived on this land for forty years. He knew every inch of these cliffs. He was like a mountain goat. I can guarantee he didn't lose his footing and fall. He was picked up and thrown. His body was found nearly thirty feet from the base of the cliff. He wouldn't have landed that far out if he had slipped by accident."

Howie wasn't convinced, but he decided to move on.

"So, what's been going on at the La Chaya rez? What did your father find out?"

"You *are* some kind of cop, aren't you? You work for the BIA?"

"I definitely don't work for the Bureau of Indian Affairs," Howie said firmly. "I told you, I'm a P.I. in San Geronimo, at the Wilder & Associate Agency. My boss is an ex-cop from California—a big shot, actually. At least, he was once."

"And you're on a case?"

Howie decided he had nothing to lose by being truthful.

"We've been hired by an anti-human trafficking organization in Washington, D.C. They want to know about the Chinese woman, just like I do. They want to know if she was being trafficked. I've taken the case on a temporary basis. I said I'd find out as much about the woman as I could in a week."

"So, what happens in a week?"

"My daughter's coming for a visit from Scotland, and once she's here, I'm canceling all my cases."

"You have a daughter in Scotland? How old is she?"

"Seventeen."

"Seventeen?" Rain repeated thoughtfully. Howie didn't like the way he said it. He had a sudden premonition that it would be wise to make certain his daughter and Rain never met.

"Let's get back to the dead Chinese woman," Howie said. "Would you say it's possible that she had been trafficked?"

Rain laughed. "Was she *trafficked*? For chrissake, dude! Do bears shit in the woods?"

Howie sighed. "So, tell me about trafficking on the La Chaya reservation."

"Look, Moon Deer, you want to know about this, you need to see it for yourself. Okay?"

"Okay," Howie answered. "I'd like to see it. That's why I'm here. Are you offering to take me?"

"Sure, why not? But tell me this. Are you a warrior?" Rain asked unexpectedly.

"Excuse me?"

"Are you a warrior? If not, I'll tell you right now, I don't have any use for pussys!"

"I am not a pussy!" said Howie. "Though that's not a word I use, frankly. I know women who would lynch you for talking like that."

Rain laughed. He gave Howie a big grin, like he knew all about women and no more need to be said.

"Are you a warrior?" he asked for the third time.

"Rain, that's a bullshit question asked by a teenage kid who hasn't lived long enough to understand that everybody is on a path all their own. I'm a warrior in ways you wouldn't begin to understand."

"Do you have a gun?"

"As a matter of fact, I do," Howie told him. "I have a 9mm Glock in my car."

"Good. We'll go in your car. It's a ways. Meanwhile, you'd better get some sleep. We'll leave here at three."

"Three?" said Howie. "This afternoon?"

Rain laughed. "Morning, dude. It's the only way to do this. Believe me, we don't want to be out in that desert in the middle of the day!"

Chapter Eleven

Howie spent the night in his sleeping bag on the hard floor of the cabin. It wasn't a long night. It seemed he had just fallen asleep when he felt Rain's hand on his shoulder shaking him awake.

"Up and at 'em, dude. We need to get on the road."

"Coffee?" Howie managed, more of a croak than a word. His voice was as groggy as the rest of his body. He hadn't slept well.

"Yeah, sure. How about a cappuccino? Maybe a double latte?"

"A shot of espresso would be great, thanks." Howie was pleasantly surprised. He liked good coffee.

The kid laughed.

"What do you think this is, Moon Deer? Starbucks? All I got is instant. But I've made up a thermos. Now let's get going."

"Give me a minute," Howie said grumpily, sitting up in his sleeping bag. He was feeling every bit his 38 years and Rain's teenage health and energy was irritating.

The night was moonless with a billion stars blinking in the black canopy overhead. Howie drove with Rain giving directions from time to time from the passenger seat. His headlights barely penetrated the darkness. Three o'clock in the morning was a lonely, introspective time.

"Damn!" he said. "I forgot! I need to buy a new phone! My old one got smashed and I need to get in touch with my office. Is there a Best Buy or Walmart in one of the towns we'll be passing?"

Rain's laugh wasn't as sarcastic as when Howie had asked for an espresso, but almost. "Let's see, we just passed Two Elk, population 97. Forget it, Moon Deer. Who needs a phone anyway?"

"*I* do." Howie told him. "There are people I need to be in touch with."

"Oh, yeah, your *office*! Come on, dude. Phones are umbilical cords that tie you into the System."

"So how do you communicate? By smoke signal?"

"Moon Deer, I have a very old cell phone. Okay? But I'm not obsessed with it."

"Good. I'm not obsessed either. But I still need to stop at an electronics store. Or maybe a supermarket—sometimes they have them."

"All right, Gallup," Rain said after a moment. "I need to stop there, too. Maybe you can find some place open at this hour to buy your electronic nipple. Though I doubt it."

It's not my electronic nipple! he wanted to say. But he let it go. He wasn't going to prolong the argument.

They drove south from Shiprock on Highway 491 and reached Gallup just as the sky was beginning to lighten to a pale gray in the east. Rain directed him onto Route 66, the historic highway that was the main road through town.

"What do you need to do here?" Howie asked.

"I need to stop at my shop."

"Your shop?"

"You'll see," said Rain.

Gallup had been built by the railroads in the 19th century, and for most travelers it was a place you hurried past on Interstate 40. People called it the Heart of Indian Country because it was on the edge of the huge Navajo reservation, which also included the Zuni and Hopi tribes. Gallup was a town of motels, gas stations, and pawn shops with bars on the windows. If the surrounding land made you think of cowboys and Indians, wagon trains and gun fights, it was due in part to the fact that many classic Hollywood Westerns were filmed here.

"Pull over," Rain told him, indicating a small, dilapidated looking store that was nestled between a motel on one side and a 7/11 on the other. A hand-painted sign over the door said WALKING RAIN TRIBAL MUSIC. Several guitars were displayed in the front window, acoustic and electric, as well as a few amps, a mixing board, and a pared-down drum set. Most of the equipment looked used. The window was partially covered with flyers announcing performances at local coffee houses and bars, and musicians looking for drummers or vocalists to fill out their bands.

"This is your place?"

"Yep," said Rain. "Tribal music is my thing. Wait in the car, I'll only be a minute."

Howie watched as the kid used his key to open the front door. He imagined a local music store like this fulfilled a community need, a meeting place for local musicians, most of whom would never progress beyond the occasional Saturday night gig in a small town like Gallup. As the owner of such a store, Rain would be a celebrity.

He returned a few minutes later, locking the store behind him. He had a black guitar gig bag slung over one shoulder and two plastic gallon jugs of water, one in each hand. He put the guitar bag and water jugs in the back seat then got back into the front next to Howie.

"You're going to serenade the snakes?" Howie asked.

"You'll see, Moon Deer. Let's go."

Gallup was just starting to wake up as they drove toward I-40, but they didn't pass anything like a Best Buy or Walmart as they headed toward the ramp.

"I'm going to need to turn around, Rain," Howie told him. "I really need that phone."

"Oh, come on—there's no cell service out here. The reservation has a few landlines, not many, but the government did that. Otherwise there's nothing. Who are you going to talk to anyway? You can buy your phone when you're back in that stink hole you call 'civilization.' "

"Rain, we're not talking about civilization—"

"Plus, we're on a schedule here, Moon Deer. We need to be places at certain times or this isn't going to work. The light has to be right. If you know what I mean."

"I have no idea what you mean."

"And if I'd have known you were going to delay us by going off on some stupid shopping trip, I wouldn't have agreed to come!"

Howie sighed. "For chrissake, Rain, I'm not going off on a shopping trip! . . . well okay, I guess I can live without a phone for a few hours. Let's keep going."

Howie had let himself be persuaded because in truth, he felt a little guilty about his reliance on his phone. It was his Little Helper, he had to admit it. It wasn't just a telephone, it was his music, his camera, his address book, and more. It held his life together. But Rain was right. It wasn't good to be addicted to an electronic device.

He needed to talk to Jack but decided it could wait a few hours.

***

Howie drove east on I-40 for nearly half an hour until Rain told him to take the next exit. The sign on the interstate said CRIPPLE CANYON RD. NO SERVICES. That was an understatement. There was nothing here, not a gas station, not a house, nothing but land and sky and a few buzzards overhead looking for their next meal.

The exit took them on an underpass beneath the freeway then headed north on a two-lane highway that wound its way through a valley that was bordered by steep red cliffs.

"Are we on La Chaya land yet?"

"We are," Rain told him. "It began as soon as we got off the free-way."

"So why aren't there any signs saying where we are?"

"They like their privacy. They're not looking for visitors."

"So, who are these La Chaya people? Do they live under rocks?"

"Like I said, they're sheep herders. Most of them live like it's one thousand B.C.E. They sell their wool to the Diné because their weaving is primitive and doesn't measure up to ours."

Howie was impressed that Rain said B.C.E., Before the Common Era, rather than simply B.C. However, it seemed a little pretentious to add that final E in casual conversation.

"There was hardly any sort of town here until a few years ago," Rain added. "You'd think that would be Edenistic. And it was, I guess, until the bad guys stepped into the vacuum to take charge."

Edenistic? Howie smiled.

"So, what kind of government do they have?"

"They don't have Chapter Houses like the Diné. Theoretically, they have elections once a year to appoint a Governor, a Lieutenant Governor, and a War Chief. It's supposed to be a democracy. But the same guys always get elected, and if you complain, you'll come home one day to find your house burned down."

"So, who are these same guys?"

"Look, Moon Deer, these are basically Indians who got corrupted by outsiders with a lot of money. The outsiders had ideas of what they could do on an Indian reservation out in the middle of nowhere, and the insiders—the small clique who run things—suddenly had a lot of cash and power. Now shut up. We're getting close and we need to pay attention."

The road had begun snaking its way upward into a high plateau of dusty piñon and juniper. The sky was blue in the early morning but the sun still hadn't risen above the hills. They climbed for some time before coming to a craggy summit—8243 feet, according to the road sign—

from where they were able to look down into a narrow river valley below.

"What the hell is that?" Howie cried.

"What does it look like?"

Howie had to shield his eyes because the morning sun was in his eyes. What he saw in the canyon below didn't seem real.

"It looks like a half-finished casino that's been set down in the middle of nowhere," Howie said.

"I told you, you needed to see this for yourself. The casino was the first get-rich-quick idea the new tribal government dreamed up. This was five years ago. They got financing from a group of shady investors in Texas. The idea was this was going to be an exclusive resort for high rollers. But the Texas investment firm went bust after the CEO in Dallas was arrested for fraud and the construction came to a stop when they ran out of money. The unfinished buildings have just been sitting here for the last few years gathering dust."

"Couldn't they get financing someplace else?"

"Not these guys. They wouldn't know how to fill out an application form. Anyway, that's when the Chinese approached them with a new idea."

"The Chinese? Are they into gambling, too?"

"No, they're into something else. You'll see. Just be patient, Moon Deer.

The road descended into the river canyon on a steep switchback. The river itself was brown and sluggish, perhaps fifty feet across, with a dozen or so small houses on both banks.

The casino and unfinished hotel were on the far shore, still in the deep morning shadow of the canyon. The casino was a multi-story, free-form structure that was supposed to look like a modern version of an

Anasazi cliff dwelling with a façade of swirls and curls in poured concrete.

Next to it stood the concrete shell of what aspired to be a fancy three-story hotel with a big swimming pool out front. Further along the road, there was a gas station and an outsized travel shop. Large free-standing signs stood by the highway, some with computerized screens, but the screens were dark. The huge parking lot by the casino was empty. The swimming pool, strangely enough, was filled with water and there were deck chairs around the edges, but Howie couldn't see a single person anywhere.

"But it's crazy to build something like this in such an out-of-the-way place!" Howie said. "They must have known it would never make money."

"The dudes on the tribal government made money, Moon Deer. And that's all they cared about. I bet some of the investors cashed in as well. People at the top pay themselves a lot of money around a project like this that never gets done. Now keep driving, Moon Deer. This isn't the time for talk. I've told you, we've got to keep an eye out."

"For what?"

"The local cops. When you've seen what they're like, you don't want to meet them again. Now drive. Not too fast, keep to the speed limit."

The road crossed a bridge and came to the casino/hotel complex. There was a large billboard by the entrance, turquoise letters against a pale background:

EVERYONE IS A WINNER
AT
THE CASINO LA CHAYA!

But one edge of the billboard was torn and there were no winners in sight. As he drove closer, he saw that the door frames had no doors, and the windows were empty of glass.

"This is a very strange place!" Howie observed.

"Keep going." Rain looked tense. "We want to get past the casino without anyone seeing us."

"There are people here?"

"You can't be sure. Sometimes the cops bring girls to the hotel."

"With no doors?"

"These guys aren't picky. Now, keep going."

Howie drove past the casino and hotel at 35 mph. The emptiness of the unfinished gambling paradise was profound. The only part of the complex that looked finished was the gas station and convenience store on the north side of the hotel, but there was nobody there either. The road continued past the buildings and came out alongside a sluggish river for another half mile, where it came to another switchback that zig-zagged up the far side of the canyon."

"Here?"

"Yeah, yeah, . . . keep going?"

Howie noticed that Rain had gotten the black guitar bag from the back seat and was holding it tightly.

"What's in the guitar bag?"

"Insurance," said Rain.

Howie shook his head. "That better not be what I think it is!"

They came out of the shadow of the canyon onto a flat plateau that was ablaze with morning sun. Howie had to squint even with his dark glasses. The road continued in a straight line toward a range of brown mountains several miles away.

"There's a dirt track coming up on your left," Rain said after a few minutes. "Turn here."

Howie slowed nearly to a stop in order to find the road. It was hardly more than a wagon track.

"I'm not going to get stuck here, am I?" Howie asked. "I don't want to wreck my car."

"Come on, Moon Deer, it's just an old Subaru!"

"It's paid for," said Howie. "And it's mine."

Howie felt defensive about his car. The Outback was bruised and battered, but it had all-wheel drive and it had been reliable transportation for more years than he wanted to count. Howie liked friendly old things. Unfortunately, it didn't have great clearance from the ground.

The wagon track was torturous going, but at least it was dry. Howie proceeded in first gear at five miles an hour up and down the terrain. There was a gully he wasn't sure he could cross, but he managed by driving with his right wheel high up on the bank.

He continued slowly for at least fifteen minutes. Peering forward through the windshield, it seemed like an hour.

"Okay, stop here," Rain said at last.

"What do you mean, stop here?" said Howie. "There's *nothing* here!"

"That's the point. This is where we get out and walk."

There was no place to pull over. Howie stopped in the middle of the track and turned off the engine.

"I can't just leave my car here."

"Sure, you can," Rain told him. "There's nobody around but the rattlesnakes. You have a day pack?"

"Yeah."

"Then empty it out. All we're going to take is water and weapons."

They got out of the car and each took one of the gallon jugs of water to put into their packs. Howie found his Glock in the glove compartment and slipped it into his pack next to the jug. Rain opened the guitar bag, pulled out an AR-15 assault rifle, and hung it by its strap across his brawny chest.

Howie shook his head. "Are these guns really necessary?" he asked.

"You bet," said Rain. He looked happy. He looked alert and fully alive. He reminded Howie of his cat, Orange, as she set off to hunt for birds and rabbits.

Howie was increasingly skeptical about this entire adventure. But it was too late to turn around now.

Chapter Twelve

It had been some time since Jack had been in a plane and he wasn't a happy passenger. He didn't like putting his life in the hands of people he didn't trust. He gripped his arm rest every time the engine changed pitch. When they hit a patch of rough air over the Grand Canyon, he groaned audibly, certain the wings were about to fall off.

"You're scared of flying?" Buzzy asked. He found this funny. The three of them were sharing a row near the rear of the plane: Buzzy on the aisle, Katya on the middle seat, and Jack by the window.

"I am *not* scared of flying!" Jack lied. "Airplanes are perfectly reliable. It's the human element that worries me. For all I know, the captain is partying in the cockpit with a stewardess on his lap!"

"They don't call them stewardesses anymore, Jack. They're flight attendants. Gender neutral and sexless."

Jack shook his head. He didn't mind gender neutral. He didn't even mind sexless. He was too old for that nonsense. But he missed life as he had once known it, the old days—the luxurious feeling of flying without any need to take off your shoes in the airport. He missed the NO SMOKING sign that turned off overhead as you rose into the air, and the pretty young women who came by with a smile to offer you a cocktail.

He knew he was old-fashioned, but frankly he hadn't been won over by the new world.

They were on the second to the last flight out of Albuquerque to San Francisco, which had left the gate at 10:25 PM and would arrive in California at 12:13 AM. It wasn't a great time to arrive in a major American city, but it was the only flight they could get at the last minute.

From the airport, they took an Uber car to the Manor Motel on Lombard Street where Buzzy had booked two rooms. The motel was in the

Marina district, centrally located, but the rate Jack remembered—$36 a night—was a thing of the past.

"Sure, Jack," said Buzzy, as he had fiddled with his phone to make the reservation. "How about $156 a night plus a hundred-dollar pet deposit for Katya. When were you there last? The Stone Age?"

Jack sighed. Had it really been that long ago? Probably it was. He realized that this jaunt to California was going to be pricey, but a motel couldn't be avoided. Two rooms were necessary since he had no intention of sharing a room with Buzzy, and he knew he was going to need to sleep before confronting Audrey at the restaurant that evening.

Jack's room overlooked Lombard Street, which was one of the city's main corridors onto the Golden Gate Bridge, so it was busy with traffic all night long. He lay in bed with the window open, inhaling the scent of the city—damp sea air, so different from New Mexico. He listened to the late night city sounds, music from car stereos, voices, laughter, trucks changing gears, often sirens going by. He had spent his childhood only a short distance from here. This was the city where he had risen from patrolman to the rank of commander in one of the great police departments of the nation.

He barely slept, his mind turning with old memories—Galileo High School, the girl he lost his virginity with Junior year, his youth, his career, meeting Emma when they were both still in their twenties, time that had somehow fled away . . .

He slept for perhaps an hour close to dawn, but woke well before seven, not at all tired, full of energy. The first thing he needed to do was phone Emma and let her know where he was. This wasn't going to be easy, but it had to be done. It was an hour later in New Mexico and Emma was an early riser. She would be up. He would assure her that he would do his best to be home in San Geronimo when he had promised, today before midnight.

Luckily, the gods were with him. Emma didn't answer so he was able to leave a message on her voicemail, which was considerably easier than speaking to her in person. Most likely, she was in the shower.

"Hi, it's me," he said. He took a deep breath and continued. "Look, I've had to make a quick trip to San Francisco—it's the case I'm working on. But I'm fine so you shouldn't worry about me. I'm with Buzzy and Katya, I have my pills, I've just spent the night at a motel, I'm taking care of myself. I only have one thing I need to do and then I'll be home. There's a young Chinese woman I need to interview and that's it. I'll be taking taxis everywhere I go. I'll get a good nap this afternoon— really, this isn't going to be any more tiring than if I was in bed at home. I wouldn't be doing this, Emma, except it concerns human trafficking and you know how I feel about that. I'm planning to be home by tomorrow at the latest. As long as there aren't any unexpected delays," he added cautiously.

Jack believed he was striking the right tone. Emma had always been a great one for civil rights and justice of every kind, and she hated human trafficking as much as he did. She would understand. Hopefully.

"Love you," he said and disconnected with a sigh of relief. Now that the hard part of the day was over, he needed to take Katya out and he thought he might combine this with breakfast at a corner coffee shop he knew on Chestnut, just one street over.

"Come on, girl!" he said, putting Katya in her harness.

He wasn't going to be foolish. He took his white cane, which he rarely used in San Geronimo, and with the cane in his left hand and Katya's harness in his right, he headed out the door, turned left on Lombard, and left again toward Chestnut.

Along the way, he stopped to let Katya use the gutter. He was particular not to let her take a poop on the sidewalk.

Nevertheless, this wasn't the new proper.

"Aren't you going to clean up after your dog?" a woman cried at him.

"I . . . I'm . . ." Jack didn't really know what to say. He hadn't brought along a doggie bag and glove. In San Geronimo, with his backyard and both Howie and Buzzy taking Katya for long walks, it wasn't something he ever thought about.

He waved his blind man's cane helplessly as the woman huffed and puffed about him breaking the law, but in the end, she let it be. Jack was mortified. "Come on," he said to Katya. "Let's get the hell out of here!"

But there was no coffee shop on Chestnut where he remembered it, and now he truly was lost. If it hadn't been for the kindness of strangers, and the fact that Katya was an unusually well-trained guide dog, he would have been in trouble. A stranger—another woman, this one more kindly—led him to a bistro where he had an absurdly expensive cappuccino and a croissant. It was a good thing he had a credit card with him.

By the time Katya got them back to the motel, retracing the route, Buzzy was in a stew, worrying about where he was.

"You didn't answer your phone, Jack!"

"Relax, Buzzy, I'm capable of getting around in a city I know by heart," Jack told him. "I heard my phone ring, but I had the cane in one hand, and Katya in the other. When I'm busy, I don't answer. I don't live my life at the beck and call of my telephone!"

"Well, don't wander off again," Buzzy said sullenly. "Emma would be really pissed if I lost you! And I'm not prepared for that."

"Yeah, yeah . . ." Jack suddenly felt exhausted. The adventure of getting back and forth to Chestnut Street had taken everything out of him, and he told Buzzy he needed to go to his room and lie down.

Jack slept for nearly three hours, and when he awoke it was late morning and he felt better. He decided to call his former right hand, Charlie—now Commander Charles Lee, who had replaced him in his old job at the SFPD. Charlie had been his protege for many years, first as a young detective, then later as a lieutenant, then captain of a precinct. It would be good to talk and catch up and see what Charlie might know about the Chinese gangs. Jack imagined lunch together at Tommy's Joynt on Geary, where they'd had lunched many times in the past. Tommy's was an old-fashioned San Francisco place that had prime rib cut from the bone, huge portions for cops.

Jack phoned the number he had for Charlie, but it had been disconnected.

Next he tried the switchboard at the police headquarters on Third Street, only to be told that Charlie had retired four years ago and they couldn't give out further personal information.

Jack took a few moments to absorb this. Another old cop friend gone. He sat with a hollow feeling and a sense of being truly old.

"Well, look at us, Katya!" he said roughly, fluffing up her ears. "We're still here, aren't we? Old-timers still chasing down the bad guys! Right, Katya?"

Katya was unable to answer, but she thumped her tail with a modest show of enthusiasm. That's what he liked about Katya. Come hell or high water, she was on his side.

***

Buzzy was relieved to find that Jack hadn't been mugged, run over, or lost. He had already received two calls from Emma—a fact he kept to himself—and when Jack went to his room to lie down, he phoned Emma again to let her know that her wandering husband had returned safely to the motel.

"There are three things you need to do," Emma told Buzzy firmly. "Make sure he takes his pills every four hours. You got that?"

"Yes," said Buzzy. "The second?"

"Don't let him walk too far. Take taxis wherever you go. And make sure he has a good long nap this afternoon. That's the third. Last, get him home tomorrow."

"That's four things. But I'll try," said Buzzy. "He's a little stubborn, as maybe you know."

"Not as stubborn as I am!" she told him. "And don't let him know we've been talking. It'll only make everything worse."

Jack looked in better shape after his three-hour sleep when they met in the motel lobby in the early afternoon. There was time to kill before they could meet Audrey Chang at the restaurant so Jack suggested a nostalgic tour of the city to revisit the haunts of his youth. This appealed to Buzzy about as much as getting run over by a cable car.

"Why don't we just hang at the motel and chill," he suggested in return.

"For chrissake, you kids today! All you want to do is lounge around and stare into your phones! We're only in San Francisco a few days so let's get out and enjoy it!"

"We're here for *one* day, not a few days, Jack," Buzzy said. "I'm going to see about getting us seats tonight on the last flight to Albuquerque. We can do the Audrey babe and get to the airport in time to make it home."

"We're not going to *do* the Audrey babe, as you put it. And as our timeline goes, we're going to keep our options open. Now book us a car for the afternoon. We're going to be tourists."

Buzzy groaned. "Jack, being a tourist is maybe the most uncool thing ever!"

"Just get a damn car!" said Jack. "I'm going to teach you something this afternoon, an important piece of cultural American history. San Francisco in the 1950s. Miles Davis at the Black Hawk . . . Ferlinghetti at City Lights . . . the Kingston Trio, folk music everywhere. No hippies yet, thank God, but beatniks in North Beach everywhere you looked!"

"You were a cop, not a beatnik," Buzzy reminded him. "Beatniks probably hated you."

"I was an enlightened cop," Jack told him. "I went to the opera."

"Because Emma made you."

Jack couldn't honestly refute the charge, so he kept quiet as he listened to Buzzy tapping on his device, reserving a car for the rest of the day and possibly for the evening. Buzzy planned to follow Emma's instructions to the letter. Above all, he wanted to avoid the spectacle of Jack dropping dead on the sidewalk.

Their first stop on Jack's grand nostalgic tour was the Caffè Trieste on the corner of Vallejo and Grant in North Beach. Jack assured him that the Trieste was ground zero for all things avant-garde, once upon a time in his youth.

"Everyone was here then," he said. "You'd walk in for a coffee and see Alan Watts, Ginsburg, Gregory Corso, Ferlinghetti, Richard Brautigan, Rexroth, the whole lot! And the girls!" Jack waxed. "Those beatnik girls in black tights were something to see!"

Buzzy wasn't impressed. Beatnik girls, as he imagined them, didn't excite him. Long black hair, bangs, huge earrings, sitting next to guys playing bongos—it wasn't his thing. The Caffè Trieste occupied a small corner storefront and there were only a few tables and a counter. The room was saturated with the aroma of coffee beans so thick in the air it was overwhelming. The only customers today were a clean-cut family with two kids who looked like they had blown in from Kansas.

Buzzy left Jack and Katya at a table and went to the counter to get Jack a double espresso and a chocolate biscotti and a latte for himself. He lowered his voice and told the barista—an attractive young Italian girl—to make Jack's espresso decaf.

"Hmm," said Jack thoughtfully as he took his first sip of his coffee. "Okay, but not as good as the old days."

"Nothing is as good as the old days," Buzzy reminded him.

Jack took another sip. "It just doesn't have the bite it used to have."

"Given time, everything falls apart," said Buzzy. "It's the Second Law of Thermodynamics."

"You know, I met Emma only a few blocks from here. 1972, I think it was," Jack said wistfully. "She had a top floor apartment in an old Victorian on Green Street and the apartment across the hall from her was burglarized. I was there making out a report, the usual procedure, and I knocked on her door to ask if she had heard or seen anything. I was just a newbie inspector in those days and I doubt if I cut much of a figure. When Emma opened the door, I could hardly get a word out, she was that lovely. There was something about her that knocked my socks off . . . something about her," he repeated.

Buzzy was only half-listening. He had just noticed a man in a dark blue windbreaker and jeans walk past the large plate-glass window that looked out onto Vallejo Street. There was nothing remarkable about this in itself. He was in his mid-thirties with short reddish-blond hair and a plain face. He didn't stand out in any way. But Buzzy had noticed him earlier on Lombard Street outside the motel as he was helping Jack into an Uber car to take them to North Beach. Buzzy watched the man jaywalk across Grant Street and enter a Kiehl's outlet on the other side. It seemed odd to see the same person twice in different parts of a large city.

". . . she was very bohemian back then," Jack was saying. "Not a hippie—she was a lot classier than that. Well-educated, well-read. Her apartment had sunlight pouring in the windows, Mozart on the phonograph, plants in clay pots, posters on the walls for dance recitals. She had just spent a year in England and she called her apartment a flat! Naturally, I was only a cop in her eyes, an oaf. I knew that. But I wasn't an idiot, and, in fact, I was able to identify the symphony she had on her turntable.

" 'Ah-ha, Mozart number forty, the G minor!' I said, hoping to impress her. 'The second movement really knocks me out.' "

" 'Knocks you out how?' she asked, giving me a skeptical look. I guess I got a little raffish at that point. 'Like a bullet to the heart,' I told her, looking her straight in the eye so she would know what she was doing to me . . ."

Across the street, the man in the blue windbreaker came out of Kiehl's with a small shopping bag in his hand. Kielh's sold expensive body lotions and stuff that Buzzy found ridiculously self-indulgent. He'd had a girlfriend briefly at Stanford who had used it. Before he was kicked out.

He watched as the man jaywalked boldly back across Grant to the Caffè Trieste, bypassing moving cars like a bullfighter. He passed by the big plate-glass window and kept going down Vallejo until he was out of sight. He wore aviator sunglasses so Buzzy couldn't see his eyes, but he was almost certain the man had glanced through the window as he had walked by to see him at the inside table with Jack and Katya. It left Buzzy with an uneasy feeling.

Jack meanwhile was still in memory land.

"Of course, I was there about the burglary so I had to ask questions about the old man across the hall, and if she had seen or heard anything. I was taking notes like this was going to be all part of my report, but I was just trying to stay as long as I could, hoping I could think of a way of asking her out. I tell you, that was the most well-researched burglary report ever written for the San Francisco Police Department!

"So naturally in the next few days, I had to return and interview her several times to make sure I got everything right. Well, Emma was never a dummy, not then, not now—she knew what I was up to. But I guess I fascinated her a little, too. I was a plainclothes cop and I knew a very different side of the city than she did. I showed it to her eventually, the joints where the hoods hung out. Emma was fascinated. I think it was a relief to her, after the very polite world of well-educated people she had grown up in. I even introduced her once to a Mafia don . . . hey, let's finish our coffee! We're just a few blocks from City Lights Bookstore. We can walk. Emma and I used to spend hours there . . ."

Buzzy didn't mind going down memory lane with Jack. He simply tuned him out. At his insistence, they didn't walk. They rode to City Lights in the Uber car he had booked. Buzzy had been to City Lights before and he liked the place. It was counterculture, and though this wasn't his bag—he was an anarchist, which was different—you could find a lot of pretty young women in the aisles, usually with a novel by Jean-Paul Sartre in their hands, and there was nothing wrong with that. Buzzy liked pretty young women who were going through a bout of existentialism.

But that's when he saw the same man with reddish-blond hair in the blue windbreaker browsing the shelves in the Religion section, and he knew it couldn't be a coincidence. The man was in the Christianity section and was pretending to be absorbed.

He didn't want to say anything to Jack, hoping to keep his blood pressure down. Emma had told him explicitly, no excitement. But somehow he and Jack had drawn unwanted attention.

They were being shadowed.

Chapter Thirteen

At 11 o'clock Wednesday morning, the day was already a scorcher on the La Chaya reservation in northern New Mexico. In mid-summer, mid-day, the desert was brutal.

Howie and Rain Walker walked in single file along a rough footpath that climbed up and down through the mesas and arroyos. Goat path was a better description of it. It was hard country with some scruffy brush but no real shade.

Rain was a dozen paces ahead with his AR-15 hanging across his back. Howie followed with a gallon jug of water and his Glock riding heavily in his daypack. The weight pulled on his shoulders. And his conscience. He knew he would need to tell Claire about this at some point in the future, and she wouldn't approve.

Howie had a San Francisco 49ers cap to give him some protection from the sun. Jack, who was a huge 49er fan, had given him the cap years ago. Every hour or so, they stopped in the shade of a boulder or a red sandstone cliff to have a drink of water. At one point they came across a rattlesnake that was sunning itself in the middle of the path. They gave it a wide miss.

They walked for several hours without a word spoken between them. At last, after climbing a steep grade to the top of a mesa, they reached a place where they could look down into a canyon a thousand feet below. Rain sank onto his knees and gestured for Howie to come up alongside him and do the same.

The canyon was broad, at least a mile across before another red rock mesa rose abruptly on the far side. A fast-moving river snaked its way along the canyon floor. Howie was surprised to see water in this parched land. The river was barely a dozen feet wide, but even at this distance, he could hear the rush of water over shallow river rocks.

That wasn't the only surprise.

On the far side of the river, on a wide plateau, there was a large metal building, rectangular, reflecting the sun. It was half the size of a football field, oddly out of place in this empty land. On the north side of the structure, maybe a hundred yards away, there were four neat rows of white tents, twenty tents in all. Beyond that, half a mile up the valley, Howie could see the reflection of sun against something shiny and man-made. It appeared to be a large greenhouse, but he wasn't sure. A dirt road came down from the upper canyon to the complex of buildings and tents.

"What the hell is down there?"

"It's a hemp operation run by slave labor," Rain told him. "That's what my dad said, at least. My guess is they probably grow the real kind of cannabis as well."

"The tribe is running this?"

"They *think* they're running it, but they're not. It's the Chinese. They're the ones with the money. There're only a few of them, but they're the boss."

"What's in the big metal warehouse?"

Rain shook his head. "Don't know. Probably it's where they keep equipment, and dry and store the hemp before they move it."

"How did you find this place?" Howie asked.

"My dad brought me here. He wanted me to see it. He found it. Like I said, he was curious about what was going on here. He thought there was more to it than hemp. He was still investigating when the fuckers killed him."

Howie also thought there must be more to it. There had to be. He couldn't imagine there would be enough money in hemp to make this outlandish encampment profitable. Of course, financially speaking, it would be a plus to have slave labor, like the White Man and the cotton fields of the Old South. Saves on the overhead, no unions to worry about. But why put a hemp farm all the way out here in this remote canyon? It didn't make sense.

"Take a look," Rain said, passing him a small pair of field binoculars that he pulled from his daypack.

Howie raised the binoculars and fiddled with the focus. The metal building came into view, but it was windowless, and he still couldn't make out anything about it.

"That's odd," Howie said. "There's an old VW camper parked in front of the building."

"What's odd about that?"

"It's like the campers the hippies liked in the Sixties."

"They're back in style again, Moon Deer. If you put in a new engine and do some work on the interior, you can get a lot of money for them."

"I know. But it seems out of place down in this canyon."

Howie scanned slightly to the right and a second van came into view, half hidden in the shadows at the side of the building. This was a more modern vehicle, light gray, no windows in the rear. He was too far away to see the make, but it looked heavy duty, like it could carry a serious load. Two men were standing near the van with their backs to Howie. He tried to sharpen the focus, but he couldn't make out anything about them.

He kept scanning northward past the rows of white tents until he came to a tower about ten feet high with a small wooden shack on top. The shack had open windows on all sides. It was a guard tower. As Howie looked more closely, he could see the dark shape of a man inside. Instinctively, he lowered himself closer to the ground.

"Jesus! This is a prison camp!"

"Yep. If you keep scanning, you'll see there are four guard towers, one at each corner of the complex."

"But where are the prisoners?"

"Working up in the greenhouses, I suppose. Most likely, they won't be brought back to the tents until tonight."

"Most likely?"

"I've never been down there, Moon Deer. So I don't know."

"Did your dad hike down into the canyon?"

Rain shook his head. "Nope. He was too old for a climb like that. But that's why he brought me here, to this spot we're sitting now. He wanted me to go down and investigate."

"So why haven't you done it yet?"

"I've been waiting for the right time," Rain replied. "I didn't want to do it alone."

"No kidding? A hot shot like you?"

"Look, Moon Deer, whatever we find out, we're going to need to document it. I need a reliable witness."

"Glad to know I'm reliable!"

Howie moved the lenses slowly along the riverbank until he came to what appeared to be two large generators, each housed in yellow trailers on wheels that must have been pulled in here by trucks. A vintage gasoline tanker with a rusty frame stood abandoned nearby.

Generators of this size would eat up a lot of gasoline, Howie imagined. A web of thick black electric lines came from the generators and passed over a few hundred feet of open land to the metal building. The generators were silent and, except for the two men standing by the van, the complex was like a ghost town.

"We'll wait until night," Rain said. "I know a way to get down there. My dad pointed it out to me, though he couldn't manage it himself. It's a butte that descends almost like stairs."

Howie doubted if it would be as simple as walking down stairs. These were vertical cliff walls where you didn't want to get too close to the edge. He looked at his watch.

"Night is seven or eight hours away. Are we just going to hang out in the open until then?"

"Nope," said Rain. "I know a cave that's a few miles away. We'll hang there."

"A cave?"

"Hey, Indian!—my ancestors lived in caves! The best spots were a hundred feet up the side of a cliff with a shelf where you could build a few dwellings. Pull up the ladder at night, and nobody can get you."

"So, this is where the dead Chinese lady came from?" Howie pondered.

"Wouldn't you say?" Rain answered.

Howie would say. He didn't understand what was going on here, but whatever it was, he sensed he was at Ground Zero of something really bad.

"So, look, Moon Deer, you don't have to do this, you know," Rain told him. In a condescending manor, Howie thought. "It's going to be dangerous. I can take you back to the car if you like. I'll come back later and go down on my own. If you're scared, you wouldn't be much help."

Howie kept scanning until he was back to the mysterious metal building. What was going on in there? he wondered. He was seriously curious.

"No, I'm coming. But listen, Rain. We're going to make sure no one sees us. We're not looking for a confrontation, okay? We're looking to be invisible. We're not going down there to get into a fight."

Rain laughed, throwing his head back to get his hair out of his eyes.

"You've got me all wrong, Moon Deer. I'm a peaceful guy! I used to have a peace sticker on my car!"

Howie didn't feel assured, but he decided he would take the chance. If this was a slave camp run by traffickers, it needed to be stopped. This wasn't something you could turn your back on. It was what he had been paid to investigate. He had to know for sure.

Chapter Fourteen

The fog was rolling in from the Pacific, ghostly against the colored lights of the store fronts, as Jack, Buzzy, and Katya arrived at the Emerald Buddha on Tuesday night. Jack felt the bone-chilling damp of the ocean that was only a few blocks away. There was something melancholy about fog at night in a coastal city. In the distance, Jack heard the deep moan of fog horns guiding shipping in and out of the Golden Gate.

Buzzy had made a reservation for 9 o'clock. The restaurant closed at 10, so this was a good time for a late dinner with a chance afterwards to meet the night manager.

A svelte young Chinese woman in a tight-fitting gold satin dress met them at the podium. She was doll-like—a very pretty doll, Buzzy thought—with red lipstick, black hair, and a smooth, pale complexion.

"I made a reservation," Buzzy told her, deepening his voice a little. "Wilder, party of two."

If Buzzy was flirting, it was so subtle, you'd need a Geiger counter to know it was happening.

The young woman smiled. "Won't you come this way?"

She led the way along a red carpet into the dining room. The Emerald Buddha was a large restaurant with a high ceiling and at least a hundred tables. There were fish tanks along the walls with future meals swimming around for customers to inspect. Red lanterns with tassels were hung from the ceiling and there were Chinese prints on the walls—misty mountains, the Great Wall on a wintry day. But beyond that, there was little attempt to create atmosphere. It was an industrial sort of restaurant, brightly lit, where you could probably feed five hundred customers at a single sitting. Buzzy imagined there would be banquet rooms down one of the hallways.

The dining room was only half-full this time of night, but Buzzy could see that this was a restaurant that did a good business. At least half the customers were gringos, as Buzzy called non-orientals like himself who were out for a night of culinary tourism. But there were also many tables of local looking Chinese families. At this end of Geary Boulevard, they were far from the tourist traps of Chinatown, and the inclusion of locals was an indication that the food was good.

"I think that's our girl," Buzzy said after the hostess had seated them and left menus. "Audrey Chang."

"Did she have a name tag?" Jack asked.

"She didn't need one. She looks like a younger version of Christine . . . only prettier," he added cautiously.

"Well, don't think about asking her out on a date," Jack said grumpily. "That's not why we're here."

"Jack, my generation doesn't date. We hang-out."

"Right. You're real romantics. Just hang-out later, please, on your own time. Now, what's on the menu?"

"There's a great deal on the menu. It's seven or eight pages long. But I'm sure they'll have your usual Chicken Kung Pao."

"What about duck with those pancakes?"

"I bet they'll have that, too, Jack. Would you like me to order it for you?"

"No, I'm feeling experimental. Read me the menu, Buzzy."

"You're kidding? All of it? There are probably two hundred items!"

"Good, I like choice. And I want to hear about them all. Look, Buzzy, we're not here to eat and run. We need to stretch this meal so we're still here after closing time. In fact, I'm aiming to be the last customers in the joint. I hope you're hungry."

***

"What a relief, *real* Chinese food!" Jack exclaimed from time to time as the multiple courses came and went.

New Mexico was the land of the burrito and green and red chile. But Chinese restaurants, forget it. You needed to be in San Francisco, L.A., or New York. Jack was in foodie heaven.

They began with the appetizer plate: wontons, pot stickers, egg rolls, some shrimp thing, minced pork in a sauce, spareribs, and something that might have been a vegetable, but not even Jack could identify it. They continued slowly, ordering one course at a time.

A fish soup followed the appetizer plate. Buzzy gave this one a miss. It consisted of an entire fish floating in broth. The head was attached with large staring eyeballs. Jack didn't seem to mind. He didn't have to look at it. He slurped the broth and proclaimed that it was "sublime."

After the soup, they had shredded garlic pork, an interesting eggplant dish, shrimp in a spicy sauce, green beans that were even spicier, sizzling beef, scallops, basil chicken, and yes, Chicken Kung Pao.

Jack had a single beer, a bottle of Tsing Tao. Buzzy had tea. He found alcohol boring. The feast tonight was overkill, more than they could possibly eat. Jack gave it a good try, his chop sticks working like greedy robotic fingers, but not even he could make much of a dent in it. There was so much food, Buzzy was able to slip the sizzling beef course to Katya under the table.

Jack was enjoying himself so much, he had a second beer.

As they ate, course after course, the dining room emptied out. At last, there were three tables left with customers, and finally, by 10:30, only themselves. The restaurant staff was beginning to give them the evil eye. Their waiter had dropped off their bill twenty minutes ago.

Jack belched as he took out his American Express card and put it on the table. The waiter, a lanky Chinese man with a stoop, appeared magically. But Jack kept his hand covering the credit card and plastic tray and wouldn't let him take it.

"Would you tell Miss Audrey Chang that I would like to have a word with her," he told the waiter. "You can say I'm a friend of her sister Christine."

"Ah, Miss Chang is in her office, she is very busy this time of night. She does not see customers. I am very sorry. But I can bring Miss Liang. She is dining room boss."

"No, it's Audrey I need. Please tell her it's important."

The waiter disappeared with a scowl on his face. It was late and Jack had still refused to let him take the credit card.

***

A woman they hadn't seen before came to their table a few minutes later and said that if they would follow her, Miss Chang would see them in her office.

"Why don't I take your credit card while I'm at it," she said with a smile. She was an attractive middle-aged Chinese woman dressed casually in slacks and a fitted shirt. She looked as though she belonged to the business side of the operation.

Audrey Chang's office was a crowded windowless room past the restrooms at the end of a long corridor. She was seated in front of a computer screen at a desk that was piled with papers. Buzzy was happy to see that, as he had suspected, Audrey was the pretty hostess who had seated them when they had first arrived. She had changed out of her slinky satin dress and was now in jeans and a white blouse.

Buzzy guided Jack to a chair facing the desk and he found a spot for himself by moving a stack of menus from a second chair.

"I know why you're here, Mr. Wilder," she said without introductions. "My sister phoned from Albuquerque and said you'd probably be coming. She told me to look out for a blind man, a guide dog, and a geeky kid—you would be easy to spot."

"Now, wait a minute!" said Buzzy.

"Did you enjoy dinner?" Audrey asked Jack, ignoring Buzzy's objection.

"We did," said Jack. "We don't have good Chinese food like this in New Mexico. Now, Audrey, since you know why we're here, let's get to the point. This is about a terrible thing that happened. My assistant was driving through an empty part of our state when a Chinese-speaking woman stepped out in front of his car and died. She'd been shot. We're trying to discover who she was and how she got out there in the middle of nowhere. Of course, we suspect she'd been trafficked. Christine said you might be able to help us."

Audrey shook her head angrily. "Excuse me, my sister told you not to contact me, that I wouldn't tell you a thing. But she didn't trust you. She wanted me to know that you might show up anyway."

"Audrey, I understand how dangerous these Tong gangs can be," Jack told her. "I'm sure a restaurant like yours couldn't stay in business if you got on their wrong side. Look, you're an artist, aren't you? Christine said you're studying at the San Francisco Art Institute, is that right?"

"Yes, I'm studying art," she said reluctantly. "I don't know if I'll ever make a living at it. Chris and I both feel the same way about restaurant work. When we were little, we swore we'd get out of it when we grew up. If I never see a wonton again it won't be too soon!"

Jack nodded sympathetically. "At one time I knew a lot of people over at the Art Institute. Teachers, students, many of them were very talented. Are you studying painting? Sculpture? What?"

"We don't have hard divisions like that anymore, Mr. Wilder. All the disciplines are interrelated. My own style . . . well, I'm still searching for it. But you don't have to soft talk me and pretend you're interested in art. I know what you're after, and I'm not going to tell you anything. I can't. First, because I don't know anything. And second, because even if I did know something, I wouldn't put my family at risk."

"Audrey—"

"But listen. I'm sick of seeing my dad pay off these gangsters every month. I don't like them and I'm willing to give you a name. Someone who might give you the information you're after."

Jack had been expecting an extensive argument, so this was a surprise. He sat back and nodded. "Okay. Who?"

"It's a second cousin of mine. He's married to the daughter of one of the Red Gecko Grand Dragons, which makes him almost untouchable. He's not in the gangs himself. He's a doctor at Stanford, a very idealistic person. But because of his marriage he hears things."

"And you'll give me his name?"

"Yes, but you must be careful. Don't go anywhere near his home. They'll be watching his wife. It's better to find him at work. He does the nightshift in ER."

"At Stanford University Hospital?"

"Yes."

"Hey, I went to Stanford for a while," Buzzy volunteered.

He waited for Jack to say the line, until he got kicked out. But this time Jack's thoughts seemed elsewhere and he let it go.

"All right," Jack said to Audrey. "Thank you very much."

Chapter Fifteen

Buzzy, Jack, and Katya spent another night at the Manor Motel and on Wednesday morning, they set out to find Dr. Thomas Yi, Audrey's second cousin who was married to the daughter of a Tong big wig.

Besides being an ER doctor at Stanford, Dr. Yi, according to Audrey, had also published slim books of poetry that had received prestigious awards. He appeared to be a Renaissance man who devoted himself selflessly to community needs. Maybe he was trying to make up for the sins of his wife's father, the Chinese gangster.

After a search online, Buzzy had discovered that Yi's wife, Beth, was the director of a community theater that called itself Woodside Live. Woodside was one of the most expensively cute little towns in the Bay Area, a seemingly rural nook snuggled against the eastern slope of the coastal mountains with multi-million-dollar country homes that were only a forty-minute drive from Silicon Valley.

To Jack, Thomas and Beth Yi sounded like rich guilty liberals who were perfect for his needs. From Lombard Street, they took an Uber car to the airport where they rented a four-door Kia that smelled like a hotel carpet and looked, in Buzzy's opinion, like a dark brown bug. They picked up the Kia on the third floor of a multi-story parking structure that had roller coaster curves leading down to the ground floor where they exited over metal forks that would tear their tires to shreds if they tried to back up.

"Renting a car isn't what it used to be," Jack observed. He rode in the passenger seat with his window open a crack. Katya was in the back with her own cracked window. They both seemed to be sniffing the air for signs and omens. Buzzy was amazed at how Jack and Katya, over the years, had grown more and more alike.

The traffic was intense getting out of the San Francisco Airport. Buzzy had to be sharp, looking everywhere at once, making sure he was in the correct lane. There were multiple exits taking you to distant parking lots and terminals of no return, and if you got on the wrong exit you could end up going in circles for hours.

"And this used to be such a small, friendly airport!" Jack said with a shake of his head.

Buzzy was ready to strangle Jack. There was something smug and narcissistic about old geezers telling young people how much better everything was when they were young. Fortunately, Buzzy had learned restraint.

"Here's a thought," he said to Jack. "What if you could live your life backward? You'd start out waking up in a coffin, then you'd climb out, and every year you'd see yourself getting younger and younger. Finally you'd get back to those wonderful days of old you keep talking about, complete with a juicy young girlfriend. And if you kept on going, you'd end up as somebody's orgasm—"

"Buzzy, please concentrate on driving. Spare me the nonsense!"

Time going backward wasn't complete nonsense, and Buzzy was about to tell Jack so. He had taken a theoretical physics class at Stanford in which the relativity of time had been discussed at great length, along with wormholes and multiple universes. But just as Buzzy was about to say that there were more things in heaven and earth, Jack, that were not dreamt of his philosophy, he noticed a gray Ford Explorer in his rear-view mirror that he didn't like.

The Explorer had appeared from one of the many feeder roads and it came up aggressively behind him. It was the sort of car that seemed anxious to beat the clock in order to win some imaginary race. Most likely, a stressed-out cyber entrepreneur, Buzzy decided. He kept going toward the Bayshore Freeway and the next time he looked in the rear-view mirror, the Explorer was gone.

But a few minutes later, there it was again as he was turning left onto the southbound freeway ramp, two cars behind him.

Buzzy needed to pay attention as he merged into a moving river of cars, trucks, and busses. He'd settled into the second lane from the right before he was able to get another good look in his rearview mirror. The gray Explorer was now two cars back.

What of it? Buzzy told himself. There were lots of cars on the road, and when he looked again, the Explorer was gone, once again.

Palo Alto wasn't far. Buzzy got off the freeway at Embarcadero Road. He was on a suburban street driving through Palo Alto when the gray Explorer appeared again in his mirror. Driving now at 35 mph, he was able to see two hulky shadows in front.

They drove forward from the shade into the sun, and now there could be no mistake. The passenger in the SUV was the guy with the red-dish/blond hair and blue windbreaker, which he hadn't bothered to change.

Buzzy looked over at Jack, who was riding comfortably leaning back against the head rest, his mouth half open. He looked like he was sleeping, but with Jack's dark glasses, you could never be sure.

Buzzy did an experiment. He made a right turn onto a side street, then another right turn that took him back to El Camino Real, and then another right turn again so that he circled around to where he had begun. When he looked in his rearview mirror, the Explorer was still two cars back.

Jack rolled his dark glasses his way. "Who's following us?"

"What?"

"You heard me. Why did you do that little maneuver, driving around in a circle? Who are you trying to shake?"

"How could you tell I did that?"

"Because I could. Now, what the hell is going on?"

Buzzy had been hoping to avoid this conversation, but there didn't seem any way out.

"Look, I wasn't sure at first, and I didn't want you to get excited. But there's, like, a gray Ford Explorer behind us, and I've seen it now a couple of times."

"*Like* a gray Ford Explorer?" Jack repeated caustically.

"Jack, gimme a break—yes, an Explorer. I wouldn't have worried, but yesterday, you see, I spotted somebody at the Caffè Trieste, and then I saw him again at City Lights, which seemed a little too much of a coincidence. He was a tall guy, mid-thirties, with reddish/blond hair."

"And you didn't think to mention this to me?"

"I didn't want to spook you, Jack. And like I said, I wasn't sure. But now with this Explorer . . . I'm starting to feel we're in somebody's sights."

Jack considered this. He knew various maneuvers to shake off a tail, but he wasn't sure he trusted Buzzy's driving.

"Pull over, Buzzy. Find some place where we can sit and think this through."

Buzzy pulled into the parking lot of a dental building, found a slot, and cut the engine.

"Do you see the Explorer?"

"No, I do not, Jack. Either he lost interest, or we lost him. But I don't see him anywhere."

Jack hated asking Buzzy to do anything illegal. You didn't want to encourage a promising young person to break the law. But there were times when you were low on options.

"Can you hack Yi's computer and get his personal information?"

"Well, sure, Jack. That's elementary. It would take maybe half an hour, unless he's set up some special firewall. But it shouldn't be hard."

"Then do it," said Jack. "I'm interested in his calendar. I want to know where he'll be, when."

***

They found a suburban park in a residential neighborhood that was used mostly by parents who brought small children to play on the swings and climbing structures.

Jack sat at a park table in the shade of a large oak and let Katya out of her harness to run loose, sniff the bushes, and use the facilities. Buzzy remained in the car with his laptop, a mysterious metal box plugged into the USB port, earphones on his head, and his phone propped up on the dashboard. He told Jack not to interrupt him, he needed to concentrate.

Jack used the time to phone Emma in San Geronimo and this time she answered. She was at work at the library and couldn't talk for long. That was okay with Jack. This was a conversation he had been dreading.

"Jack!" she said wearily. "Are you crazy? Do you want to die?"

"It's not like that," he answered. "I'm taking it easy, getting plenty of rest. There are a few people I needed to talk to here, that's all. Honestly, I would have gone crazy lying in bed at home doing nothing."

"I'm not going to argue with you, Jack. I've tried my best, the rest is up to you."

"I'm going to be fine, Emma. Buzzy is driving me everywhere—it's like being in a traveling bed. Right now, I'm sitting at a shaded table in a lovely park and I'll be home tomorrow at the latest. You know what we did yesterday? We went to the Caffè Trieste. Remember all the times—"

"Jack, I don't want to hear it. You're seventy-seven years old, you've just had heart surgery, and you're acting like some naughty teenager!"

He was considering how to answer this when a woman accosted him from a few feet away.

"Sir, is that your dog?" she demanded.

"Hold on a sec, Emma . . . yes, she is," he told the woman. "I'm blind, madam. She's my guide dog."

"It doesn't matter if she's a guide dog. You can't let her run loose!"

"Yes, okay . . . I'll get her as soon as I finish this call."

"And she just pooped on the grass!"

"Dogs do that, you see."

"Then clean up after her!"

"I will . . . now if you don't mind, I'm talking with my wife . . . Emma, are you still there?"

"Jack, I don't believe you! You let Katya loose in a park?"

"Well, sure. She needs to run around."

"Oh, Jack, you can't let dogs do that anymore. Dogs have to be on a leash."

He sighed. There seemed to be so many more rules than there used to be. "I'll take care of it, Emma. I'll clean up after her. But honestly, I've got more important things on my mind!"

"Sure, you do. Well, go ahead, do what you have to . . . but just get home tomorrow please!"

"I will," he promised. "Katya! . . . Katya, come here . . . I love you, Emma!"

Emma sighed and disconnected. Jack was putting Katya back in her harness when Buzzy came out from the car and joined him at the picnic table.

"Okay, I hacked into his calendar. Yi won't be at the hospital tonight. This is one of his two days off. But I know where he'll be this afternoon—at a polo practice."

"Polo? You're kidding! *Horse* polo?"

"It's not water polo. The field's just a few miles from here. The practice is going on now, but we can catch him if we hurry."

Jack was surprised people still played polo. It was a sport from another world, another time.

"Is there any sign of the gray Explorer?"

"I don't see it. Maybe we've lost them."

"Okay, let's catch the end of their polo practice. But Buzzy . . . Katya, well, you know how dogs are. Do you think you could clean up her mess?"

"You know, Jack, you sure do expect a lot from me for what you pay."

"And I'm grateful, Buzzy. I truly am. And in fact, you're getting a raise. As of now, I'm giving you a dollar an hour more. How about that?"

Buzzy couldn't think of an adequate response.

***

The Woodside Equestrian Centre was located in a languid green valley that felt like you had been transported to a perfect rural yesteryear.

Buzzy noted the spelling of "centre" as he approached the gatehouse. The horsey set in Woodside was avidly Anglophile. There were English saddles only at the Woodside Equestrian Centre, and riders were dressed in jodhpurs and boots and red jackets, the full regalia. It was obvious that you needed a lot of money to pretend you were English gentry from a hundred years ago. The Equestrian Centre was a private club and you had to be either a member or on a member's guest list in order to gain entry.

Buzzy looked up at the uniformed security guard in the booth by the entrance.

"We're guests of Dr. Thomas Yi," he said with confidence.

The guard turned to his computer screen. "And your names, please?"

"John Sacco and Peter Vanzetti," he answered.

"Yes, here you are." The guard handed them two guest passes and a card they were to place on their dashboard. Buzzy and Jack were on Dr. Yi's guest list due to a bit of hacking on Buzzy's part.

"Jesus!" Jack muttered as they continued down a pleasantly wooded lane. "Sacco and Vanzetti! You don't give up, do you?"

"It was spur of the moment, Jack—I hope you don't mind. I couldn't bear the club's website. It was so snooty, it made you want to plant a bomb."

"Sure, Buzzy. Stifle your inclinations, please."

They parked by the clubhouse, which was an attractive redwood building set in a well-shaded garden with floor to ceiling glass on all sides and a deck with tables and umbrellas. From here they needed to walk to the stables, riding rings, and finally the polo field, which was a few hundred yards away.

Everything was well-maintained. Everything was pretty. The members standing near the jumping structures were mostly youngish women, and they were as well-maintained and pretty as their surroundings. Their cheeks were rosy with good health.

The polo field, green as an emerald, was surrounded by a white wooden fence with bleachers on one side. Six horsemen were on the far end of the field practicing, one at a time, riding up toward a ball with their mallets raised and knocking the ball into the goal.

"Describe, please," said Jack impatiently.

This was the hardest part of Buzzy's job, describing things to Jack, but he had been getting better at it. He did his best now with the polo field and the horsemen. Looking more closely, he saw that one of the players was a woman, and he mentioned this to Jack. This was gender-neutral California polo.

"They all have white pants and green jerseys," Buzzy said. "I'm not sure I see Dr. Yi . . . no, that has to be him. He's batting now, if that's what they call it. He's the only Asian-looking guy on the field. The rest are gringo to the max."

The practice went on for some time. Jack, Buzzy, and Katya sat in the bleachers while Buzzy narrated what was happening on the field. After practicing whacking the ball through the goal posts, they spent another half hour galloping up and down the field passing the ball to each other. It didn't look easy.

Jack raised his face to the sun and imagined polo horses on a green field. It was a peaceful image. The sun was warm and almost put him to sleep.

"They're finishing up, Jack," Buzzy said at last. "Yi just climbed down from his horse and he's leading him to a gate at the far end of the field."

"Let's intercept him," Jack said.

Thomas Yi was a handsome, erect, athletically built man in his late thirties. Walking with his horse beside him on a lead, he looked like he had the world in his pocket.

"Dr. Yi!" Buzzy called out when they were closer. "Could we have a word?"

Jack was nearly overwhelmed by the musky odor of horse. A horse that had been running hard and was breathing like a fire engine only a few feet away.

"Dr. Yi, I'm Commander Jack Wilder from the San Francisco police." Jack smiled slightly. "That's my former title, before I lost my eyesight. These days I'm a private investigator in a small New Mexico town."

"I've skied in San Geronimo, Mr. Wilder, and I know who you are. My cousin Audrey phoned me this morning, so I've been expecting you."

Jack was impressed by how Chinese families stuck together. They were like an aspen forest with all their roots connected beneath the soil.

"Then you know what I've come to ask?"

"I do, and putting an end to human trafficking is a worthy cause. But I'm sorry, there's nothing I can tell you. I'm sure you've heard this before, but I will never put my family in danger. However, if you want to keep me company while I cool down Beowulf, perhaps there's something I can do for you."

Beowulf seemed to Jack a fancy name for a horse. Buzzy guided him on one side, Katya on the other, keeping him in a straight line as he walked alongside Dr. Yi.

"I used to watch polo in Golden Gate Park," Jack told him. "A wonderful game, but a bit pricey to play, I've been told."

"It's not cheap," Yi admitted. "But once you're hooked, you're hooked. I'm sure it sounds frivolous, but it's a thrill to gallop down a field after a ball."

"I can imagine," said Jack. "And I bet it's a good way to release the stress of working in an emergency room in a busy hospital. So how can you help me?"

Dr. Yi paused to give Jack a long look.

"I've thought about this all morning. I've decided to give you the name of probably the only person on the West Coast who's in a position to tell you what you want to know without worrying about his personal safety. He's an old man now, and I can't guarantee that he will talk to you."

"I'd like to meet him," Jack said. "I'll keep your name out of it."

"It doesn't really matter. He's my uncle. He'll guess immediately."

"I see," said Jack. "Doesn't that put you in danger?"

"In this case, no. My uncle is very fond of me, as I am of him. He's Abbot Longwei of the Taktsang Buddhist Monastery in Big Sur."

"A Buddist monk?"

"Yes, he is. He's a very holy man."

"Great, I envy him. But how does a holy man know about human trafficking in New Mexico?"

"Because he knows everything. Before he retired to devote what was left of his life to meditation, he was the Grand Dragon of Red Gecko, the most powerful Tong on the West Coast."

"You're serious? A gangster who retires to become a Buddhist monk?"

"It's not that uncommon. You can take it or leave it, Mr. Wilder. This is the best I can do for you. As I said, whether Abbot Longwei will talk with you or not, I don't know."

Without a further word, Thomas Yi disappeared with his horse inside the stable.

Jack stood wondering whether to take the bait. On the negative side, Emma was expecting him home quickly. Also, this could very well be a trap, a way to make two people asking dangerous questions disappear. The mountains that rose from the Big Sur coast were rough and wild.

In the plus column: Big Sur was only a few hours away and this felt like it could be his best lead yet.

Chapter Sixteen

The cave where Howie and Rain Walker spent Wednesday afternoon, waiting for nightfall and sheltering from the New Mexico sun, wasn't terrible as caves went. There were no bats. Still, Howie found it a little creepy.

The entrance was a wide mouth fifty feet up a steep sandstone cliff, accessible only by a narrow trail that involved some climbing. Indians had obviously used this cave since time immemorial. The back wall was scorched black from old fires, and there were several faded petroglyphs near the entrance, more ancient still. The petroglyphs were abstract designs, spirals and markings that looked like they might be stars.

Rain curled up near the fire-blackened wall and slept for hours. Howie tried to sleep as well, using his daypack as a pillow, but the ground was too uncomfortable.

After the sun set, the day cooled quickly. Sitting near the entrance, he could see for miles over the mesas and arroyos without spotting any trace of humanity. It was a profound view, but the vastness was also a little frightening.

"We'll wait until midnight," Rain said, sitting up at last. "I got some energy bars—want one?"

"Thanks," said Howie.

"You're what I'd call a city Indian, aren't you?"

Howie was surprised by the bluntness of the question. It made him frown, defensively. But he gave it some thought.

"Yes and no," he answered. "I like living close to nature, but city life has a lot to offer. Civilization has its good points."

Rain laughed, his handsome teeth glinting in the day's last light. "Civilization!" he said scornfully. "That's what brought this planet to the edge of destruction! The White Man's cities are nothing but garbage dumps full of greed!"

"I wouldn't describe Paris as a garbage dump," Howie said. "Or New York either. The restaurants are pretty good, too."

"Restaurants!" Rain scoffed. "I know you're joking, Moon Deer, but gimme a break! We Indians need to go back to the Old Ways, period. That's the only thing that'll save us. We need to be warriors again!"

He said this fiercely, which was worrisome. Howie kept his thoughts to himself. He understood the virtues of old Indian ways, as imagined by a 19-year-old reservation kid today. Rain was angry, Howie understood that. Angry and idealistic and young—which were dangerous combinations.

"I think we all need to find our own way of becoming warriors," he said after a while. "Each to his own. That's the key, Rain. You can be a warrior sitting in a library reading a book."

Rain shook his head. For him there was only one way. His way, obviously.

Midnight was a long time coming. Howie somehow had managed to fall asleep in a sitting position, propped up against the back wall of the cave, when he felt Rain shaking him awake.

"Time to go."

***

The night sky was mostly clear overhead, with heavy clouds brooding over the mountains to the west, their fringes silvery in the light of the moon that was almost full. Flashes of silent lightning lit the mountains, too far away for the thunder to follow.

It was nearly an hour trek from the cave to the rim of the canyon where the compound was located. They hiked single file in silence,

Howie in the rear. The moon came in and out of the clouds to show the way.

From the canyon edge, the valley floor looked a long way down. They could just make out the compound. There were several lights shining at the corners of the large metal building and also at the perimeters of the tents, but otherwise the compound was dark. The laborers, whoever they were, were most likely asleep, leaving a few guards in place.

"The guards won't be looking for anyone to arrive from the outside. That's the good news," Rain said. "Their attention will be on the tents, making sure none of the prisoners escape."

"What's the bad news?"

"If they spot us, they'll shoot to kill."

Howie sighed. He couldn't afford to be killed, not with his daughter about to arrive. He paused to survey the compound below wondering if he should back out. It would be embarrassing. Rain would deem him a coward, not a gung-ho warrior from the days of old. But at least he would get out of this alive.

"We'll just need to make sure they don't spot us," he said finally. "Look, once we're down in the canyon, we'll take a look at the metal building. That's what I'm most curious about. Then we'll bypass the tents and guard towers and make our way along the river to where we saw those greenhouses. I'm curious if they're doing anything in there besides growing hemp. If we stick close to the river, we'll be a good distance from the towers, and they won't be able to see us. We'll return the same way and they'll never know we were there. Okay?"

"Sure, bro. We won't take any chances."

"That's right," Howie told him sternly.

"Okay, let's get going.

Rain led the way along the rim of the canyon to a shoulder of descending rock which fell away gradually into the canyon. The shoulder was shaped something like a medieval buttress supporting a cathedral wall. Howie saw that it should be possible to hike down the spine.

"Is there an actual trail?" he asked.

"No, but it shouldn't be too difficult. Just watch your step."

Once again, Rain led the way, stopping occasionally to scope out the terrain. He scampered around boulders and brush, a lithe figure bobbing up and down in Howie's vision with his AR-15 strapped across his back. Howie followed more cautiously, making sure he had a good foothold before moving on. He thought himself in pretty good shape. He had skied hard much of last winter and then had done construction work on his property in the spring and early summer that included a good deal of heavy lifting. But that was pleasant work. Climbing down a shoulder of loose rock, with sheer drops to the valley below, was something else. After twenty minutes, halfway down, Howie's thigh muscles were burning, and his hands were raw from gripping rocks and roots. He knew that one false move and he would slip to his death.

Rain occasionally stopped and looked back uphill to where Howie was coming down. The look on his face was scornful. Howie kept his concentration on what he was doing. He had reached a stretch of steep scree where all he could think to do was slide down on his butt, using his arms and legs like a large spider. It wasn't graceful.

The moon had been coming in and out of the clouds all night, but when they reached the valley, the clouds thickened, there was a rush of wind, and the light of the moon vanished as though a switch had been turned off. Howie was glad that this would help to conceal their presence, but he wished they had a flashlight. Rain reached the valley floor first and stopped for Howie to catch up.

"No talking from this point on," he whispered.

"Fine," said Howie. "And let's remember what we're here for. We're just going to take a look around. We're not going to be taking any scalps, okay?"

Rain smiled. "Fine," he agreed.

***

The summer storm, when it came, began slowly. A few heavy drops, widely spaced, from a black sky.

Howie and Rain were making their way cautiously along the canyon floor toward the metal building when the sky exploded in lightning. The clouds themselves had become a huge filament, causing a diffuse flash that lit up the warehouse, the rows of white tents, and the guard towers. The entire valley came into view for just a moment, leaving Howie and Rain suddenly exposed. They both dropped instantly onto their hands and knees.

The growl of thunder arrived seconds later, still some distance away. The weather in New Mexico was unpredictable this time of year, often changing quickly. Howie looked over at Rain, who appeared to be enjoying himself. This was his warrior fantasy come true, his chance to be an action hero.

"You know, I don't think there are more than three or four guards up in those towers. We could take them out easily then let those trafficked people loose!" Rain whispered. "They're not expecting an attack!"

Howie shook his head. "And once they're loose, what are we going to do with them? Look, Rain, we discussed this. We're not going to attack anybody. We're here only to reconnoiter."

Howie hoped the word reconnoiter had enough of a military ring to it that Rain would be satisfied.

"Let's check out the warehouse," Howie whispered. "Come on, let's go."

Howie took the lead, rising from his hands and knees and running in a crouch toward the dark outline of the building. He was glad to hear Rain coming up behind him.

The sky flashed as they ran, and once again they fell to the ground. The thunder was longer in coming, which meant—possibly—that the storm cell was moving away. Howie was glad when they reached the side of the warehouse and they weren't so exposed.

The rectangular metal building was at least two stories high, big enough to house an airplane. Both the VW camper and the gray van he had seen earlier were gone.

It took Howie and Rain nearly ten minutes to walk around the perimeter searching for a door or a window. But the sides of the building were unbroken metal concealing whatever was inside. They found only a single door. It was at the far end of the structure, industrial sized, a double door at least eighteen feet high that was attached to rails at the top. But there were no handles, nothing to indicate how it might be opened, and it appeared to be securely locked.

"There must be some way we can get inside," Howie mused. "What do you think?"

Rain didn't answer. Howie turned from studying the door to find that the kid was no longer by his side.

He moved back from the building and saw the outline of Rain more than a dozen feet away. He was in a crouch jogging toward the tents.

"Damnit!" Howie hissed. He wanted to call out to Rain to come back, but it was too late. He couldn't make noise.

With dread, reluctance, and anger at the teenage prima donna, Howie followed after him, determined to stop a situation that was quickly slipping out of control.

Chapter Seventeen

Chasing after Rain, Howie hurried in a fast walk that wasn't as silent as he'd like, but he couldn't seem to catch up.

With the cloud cover, the night was dark and velvety and dense. Ahead, Rain moved easily across the landscape, like a dancer, until he was engulfed in the darkness and disappeared.

Howie swore to himself, thinking he had lost him. Then there was a flash of lightning, a phosphorescent glow that lit the landscape like a black and white negative. In the flash, he saw Rain kneeling by one of the tents, about to crawl in beneath the bottom edge.

In an instant he was gone.

The thunder came a moment later, an earthquake roar, very close. Howie ran the final distance to the tent and hesitated. If this teenage kid, believing himself immortal, was foolish enough to get himself killed, Howie didn't have to follow. He thought about simply turning around and getting the hell out of there. But there were two quick things to weigh:

First, it would be on Howie's conscience if he didn't at least try to help the idiot.

And second, there was a practical side. He wasn't sure he knew the way across the desert back to his car. Like it or not, he needed Rain to be his guide.

Howie found that his Glock was in his hand, though he didn't remember putting it there.

As quickly as he could, he knelt by the bottom edge of the canvas, found some space, and crawled inside. He wasn't as slim as Rain, and for a bad moment he thought he was going to get stuck between the canvas and the ground.

With an effort, he wiggled his way through until he came out in the tent. It was a bardo of hell he wouldn't soon forget.

***

A single dim lightbulb hung from a cord in the center of the tent.

There were at least fifty cots crowded inside the tent, which was probably designed for twenty. Sleeping bodies were everywhere under thin blankets. The smell was a terrible mixture of sweat and excrement.

There were no windows and Howie imagined it would be intolerably hot inside here in the daytime. Of course, during the day everyone would be outside working. These were slave quarters.

In the dim light, Howie could see Rain near the door kneeling by one of the cots speaking with a woman. As far as he could tell, all the people in this tent were women.

As Howie stood gaping, a hand reached out from one of the cots and took his wrist. Howie was so surprised, he jumped.

It was a woman, Chinese he thought, no longer young. She had a worn face of many wrinkles and dark skin.

"You bad man to come here and rape girls!" she said in stilted English. "You very bad man!"

"I'm . . ." It took Howie a moment to get over his surprise. "No, I'm not one of the guards. I'm here to rescue you. Not tonight but soon. I will come back with many policemen, and we will get you out!"

She looked at him without expression. He had no idea if she had understood a word he said.

In the next cot over, a woman sat up and looked at him. She was younger, but even more ravaged by hardship. Her lips were cracked. Her eyes were dull with misery. Howie had never felt as angry or as helpless in his life.

145

"We will get you out!" he said more firmly.

But how?

On the far side of the tent, Rain seemed to be having a similar encounter with one of the women. Howie wanted to get his attention. They needed to get away from here. Rain obviously wanted to free these poor people. Howie would have liked that too, but he didn't see how it was possible. These people didn't look up for a long hike.

What they needed to do was climb out of the canyon without being seen and report this to the authorities who could launch a proper rescue with medical support to liberate the camp. Howie was about to hiss at Rain that it was time to go, when the tent door pulled open and two guards came in with flashlights.

"Who the hell are you?" one demanded, pointing his light at Rain.

Both guards had pistols in holsters on their hips, but they weren't fast enough. Rain had already slid his rifle from his shoulder and he fired a volley into their bodies from only a few feet away. The noise was terrible. The women screamed.

"Rain!" he shouted. "That's it! Now we get the hell out of here!"

Rain appeared to have come to the same conclusion. He ran across the tent to where Howie was already on his knees about to slip outside.

"We will return!" Rain shouted to the women, heroically, just before they scampered out into the night.

***

Howie took off running as fast as he could down the canyon toward the buttress rock about half a mile away, their staircase out of here. He heard Rain not far behind him.

Flood lights came on suddenly from the compound, bathing the desert in light. Howie had never been much of a jogger, but panic gave him a surge of energy. He nearly doubled his speed as he leapt over sage-brush and gullies.

"Faster!" Rain called out to Howie as he rushed past.

Screw you! would have been Howie's response, if he hadn't been gasping for breath. He was going as fast as he could.

Gunfire erupted from the compound, a volley of shots that was like a string of firecrackers. If there was any doubt that this was live ammunition, a bullet zinged overhead.

Gunfire followed Howie and Rain sporadically as they ran along the canyon floor, but the shots were wild, and soon they were beyond the reach of the flood lights. The guards at the compound hadn't been expecting them. They had thought their hidden prison camp secure, and it had made them lazy and sloppy.

Howie and Rain reached the buttress and scampered upward, using their hands and feet. The clouds blew by overhead, sometimes revealing the white light of the moon, other times enclosing them in darkness. Every few minutes a flash of distant lightning lit the night.

It took a strenuous half hour to climb the buttress to higher ground. Dawn had begun to light the sky. Howie collapsed on the mesa, breathing hard, exhausted. When he caught his breath, he sat up and was surprised to see Rain on the ground a few feet away groaning in pain.

Howie didn't care if Rain was hurt. He was furious.

"Goddamnit, look what you did! You shot those guards! I told you not to go near those tents! What kind of idiot are you?"

"Got a muscle cramp . . . gimme a second," Rain answered in a strained voice. "Gimme some water."

"Drink your own damn water!"

"Didn't bring any . . . I'm training . . ."

"Yeah? Training for what? To be an asshole?"

"I'm going to be sick!"

147

Robert Westbrook

It took Howie a moment to get the story. Rain had been training not to need water. For the past month, he had been steadily decreasing his water intake until he was drinking only half a cup a day. This was part of his warrior regime apparently, so that he could be some superhuman out of a Marvel comic book, someone who could go for days and weeks without water or food. Now, with all the running and climbing of the past few hours, his foolishness had caught up with him. He was seriously dehydrated.

They had set out yesterday with two plastic gallon jugs of water, but Rain had left his jug untouched in the cave where they had spent the afternoon. Howie's jug, with only a few inches of water, was where he had left it on the canyon rim. He had taken only his gun into the canyon, pushed down into the front of his pants, not wanting to make the climb with an awkward pack.

He found the daypack where he had left it and gave Rain a drink.

"Remind me never to go anywhere with *you* again!" Howie muttered. "Now let's get out of here before those guards come after us!"

It took Rain another few minutes before they were able to set off. He massaged the cramp in his leg and gradually got himself together. But now it was Howie in the lead with Rain struggling to catch up. Howie refused to slow down. As far as he was concerned, the kid deserved all the suffering he could get.

The morning sun was rising when at last they came over a hill and climbed down to where his car was waiting. Howie had never been so glad to see his dusty old Subaru. He unlocked the doors and climbed wearily into the driver's seat.

"Talk about a totally wasted venture!" he complained as he started the engine. "We could have gotten in and out of that canyon without any trouble if you had only done what I told you!"

"I didn't have a choice, Moon Deer. The guys were reaching for their guns. Anyway, we found out what we wanted to know. It's a prison camp for trafficked migrants. What else is there?"

"Listen, all we did was stir up a hell of a hornet's nest. We didn't even get to see what was in those greenhouses. Now they're going to be much more on guard. And if they catch us, it's going to be a murder charge."

"If they catch us, they'll kill us first," said Rain. This was supposed to be an optimistic take on their situation

Howie drove cautiously until they reached the main dirt road. The sun had risen high in the sky and he was starting to think of his stomach. He was wondering where they might find breakfast when Rain tapped his shoulder.

"Better look in your mirror, Moon Deer. We have company."

Howie glanced up into his rearview mirror and groaned. Behind him on the road, perhaps a half mile away, a large dust plume rose into the sky from a vehicle that was coming up on them fast. It was a cop car. Even at this distance, he could see the flashing red and blue lights.

He put his foot on the gas and accelerated sharply to 60 mph. He wasn't sure he could push his old Subaru faster than that on the uneven dirt road. His goal was to get clear of the reservation before the tribal cops caught them. At this point, they would have a better chance of survival with nonnative law enforcement.

"They're gaining on us!" said Rain.

Howie could hear the siren wailing not far behind them. He pressed harder on the gas and saw the speedometer rise to 75. At this speed, any mistake—any bump—would send them careening into the desert.

"Relax, Moon Deer. It's a good day to die."

"You know what, Rain? It is *not* a good day to die. I have things to do!"

149

"Yeah, you need to phone into the office! I mean, what kind of Indian are you, bro?"

Howie and Rain had been arguing about this in one way or another ever since they had met, who was a real Indian and who was not. Howie found the question itself ridiculous and he didn't answer. He needed all his concentration to stay on the road.

There was a series of crackling sounds and a bullet thudded into the rear hatch. The Subaru edged up to 80 mph without Howie consciously pressing the pedal.

The road was fairly decent as dirt roads went, wide and straight. Howie was starting to think they might get away when he saw trouble ahead, two vehicles with flashing red and blue lights blocking off the road. Howie took his foot off the accelerator and the speedometer fell to 60.

"What are you doing?" Rain demanded.

"We don't have a choice. I'm going to make it look like I'm going to stop, then I'll go off-road and get around them. Hang on."

"Okay." Rain nodded approvingly. "That might work."

Howie slowed to thirty as he approached the two white vans that were blocking the road. The cop car that had been chasing them was now only a dozen feet away, but the shooting had stopped. The cops seemed to believe they had won the contest.

He slowed almost to a stop as he approached the vans. A man was standing in the road with a shotgun in his hands. Howie was about to swerve off into the desert when he saw who it was.

He came to a full stop.

"What the hell!" Rain cried.

The man with the shotgun stepped their way.

"It's okay, Rain. And for chrissake, ditch your damn gun before he opens fire. I know this guy."

Howie lowered his window obligingly.

"Well, Moon Deer," said the man. He was utterly average, neither tall nor short. The only unusual thing about him were the fancy cowboy boots he wore.

"I seem to have a way of arriving just in the nick of time, don't I?"

Howie managed a weak smile. It was the U.S. Marshal who had saved him once before only a few miles from here, on his shortcut from hell.

It was amazing luck to find the Marshal here. At least, he hoped it was.

Chapter Eighteen

The Pacific Coast Highway!

Driving south on Thursday morning along the ocean with the window open, Jack inhaled the smell and it brought back a rush of memories so strong they carried him back to another time.

The scent was indescribable. Damp, salty, fresh, somehow restoring. Jack and Emma had driven down the coast to Santa Cruz many times in their early days, to wander hand in hand through the amusement park along the boardwalk and onto the pier where they had a favorite restaurant to eat crab.

Jack was about to tell Buzzy about the time he'd gotten Emma, after a bottle of champagne, to take the scary old-fashioned roller coaster, but he stopped himself. He was starting to suspect that Buzzy wasn't really interested in the old days.

Buzzy had taken them on the inland route to San Jose, then Highway 17 to Santa Cruz, where they got entangled in a traffic jam that delayed them for nearly an hour.

"This can't be Santa Cruz!" Jack objected. "There never used to be any traffic here! It was just a little coastal town with a few scruffy surfers and hippies hanging out!"

Buzzy didn't say a word. He didn't need to.

Monterey, fifty miles further south, was another snarl of traffic which took nearly forty minutes to get through. The town had come a long way since John Steinbeck wrote about working people on Cannery Row. Today the workers had to commute from far away, and those who lived here had big money.

Big Sur was another thirty miles down the coast, a slow drive on a winding two-lane highway across spectacular bridges into an increasingly enchanted land of steep ocean cliffs, wild green mountains, and roaring surf. Buzzy had to slow to 20 mph to make the hairpin turns.

"Is it as beautiful as it used to be?" Jack asked.

"Sure, it's beautiful," Buzzy told him. "Beauty for billionaires!"

"Buzzy, you're much too cynical for your age. This is the time in your life to be idealistic."

Buzzy only smiled and shook his head.

As they drove into the small community of Big Sur, Jack made Buzzy describe everything. They passed the Big Sur Inn, where he and Emma had stayed, and Nepenthe, the famous restaurant perched high above the ocean where they had often eaten.

Not far after Nepenthe, Buzzy took a left turn from the coast highway onto a narrow, barely paved road that led up into the hills.

"You sure that was the right place to turn?"

"My GPS doesn't lie, Jack."

The hills climbed so high from the ocean that Jack felt his ears pop. It seemed to him that they were spiraling upward into the sky. Buzzy had to put the Kia's automatic transmission into low. At last, the road leveled out and they descended into a valley.

"We're here," Buzzy said at last, coming to a stop by an elaborately carved wooden gate. There was a sign that he read aloud to Jack: "The Taktsang Buddhist Monastery."

Jack inhaled a mountain scent of warm midsummer meadows and wildflowers. In the distance, he heard the resonant gong of a temple bell coming from some distance away. Each tone gradually faded in the air. The peace here was pervasive.

Which made it an odd place to come in search of a crime lord.

***

The long unpaved driveway descended into a grassy parking area next to a quaint one-story redwood building that stood in the shade of several huge old oak trees. The parking area contained several vehicles—a Tesla, a BMW station wagon, a golf cart, and several bicycles. Buddha, apparently, moved in mysterious ways.

There was another sign at the head of the path that led to a redwood building.

"Welcome to Taktsang Monastery," Buzzy read aloud. "Visitors welcome for Sunday meditation 1PM—4PM. Visitors must register in the office. Please respect the Great Silence. May all beings benefit!"

"It's not Sunday, Jack, so I'm not sure they'll let us in. Probably everybody is in their cave levitating."

Katya led the way along a pretty path to the front door. Buzzy followed last to make sure Jack didn't get lost.

A small sign on the front door said ENTER! The exclamation point seemed excessive.

A young man in loose white clothing sat at a comfortable old desk studying a Buddhist text. An acolyte, Buzzy decided. He was Nordic with blond hair. The room was darkly paneled with aged redwood. A golden light came through the curtained windows.

"Hello!" he said. He was fiendishly friendly. "I'm afraid visitors are only allowed on Sunday afternoons. But you may sign the guest book! You'll see there are many pithy entries. And I would be happy to give you some literature."

Buzzy was trying to find the right word to describe this guy. Obnoxious, came to mind.

Jack took over.

"We're here from New Mexico on quite a serious matter to see Abbot Longwei. Would you please send word that Mr. Jack Wilder would appreciate an audience."

"Oh, I'm sorry, sir. Very sorry. But that won't be possible. The Abbot is in retreat in his cell, no visitors. This is a monastery, Mr. Wilder."

"Yes, I understand. But occasionally the woes of the real world call and this is one of those times. Please send word to Abbot Longwei. There's a serious police matter I must speak to him about."

"Some would say *our* world was the *real* world, Mr. Wilder," the apprentice monk said virtuously. "But I'll send someone to the Abbot, if you will please wait."

***

Jack and Buzzy waited more than fifteen minutes on a hard wooden bench against the far wall. Even Katya, stretched out on the floor by Jack's feet, was starting to get impatient. After the long drive, she was looking forward to a good run and sniff in the bushes.

The acolyte in the loose white clothing went back to his Buddhist text. At last, an impressively large monk, Chinese, in a maroon robe came into the room from a side door. He had massive arms and hardly any neck. He stopped to take a good look at Jack, then Katya, and finally Buzzy. His eyes returned to Jack.

"May I inquire, Mr. Wilder, if you are in fact Commander Wilder of the San Francisco Police Department?"

"I was," Jack answered. "As you can see, I've lost my eyesight and I'm retired."

"If you're retired, why are you inquiring about a serious police matter, as you have put it?"

"I can only discuss that with Abbot Longwei."

"I see. If you will kindly wait, I will seek instruction."

The massive monk turned and left by the door he had entered, leaving Jack and Buzzy waiting once again, this time for a full twenty minutes.

The acolyte didn't look up from his text.

At last, the monk returned.

"Commander Wilder," he asked, "is it true that you now run a private investigation agency in New Mexico?"

"It is. I see you've found me online."

"Are you here on behalf of a client?"

"I'm here on behalf of a foundation. I won't tell you its name, but you can inform Abbot Longwei that it's a non-profit foundation that does good work around the world."

The monk turned his focus on Buzzy.

"And who are you, please?"

"I'm Jack's eyes. I drove us here. My name's Buzzy Hurston . . . I got kicked out of Stanford," he added, knowing it would come out anyway.

"I see. If you will kindly wait . . ."

The monk left them waiting on the bench yet again. It was maddening, a test of patience. This time, however, he returned after a few minutes.

"Please, Mr. Wilder, Mr. Hurston, you may follow me," he said. "But your guide dog, I'm afraid must remain here with Peter."

The acolyte looked up from his book, barely able to hide his irritation at being interrupted from the pursuit of enlightenment to look after a dog.

Chapter Nineteen

In Buzzy's opinion, the Taktsang Monastery was too idyllic. You almost expected Bambi to wander out from the forest with Thumper by his side. Who wouldn't be happy here? But would you retain that peaceful state of mind if you found yourself in a big city slum?

The massive monk led the way on a path past forest grottos and gently sloped meadows. There were a number of pretty little cabins tucked away in the trees. Cells, he imagined, where the monks lived. He had a glimpse of a larger building deep in the shadows of the forest that looked like a temple.

The Abbot's cabin sat at the edge of the forest on a meadow that overlooked the huge blue vista of the Pacific Ocean more than three miles away. A redwood deck radiated outward from the front of the cabin in a semi-circle. They found Abbot Longwei on the deck seated on a throne of cushions beneath a yellow umbrella that shaded him from the sun. He was a small, old, wizardly-looking man in a finely made maroon robe.

"Please have a seat, Commander," he said, indicating several cushions that had been placed on the deck. He looked like something from an old Chinese print, but his English was without accent.

Jack turned about on the deck not sure what he was expected to do.

"You know, a chair would probably work better for Jack than a cushion," Buzzy said to the Abbot. "Me, I'm fine."

The Abbot gave Buzzy a closer look as he picked up a small bell and rang it. A young monk appeared almost instantly.

"Please bring Commander Wilder a chair," the Abbot told him.

When the chair arrived, Jack sat down with a sigh. His legs were hurting him.

"Thank you for seeing us, Abbot. May I ask how you happened to know who I am? Commander Wilder is a person from a long time ago."

"Oh, but I'm from a long time ago, too!" he said. "Our paths have crossed before, you see. I followed your rise in the San Francisco police with considerable interest. Lieutenant, captain, major, commander, up and up. We all believed you would have become chief eventually if a bullet hadn't destroyed your eyesight. You shouldn't have been on the street that day to save that kidnapped child, you know. You should have trusted your SWAT team to do the job. That's what they all said afterwards. That you flunked it. It's what happens when you allow ego and anger to get the better of you."

Jack had to suppress a sigh. The Abbot was right, of course. He knew that now in retrospect. The rank of commander in a big city police force was impressive, but it was an office job. He shouldn't have interfered in a dangerous operation.

But this wasn't why he was here today.

"I feel at a disadvantage, Abbot. You seem to know all about me, but I know nothing of you, except you were once the head of the Red Gecko Tong. The Dragon Master, I believe it's called."

"Ah, this is long ago as well! Why turn over a dead log? The past is gone for both of us."

"I'm curious, Abbot, how a Dragon Master of a San Francisco Tong became a Buddhist Abbot?"

The Abbot laughed softly. "Is there such a difference, my friend?"

"Sure, there is," said Jack. "Gangsters kill people who get in their way. Buddhist monks, if I understand correctly, are big on love and light."

The Abbot appeared to enjoy the question.

"First, to call the Red Geckos gangsters is a mistake. The Red Gecko Tong was founded nearly two thousand years ago in what today is

Mongolia. It has always been concerned with the spirituality of the Taoist warrior. Buddhism came later in our history," he explained. "We are descendants of an extraordinarily sophisticated tradition. We were never the ching-chong Chinamen sitting on a rail, as you white men would have it."

"Of course not," Jack agreed. "And I know you faced a lot of racism in California, Abbot. However, though you might have begun in Mongolia, you ended up in Hong Kong, and when the Chinese started flooding into America in the 19ᵗʰ century, the Triads were quick to follow. You came to peddle drugs and prostitution and suck your own people dry."

"No, you don't see this fully," the Abbot said patiently. "And half a truth is no truth at all."

Buzzy was watching the old Abbot closely. His face so deeply wrinkled you could hardly see his eyes in the folds of skin. He looked frail yet tough as leather, all at the same time. Oddly, though he was dressed in a traditional monk's robe, he wore a San Francisco Giants cap.

"Then tell me the whole truth," said Jack, who could be tough himself.

"First of all, it's a mistake to call the Tongs gangsters. These societies were in fact the only civic structure the immigrants had. The white men were brutal to the Chinese and it was left to the Tongs to keep some sort of order. The Chinese were the cheap labor you needed to build the infrastructure for your new country. We made the railroads that connected the East Coast to the West. You couldn't have had this country without us. Yet you treated us worse than dogs. You cheated us, you fined us unreasonable taxes, you made life a misery. For the Japanese too, of course. For all the Asians."

"You came to America because you were starving back home," Jack interjected.

The Abbot nodded. "Yes, many, many were starving back home. And those who sailed from the southern cities of China were mostly uneducated, so they were easily cheated. Almost all the immigrants believed pie-in-the sky promises of better lives in the New World. They couldn't imagine how many of them would die, and how harshly they would be treated. The societies were the only support our people had."

"And you gouged them."

"No, you have a white man's understanding of history," the Abbot said. "Yes, the societies were tough, they had to be. But they ruled by firm principals. Everyone paid a tax, of course they did. The money was needed to keep order. But it was a small tax, much smaller than the punitive California tax laws that were passed against the Chinese."

Jack wasn't prepared to argue a history in which he knew he would lose. From the Chinese Exclusion Law to the concentration camps set up for Japanese American citizens during World War Two, Oriental immigrants suffered profound racism. However, that didn't excuse this Tong chief who was now a Buddhist monk. Jack had seen firsthand what the Chinese gangs did. They killed, they extorted poor shop owners, they were every bit as bad as the Italian mafia.

Jack leaned forward and lowered his voice. "Look, you said our paths crossed when we were both in San Francisco. Who are you?"

"Don't you recognize my voice? I've been told that blind people have a wonderful sense of hearing."

Jack had been listening closely to the Abbot's voice, but it stirred no memory.

"Hearing is one thing, memory quite another," he said. "I'm sorry to say that my own memory has become a bit patchy. Where did we meet?"

"Oh, no, Inspector—you have to guess!"

It was the title, Inspector, that brought back the memory. Jack had just made detective, a rank in San Francisco that is called inspector.

The name eluded him for a moment. Then it came.

"Henry Liu! The fishmonger!"

"Fresh fish today! Bravo!" said the Abbot happily.

"So, at the same time you were making a modest living selling fish to me and my wife, you were the Dragon Master of the Red Gecko Tong?"

"Bravo again," said the Abbot. "It is considered a very good thing in the Chinese societies to keep a modest profile. To be a fishmonger is a useful trade."

Jack was starting to remember.

"I helped you once back then, didn't I?"

"You did, Inspector. You saved my son's life."

***

It was an incident from more than thirty years ago. An incident among many others, as life goes for a big city cop. But Jack remembered it well.

That year, he and Emma had been living in an apartment on Hyde Street, a pleasant twenty-minute walk over Russian Hill to the edge of Chinatown. They often did their shopping in Chinatown for vegetables at the teeming stalls, and seafood at the Seven Seas Fish Market. Emma was a vegetarian then, no red meat, no chicken, but she ate fish and the Seven Seas had what Jack considered to be the freshest, best selection in the city.

Henry Liu was the proprietor.

Jack often stopped to chat with Henry, who knew he was a detective and was friendly because of it. When you were a small business owner, it was wise to befriend cops and Jack often had to insist on paying for what he bought. Nevertheless, Henry always managed to slip him a few free scallops or prawns, sometimes an entire Dungeness crab. In San Francisco at that time, romantic couples like Jack and Emma enjoyed taking a crab, a bottle of good white wine, and a freshly baked loaf of French bread down to the Wharf to have a picnic on the breakwater by the Bay.

Henry seemed old even then—ageless—and to Jack he appeared unusually knowledgeable and well-travelled for a fishmonger. He once mentioned, while discussing a good white wine sauce for sole, that he had spent a year in France. Occasionally, they discussed city politics and Henry always had brief but perceptive comments. Jack, of course, had no idea that this pleasant fishmonger was also the chief of a Chinese gang which his department was doing its best to close down.

Henry had a teenage son, Charlie, who helped in the store and was nearly as likable as his father. One rainy winter evening, Jack stopped off at the Seven Seas after work to pick up a pound of littleneck clams for Emma's dinner that night, spaghetti alla vongole. Charlie was at the cash register, Henry was in the office, when two men in raincoats came into the store with guns.

Jack had just paid for his clams when he saw trouble. He was armed with a service revolver, but it was in a holster beneath his belted London Fog trench coat with a brown corduroy sports jacket under that, buried deep. He backed away and pressed himself up against a wall, hoping to make himself invisible.

To get to his gun, first he had to transfer the bag of littleneck clams, still alive, from his right hand to his left hand. Then he needed to open the belt of his trench coat, which was tied loosely.

Jack assumed this was a holdup. He had already taken note of the fact that the men with guns weren't Asian. They looked Italian to him. But there wasn't time to ponder that. An elderly Chinese man walked out from the back office, unprepared for what was happening in the store. It was Henry's maternal uncle, Jack discovered later. He was an old man, gaunt and wrinkled.

The two holdup men were standing sideways to Jack. If they noticed him, they didn't take him seriously. He was only a frightened bystander. From that point, everything happened fast. The gunman on the left raised his hand very slightly and shot Henry's uncle in the chest. The old man collapsed like an empty bag of clothes. The autopsy later showed a direct hit to the heart.

"And this is for you, you fucking Chink!" said the gunman raising his semiautomatic pistol with the intention of killing Charlie, Henry's son.

Jack was young then, and his vision was perfect. In one motion, he had his gun out and fired one shot into the gunman's head, killing him instantly before he could pull his own trigger and shoot Charlie.

But there was still one more gunman.

Jack's hand was in motion, sweeping left to get a shot at the second gunman. He knew he was a fraction slow, and a fraction in a situation like this could get him killed.

But now another figure appeared from the back office. It was Henry. He was moving fast and silently.

Whack! There was a terrible thud as Henry swung something big and hard at the side of the gunman's head, which cracked and burst open.

This happened so quickly that it took a moment for Jack to take it in. He had supposed Henry had killed the gunman with something like a baseball bat, but it was a fish—a large bonita, the entire fish, all 13.4 pounds of it (as later noted in the forensic lab).

Jack couldn't believe it! Henry held the fish hanging down by its tail from his hand. It was ridiculous, and after the stress of nearly dying, all Jack could do was laugh.

Henry looked down at the fish he was holding and burst into laughter too. When they were more settled, Henry told his son that Jack had saved his life and he needed to thank him, which Charlie did with a formality that Jack found embarrassing. He aw-shucked the entire thing, claiming this was just the usual sort of stunt that happened when you were a San Francisco cop.

After this incident, Jack never had to pay for fish again at the Seven Seas Fish Market. His money was refused. But this made Jack uneasy and he stopped shopping there. After two times when his money was refused, he took his seafood business to a place a few blocks from Fisherman's Wharf that was nearly as good, and he never saw Henry Liu again.

Until today.

Afterwards, he had wondered, of course, if what he had witnessed really had been an attempted holdup. He was bothered by several things, but mostly what the gunman had said just before he was about to shoot Charlie: *And this is for you, you fucking Chink!* That made it personal, revenge possibly, or a warning—not about the cash in the register.

The two dead gunmen were quickly identified by the SFPD, and they were Italian, as Jack had thought. In the end, he suspected that what had happened wasn't either robbery or revenge. With other cases like this happening in the city, he believed that what he had witnessed was part of the ongoing war between Chinese and Italian factions in San Francisco. Chinatown had been expanding across Broadway into North Beach, and there were Italian interests that didn't like it. The Italians wanted to be the ones who controlled drugs and prostitution, not the Chinese.

But as the Abbot had said, this was a long time ago. And frankly, in Jack's long career, not really a big thing.

He hadn't thought of it in years. Now it made him smile.

"You were holding that fish!" he said. "Do you know how ridiculous you looked?"

"I've never eaten bonito again!" the Abbot exploded, laughing freely.

Jack felt himself relax. Whether it was luck, or perhaps the Abbot would call it karma, he felt he was finally going to get some answers as to what Chinese gangs were doing in New Mexico.

***

Jack proceeded delicately. In his experience, the Chinese liked to observe the formalities, and he didn't want to push too hard. They talked for a while about San Francisco in the old days—their old days, that is— about restaurants and places and people long gone, and the city they knew before everything became so expensive. Eventually, he got to the matter that had brought him here.

"The reason I'm here," said Jack, "is I'm investigating a human trafficking case in New Mexico, where I live these days. My associate came upon a dying Chinese woman in a remote corner of the state, on an Indian reservation. And we've been hired—my private detective agency, that is, Wilder & Associate—to discover who this woman was, where she came from, and what she was doing out there."

Jack recounted Howie's experience in some detail, his shortcut from hell. He did his best to bring it alive: the unfortunate woman, bleeding from a bullet wound, who stepped out of the desert in front of Howie's car.

Abbot Longwei listened attentively. "Yes, slavery is a terrible thing!" he said at last. "But this is an evil that's gone on for thousands of years, perhaps as long as there have been humans, far, far into our pre-history. Sometimes change happens slowly."

165

"Sometimes you have to give change a push," said Jack.

"Ah! But you see, we Buddhists don't push!" the old man said with a smile. "But now you must tell me what I can do for you. Why have you come to me with this matter?"

"Let me explain. I only want one thing. I want to know what's going on in New Mexico. I want to know who's running a trafficking operation on the La Chaya reservation, and I want to stop it. I don't want this happening in my new home state. I like New Mexico. And I like Native Americans, too—this isn't fair to them either. I want to shut this down."

"Commendable," said the Abbot. "But again, why have you come to me?"

"I want a name. I want to know who I'm after. There must be a local kingpin, somebody or some organization that's on the scene there. Those are the people I want to take down. And I want to do it in a way that will cause any criminal organization in the future to pause before they try something like this again in New Mexico."

"But are you certain it's a Chinese Tong behind this?"

"That's what my information is so far. I've also been told that there's Hong Kong money involved, and if it's true, I want to know that, too."

The Abbot laughed. "You want to know a great deal! And sadly, I am no longer a figure of importance, so I'm not sure how much I can help. No one consults me anymore, I'm old and forgotten. To be honest, I don't mind. I was more than ready to leave worldly things behind. But I tell you what, I will ask around."

"I would appreciate that very much," said Jack.

"But this will take time. You'll need to spend a few days here at the monastery, I'm afraid. If I may speak frankly, you look exhausted, my old friend. I think the rest will do you good."

"I really can't—"

"Nonsense! I'll have the guest cottage made up for you."

***

The monastery guest cottage was a good twenty-minute walk along a well-groomed gravel path, off by itself on a hilltop at the edge of a forest. Jack could only imagine the view from here of rolling meadows and redwood forests descending, often very sharply, to the glittering ocean that filled the horizon.

The cottage had no electricity. At night, Buzzy needed to light kerosene lanterns and candles. He had lived this way as a child on the utopian commune where he had grown up, but living rough in nature was something he had been glad to leave behind. More concerning, there was no cell service on the mountain, no Internet, and the only place where he could charge his phone was in the rental car with the engine running. For Buzzy, it felt like he had fallen into an electronic black hole.

The days flowed by in a timeless succession so that Jack soon lost track of whether it was a Saturday or a Monday. They spent a week at the monastery waiting for the Abbot to complete his probe. Nobody was in a hurry here. The Abbot apparently had a satellite phone, but Buzzy needed to find an excuse once a day to drive down to the coast where he was able to call Emma and keep her up to date.

"Jack's doing well," he told her each time he called. "There's nothing to do here but listen to the wind in the trees, so he's getting lots of rest."

"He's not going crazy with nothing to do?"

"He seems okay, Emma. He sits for hours on the sundeck outside the cabin with an odd look on his face. I don't know what he's thinking, he doesn't tell me. But I almost suspect he's meditating."

Emma laughed. "Oh, come now, Buzzy! The only meditation Jack does is when he's thinking hard about some gruesome crime!"

Buzzy was the one who was going stir crazy. This wasn't his idea of bliss. But then on the third day, he was walking toward the parking area by the administration center to make his daily drive to the coast when he met two young women in loose white clothing on the same path. They were Swedish, he discovered quickly. One was blonde, the other had light brown hair, and they couldn't have been more than nineteen. They were very pretty.

"Hello!" the brunette called merrily. "Isn't it a lovely day!"

Buzzy agreed it was. "Are you headed to the meditation hall?" he asked, as though this might be his destination too.

"No, no!" said the blonde. "We are going to the hot springs!"

"There's a hot springs here?"

"Oh, yes! And it's very nice, very natural. Would you like to come with us? We will show you the way!"

Yes, he would definitely like to join them, he answered. Hot springs were just his thing. Especially the natural kind.

By the end of the day, he had decided this was his kind of monastery. As far as he was concerned, if he ever took up religion, Buddhism, California style, was the way to go. Who cared if there was no electricity?

***

As for Jack, he wasn't certain whether they were guests or prisoners, but for the moment he was grateful to rest. He hadn't realized quite how tired he was.

He felt as though he had stepped off the busy planet into another realm. Temple bells rang through the forest at certain times of day, an irresistible summons. At night, an owl hooted from a nearby grove of redwood trees. As a stress addict, Jack fought it at first, but in spite of himself, peace descended on him slowly.

With nothing to do, Jack simply sat outside bathing in the warm rays of the sun. Memories flashed by his entire life in a series of vivid pictures. He relived a July 4th on Stinson Beach when he was seven . . . a girl in high school he'd had a crush on . . . meeting Emma . . . the really difficult cases he had handled as a cop. In an odd way it was like they were all present at once, right now, like a gallery of photographs he could wander through. Year after year, he saw his life in full.

"Goddamn!" said Jack, shaking his head in astonishment.

"Are you all right, Jack?" Buzzy asked coming up the path.

"I'm fine, Buzzy, just fine."

"You said, goddamn. So, I was just wondering."

"It's okay, Buzzy. Don't worry about it."

"Sure, Jack. I mean, it's cool with me if you want to go around muttering to yourself. Hey, I'd like you to meet Eva and Joëlle," he said. "They're from Sweden. They've come all the way to California in search of enlightenment. They've been showing me around a bit . . . Eva, Joëlle, say hello to Jack."

"Hello, Jack!" the girls said in unison. They sounded like a chipmunk chorus. Buzzy, for his part, sounded like a young guy in heat.

Jack could only shake his head. There were times when he was glad not to be young anymore.

The week passed slowly. Meals were left on their doorstep, pots of steaming rice, vegetables and tofu cooked in unusual ways, often spicy. Jack knew Emma would love it here. She was a great fan of tofu. As for himself, all he could say about tofu was that he didn't mind it too much. If you baked the hell out of it, it almost tasted like bacon.

He slept a great deal during this time, often three or four naps a day. It seemed he was always sleepy.

On the seventh day, Abbot Longwei sent for them.

"Well, old friend, I have learned a few things. Enough to suggest you leave this particular can of worms alone. The situation your associate encountered in the desert is more dangerous than at first it may have appeared."

Jack was taken aback. "More dangerous than human trafficking?" He thought for a moment. "So, Hong Kong money's involved?"

"Not Hong Kong. Mainland money," said the Abbot. "Beijing."

This was more than Jack had bargained for, but after coming all the way to California, he wasn't going to be put off now.

"Okay, I get it. International politics. But I still want to know what's happening on that Indian reservation. This may involve governments, but it still boils down to some local people who are involved. I want to know who I'm after."

Abbot Longwei hesitated, but in the end, he gave Jack a name and told him a story.

Chapter Twenty

On Thursday, while Jack was discovering tranquility in Big Sur, Howie was in Farmington, New Mexico, being grilled by U.S. Inspector Elliot Borello. Roasted might be a better word. Barbecued. It wasn't a peaceful experience.

Probably it had been a mistake to stop at the roadblock on the dirt road where he had been racing to get off La Chaya land. Rain obviously thought so. "Go, go!" Rain had shouted. But the Inspector was a semi-familiar face to Howie. He had a shotgun cradled in his arms, and stopping at the urging of a federal officer seemed the wiser choice.

As soon as Howie opened his car door, strong hands reached out and dragged him toward one of the white vans that were blocking the road. Before they tossed him inside, he had a glimpse of Rain being carried forcibly toward the second van. What happened to Rain from that point on, he didn't know. They were kept apart.

Howie was taken to Farmington and put in a room that had two chairs, a desk, and no windows. The building was in a semi-suburban neighborhood that was half rural, with chicken sheds and often horses in the backyards. It was the sort of place, he imagined, where you could scream your head off in a back room and no one would ever hear you.

Howie didn't see any reason to hold back. He told Inspector Borello everything he knew, all that had happened, including how Rain had shot the two camp guards in the canyon. Though he didn't feel particularly kindly toward Rain, he did his best to present the shootings as self-defense. The guards were reaching for their guns, after all. He didn't mention that he had told Rain to bypass the tents rather than go inside. He hoped that Rain, wherever he was, was telling the same story.

The interrogation continued for many hours, with only occasional breaks. Howie repeated his account again and again, until it seemed to him only a garble of words. At least, they fed him a Happy Meal from McDonald's. Howie hadn't gone to a McDonald's for years and he was impressed with how tasty his Big Mac was. He was so hungry, he could have eaten several more.

When he was talked out, and there was no more talk to give, Inspector Borello let him go with the warning that he was to stay clear and leave everything from then on to the Justice Department. Howie was glad to comply. Frankly, he'd had it with the La Chaya reservation. One of the federal marshals had driven his Subaru from the roadblock to Farmington, and as soon as he was free, he filled his gas tank and headed home to San Geronimo.

It was dawn Friday morning when Howie pulled up to his land and dragged himself up the wooded path to his pod. He was so tired he could barely keep his eyes open. Orange greeted him with a sullen meow. Howie managed to feed her, then he shed his clothes on the floor, climbed up the ladder to his loft, and fell into a deep sleep.

He slept around the clock, more than twelve hours. He got out of bed long enough to make himself a huge omelette stuffed with avocado, ham, mushrooms, cheddar cheese, green pepper, part of an over-ripe tomato, half a jalapeño—everything he could find in his refrigerator that hadn't gone off. The cheese needed some scraping off of the green parts. Once he had eaten, he thought he might climb back upstairs and sleep another few hours.

But then he glanced at the calendar on his computer nook and realized that his daughter, Georgina, would be arriving in five days' time, flying from Glasgow to Denver where he needed to pick her up. Howie had completely lost track of time. He experienced a major panic attack.

Five days!

***

A list!

He needed to start making up lists, what to do, when.

Howie knew his organizational skills were nothing to brag about. In fact—he could admit it—he was disorganized and easily distracted, starting one thing then moving to another. Making lists was the only way he could stay on track. Unfortunately, he often left his lists behind on his desk, which canceled their benefit.

In this case, he took two blank pages of computer paper and made two lists. One was for the final preparations for Georgie—he had to buy a new vacuum cleaner at Walmart, toilet paper, soap, and things like that.

The second list he labeled WORK, underlining the word several times. The most important item here was he needed to make a full written report to Lydia Cordell-Smith to tell her what he had discovered on the La Chaya reservation. He hadn't learned everything, that was true. But the U.S. Marshals could take it from here. They had the helicopters and armed officers needed to raid the compound. Meanwhile, Howie was formally taking himself off the case.

He decided this was a good night to stay home and write up the report. But first he needed to check-in with Jack.

Howie was frankly dreading reporting to Jack on his escapades of the past several days. Jack was going to be sarcastic, at the very least, possibly angry. He had always made it clear to Howie that he was no action hero, a role for which he had never been trained, and that the number one rule was *never* to get himself involved in the violent side of detective work.

Leave that part to Jack.

Dream on!

Howie had a satellite phone at home because none of the commercial servers had much interest in his ten acres of forest in the foothills of the Sangre de Cristo mountains.

He hit speed dial for Jack and listened to the phone ring six times, unanswered, before voice mail kicked in.

"Hey, Jack, it's me. I'm back in San Geronimo and I just wanted to check in. I've finished the trafficking case for the nice lady. I'll tell you all about it when we talk. In some ways the investigation was successful, and in other ways not," Howie said cautiously. "But now I'm getting ready for Georgie. I'll be in and out of the office over the next few days—I'll make sure Buzzy and Ruth know how to deal with the ongoing cases. As of Wednesday, Jack, I'll be officially on my three-week vacation. I won't be available."

He disconnected hoping that Jack remembered his daughter's upcoming visit, as well as Howie's three weeks off. It was hard to know sometimes with Jack's aging cognition.

Howie set up a pot of strong coffee and while it was dripping into the carafe, he made a quick tour of his land to see how much his neighbors, Ocean and Sage, had managed to finish in his absence.

At first sight, everything looked good. The cabin, the tepee on the far side of the creek, the new solar panels, the expanded pipe and filter system that brought water from the creek to an actual flushing toilet and shower in the studio.

Howie would need to take a final look at the plumbing tomorrow, to make sure everything worked. He'd been in touch with Georgie several times in the past month on Skype, warning her that New Mexico was going to be "rustic." But he wanted to make sure she had privacy and wouldn't be grossed out by a primitive bathroom.

He defrosted a boneless chicken breast and made an easy dinner, giving the chicken a squeeze of lemon, two cloves of minced garlic, and fresh thyme from his garden. After dinner, he cleaned up and spent the next three hours writing up his final report for Lydia Cordell-Smith. He gave her the location of the immigrant camp from which he believed the Chinese woman had escaped, and he detailed the conditions there, as well as his harrowing nighttime visit down into the canyon with his teenage Navajo guide, Rain Walker.

He wrote, as dispassionately as he was able, informing her that Rain had shot two guards so that they could escape and was now, as far as he knew, in the custody of U.S. Inspector Elliot Borello. Howie felt bad about Rain. They had shared a dangerous adventure, and in an odd way he had come to like the kid. But he could only shake his head at how it had ended. The fact that their foray into the canyon had been discovered, with two guards dead, would obviously change the situation on the ground.

Howie ended his report with the hope that U.S. Marshals would quickly organize a raid on the compound, release the trafficked prisoners, and solve the mystery of the large metal shed. This was no longer a matter for a small private investigation agency, but he hoped that his actions would quicken the end of slavery in the Southwest.

He indicated that Ruth, the agency secretary, would be sending a bill for work done.

Respectively submitted, Howard Moon Deer.

***

The next four days were busy for Howie as he bustled back and forth from town.

He managed to deal with pretty much everything on his two lists, including buying himself a new iPhone. Lydia Cordell-Smith, he discovered, had returned to Washington, but they had a virtual meeting on Zoom in which he told her the gist of his report. She appeared grimly satisfied with his description of the "slave camp," as she called it—it was exactly what she had been looking for! Evil incarnate in the heart of the American Southwest! She had been certain of its existence, and Howie had found it for her.

"Yes, Howard, it's time for the federal government to take over," she said solemnly. "But you've done a terrific job and I'll be sending you the full payment that we discussed."

Howie demurred—unwisely, Ruth told him later—that he hadn't earned $40,000. Above all, he hadn't found a name for the poor woman who had died in the desert. He suggested $15,000 would be satisfactory, which was only somewhat more than the fee he had proposed at the start of the job, $250 an hour plus expenses. But Lydia wouldn't hear of it. They settled on $30,000.

Between shopping in town for last minute items and putting the agency on hold for three weeks under Ruth's direction, the days were full. Emma, with whom he had several conversations, told him that Jack, Buzzy, and Katya were off in California in search of a Chinese gang lord who supposedly knew about human trafficking in New Mexico, and somehow he and Buzzy had ended up at a Buddhist monastery in the mountains above Big Sur where there was no cell service. Buzzy apparently had to sneak off each day in their rental car to a place where he could phone Emma with updates.

Howie had a good laugh picturing Jack in a monastery. But it wasn't something he dwelled on. As the visit drew near, his entire focus was on his 17-year-old daughter, Georgie.

Chapter Twenty-One

On Wednesday, Howie drove to Denver to pick up his daughter.

Georgie was arriving on a twelve-hour British Airways flight from Glasgow, with one stop in London. With the seven-hour time difference, she was scheduled to arrive at 10:20 that evening.

It was only a five-hour drive from San Geronimo to Denver, but Howie left home at eleven that morning to make certain he wasn't late. He wanted to allow for bad traffic, highway construction, wildfires, pandemics, maybe a monsoon. You never knew.

He arrived at DIA, Denver International Airport, at shortly before five in the afternoon, which meant a five-hour wait before Georgie's plane arrived. He didn't mind. Hopefully, it would give him time to compose himself.

He had already phoned Claire twice on the way driving to Denver. Claire had accompanied Georgie to the airport in Scotland along with her adoptive parents, Ray and Carol.

"Was she nervous?" Howie wanted to know. "I don't think she's ever flown before!"

"Howie, she was fine. Georgie is a very self-possessed young woman. *You're* the one who's nervous!" Claire said. "Relax!"

Relax? Howie was about to be a father! Howie couldn't relax! He was terrified!

Fortunately, the Denver airport was huge, an entire city, and you could pace forever up and down endless corridors that all looked the same. Every now and then, he took a ride on a moving sidewalk.

At nine o'clock, he parked himself on a seat outside the customs area from which Georgie would emerge. He still had an hour to go, but he wanted to make sure he was there in case her flight came in early.

The minutes crept by. From where he sat, he could keep an eye on the electronic Arrivals/Departures board. Each time he looked, he was relieved to see that Georgie's plane was on time.

BA1282 landed five minutes early. Howie knew it would be at least another half hour before Georgie passed through passport control and customs, but he was too excited to stay seated. He walked to the cordoned-off area by the sliding doors and joined a small crowd of people who were waiting for friends and family from different parts of the globe.

And finally, finally—after nearly an hour—there she was!

His daughter came out from customs dressed in black jeans that had rips in the knees and a stylish black shirt that had spangles on it. Her long black hair flowed over her shoulders. She had a daypack on her back and she pulled a small blue overnight case on wheels.

When he saw her last—the only time he saw her in person—she was fifteen, overweight, and gawky. She wasn't like that anymore. She had grown several inches since then. She was seventeen, slim, and lovely.

"Georgie! Welcome!" he gushed, stumbling forward to give her an awkward hug.

As he held her, he was overcome with feeling. *My daughter!* he said to himself, like a prayer.

***

It took a few hours for Howie and his daughter to relax with one another, but he believed they were going to be friends. He liked her. She was smart, poised, and very much her own person. She didn't say much about herself. She was a quiet girl. But she listened well.

Georgie's biological mother, Grace Stanton, had been Howie's first love when he was nineteen. She had been blonde and stunningly beautiful, a rich girl whose father was a U.S. Senator. She had everything, looks, talent, money, the works. How Howie, with neither looks nor money, had become her lover was a long story.

Physically, Georgie had ended up with his genes rather than her mother's. You could tell she was Howie's daughter just by looking at the two of them together. She had his round, moonish face. Though she was Scottish, she could have moved to Rosebud and be mistaken for Lakota as long as she didn't open her mouth. She had a thick Glasgow accent and often came out with expressions like donnae and wee.

"I donnae if I'll live in Glasgow after university," she told him on their second day together. "The weather's a wee bit wet."

This was an understatement. Scotland was wonderful, but you needed gills and fins to live there.

By some magic, despite her resemblance to Howie, Georgie had become a beautiful young woman. Not blatantly beautiful, as Grace had been, but more subtly so. Of course, Howie loved her from the first moment. Now it was just a matter of getting to know her.

They spent the first night in a Hilton Express near the airport. Howie was certain she would be exhausted after a twelve-hour flight and the seven-hour time change, but she said she had slept on the plane and wasn't tired in the least.

He wanted to show her the Rockies, so they took the long way home to New Mexico, west on I-70 and then a meandering course south on Highway 24 through the mountains. Each time they passed a ski resort, he promised he would teach her to ski one winter soon at San Geronimo Peak, which he claimed was better skiing than they had in Colorado. Unfortunately, this would need to wait a few years. Cambridge would be her focus for some time to come. Along with Howie's looks, she had inherited his inclination for academia.

She was planning to study biology and chemistry, thinking she might want to be a doctor. Though perhaps she would switch to art history, she wasn't sure. For a young person, she seemed very earnest. Georgie's adoptive parents—Ray and Carol—were both teachers, and growing up in Glasgow, she had come from a very cultured background.

Don't forget that! Howie told himself. Don't talk down to her!

Though she spoke sparingly, she wasn't in any way a sullen teenager. Driving through Colorado, she gradually opened up and told him her opinions about politics, art, music, and movies, but gave away very little about herself. Howie understood that he would have to earn her confidence.

They stayed the second night at a mountain lodge on a river, and in the morning, as they sat in a roadside coffee shop eating breakfast, she asked him the one question he had been dreading.

She asked about her biological mother. The beautiful Grace Stanton, the Senator's daughter. Howie didn't want to lie to her, so he told the difficult truth.

"She's dead, I'm afraid."

Georgie was stunned. "But I thought . . . I thought she was in prison. That's what I was told."

"She *was* in prison." Howie had been about to attack a stack of pancakes, but he put down his fork. He forced himself to continue. "She committed suicide. She hanged herself in her cell. Two months ago."

Georgie shook her head and her mouth fell open. She seemed more upset than Howie would have thought, mourning a mother she had never known.

"I'm sorry," he said. "I wasn't sure how to tell you. It's a complicated story, and a sad one. Your mother . . . she was talented, she was beautiful, but she was also a little mad."

Little was putting it mildly. By the end, Grace Stanton had been crazy as a cuckoo clock.

Georgie wanted to hear the story, and Howie believed she had the right. This was her mother, after all. He told the story as simply as he could, starting with how he had won a scholarship to Dartmouth when he was 17 and found himself rooming with Grace's brother, Nicolas Stanton—charismatic, brilliant, and as mad as his sister. Nick had been Howie's best friend during his undergraduate years, until he had become an eco-terrorist wanted by the FBI and they went their separate ways. He was dead now too, unfortunately.

Georgie listened with rapt attention, never taking her eyes off Howie as he spoke. This was a family story of murder and mayhem that must have come as a shock to a nice Scottish girl freshly arrived in America.

"I wonder if I will end up a wee bit mad myself?" she said softly. "It's in the genes, isn't it?"

"No, you're *not* going to end up like your mother!" he said firmly. "Your mother's problem had little to do with genes. She was a victim of her own privilege and narcissism. She was so enclosed in her selfishness that no fresh air got in. If you see what I mean."

"I think so. But it must be lovely to have so much money!"

"Not always," said Howie. "She was raised in a world of secrets and lies. Her father was a terrible man."

"A U.S. Senator!" she said wonderingly. "My grandfather!"

They left the café and continued south along the mountain highway that would take them into New Mexico. Georgie was silent in the car for nearly an hour, and Howie left her alone. He imagined she was absorbing what she had just learned.

"Did you love her?" she asked suddenly, turning his way.

"I did," he answered. "Or at least, I thought I did. I was very young. I made a lot of projections onto her that turned out to be wrong. Do you know what I mean by projections?"

"Projecting your needs onto another person, without bothering to find out who they really are?"

"Exactly. It was a case of mistaken identity. Look, Georgie—looking back, I'm not entirely happy with my part in this story. I was a poor scholarship Indian in a fancy East Coast school, and at first I had a very romantic picture of the Stantons. Your mother in particular. You should have seen her in her bright yellow two-seater sports car, the top down, driving with her blonde hair blowing in the wind! I fell in love with a mirage."

"Then you didn't really love her?"

Howie had to think before he answered. "No, I did. I loved her with all my heart, and in a way that I will never love again."

She broke my heart, Howie left unsaid.

They continued talking on and off as they drove south into New Mexico. In the end, Georgie knew a lot more about him than he knew about her. It was curious, he thought, how little she had revealed about herself.

***

They arrived in San Geronimo on Friday evening at only a few minutes past seven, in time for burritos at Angie's Food Cart, currently *the* food cart in town.

It wasn't fancy. Sitting at a picnic table by the main highway through town, he watched to see what his daughter would think about a really good New Mexican burrito with green chile sauce on one end, and red chile sauce on the other.

182

"It's not like the Mexican restaurants in Glasgow," was her only comment.

"Mexican restaurants have morphed as they've spread around the world. In Thailand, I once had a taco with pad thai noodles in it. But what you're eating now is the real thing. The Spanish have been in this part of New Mexico for five hundred years."

He hurried her along because he wanted to get back to his land before it was dark, so she could get an idea of where she was. She took half her burrito in a bag to go.

"My house is somewhat unconventional," Howie warned as they were pulling up onto the gravel parking area at the edge of his land.

She smiled politely. He had no idea whether unconventional was okay with Georgie.

She took her daypack and the small overnight suitcase with wheels, and he took the larger suitcase that she had checked through. It too had wheels, which was a good thing because it was heavy.

Howie led the way along the narrow forest path that wound up and down across his land for several hundred yards. The summer light was fading through the trees, casting a pleasant speckling of green. Just before they reached his pod, they crossed the creek on a pretty wooden foot bridge that he had completed earlier in the spring.

They turned a corner from where Howie's eco-pod could be seen for the first time: his giant egg that rested on metallic chicken legs. The top of the egg bristled with satellite dishes and antennae.

Georgie gaped at it.

Howie was about to explain that the pod came from a kit designed by two German architects, but his words died unsaid.

As both Howie and Georgie's eyes panned downward to the egg's base, they saw a young man sitting on the steps by the front hatch.

It was Rain Walker.

The kid.

He flicked his head to get the hair from his eyes so he could give Georgie a better look.

Chapter Twenty-Two

"They had me in a cell in Farmington in this totally redneck jail," Rain told them. "But I escaped, *no problema.*"

Rain seemed immensely proud of himself.

"The bastards wouldn't even let me call a lawyer," he continued, turning his focus on Georgie. "You see, Indians have no rights, none at all, even though this was our country long before it got to be theirs. They treat us like dogs! You know how I got out?"

He didn't wait for an answer.

"One of the guards came to open the cell door. He was going to take me to some room to be questioned, but I was ready. As soon as I heard the lock open, I flung myself at the door. I pushed him backward so hard he fell on his ass! I ran right over him, right out of that damn jail into the woods across the street!"

"Didn't they come after you?" Georgie asked. She was regarding Rain with astonishment.

"Sure they did. But I was too quick. You see, there's an old Indian trick where you move so fast you're invisible. It's all mental. You have to be initiated to be able to do it. You really have to *be* there, if you know what I mean."

"Sure," said Howie. "So how did you get to San Geronimo? Did you run all the way from Farmington?"

"No, man. I stole a car."

"Right," said Howie.

"It was a funky old Subaru. Even older than yours," Rain told them. "A real clunker. It broke down near Chama and I had to hitch to get up here. An Indian picked me up, a real nice guy. He drove me all the way to your land . . . Indians are the only people who'll stop for you on the road," Rain explained to Georgie. "Since you're from Scotland, you probably don't know these things. The White Man really sucks. They'll roar by in their gas-guzzling SUVs, won't even give you a look."

"How did you find out where I live?" Howie asked. "I didn't give you my address."

"The Indian who picked me up knew who you are. He said he's delivered firewood to you here."

"Tom Day Bird? Did he have a beat-up Chevy pickup truck?"

"I forget his name. I wasn't paying attention. The truck was pretty damn funky, though."

"But why did they arrest you in the first place?" Georgie asked.

He lowered his voice. "I got into a fight, that's all. I'm a peaceful person, Georgie, I want you to know that. But we were in a tent full of trafficked workers, and we were trying to get them out when these guys came in with guns. I had to protect us, I didn't have a choice. I wasn't worried so much about myself as about your father."

"Hold on!" said Howie. "We were only there to investigate. There wasn't supposed to be any violence. And there wouldn't have been, if you weren't so hot-headed!"

"Well, sometimes you just have to do what you have to do," Rain said devoutly. He gave Georgie a look Rudolf Valentino would have been proud of.

He proceeded to tell her a tale of epic proportions, how he and Howie had climbed down into a remote canyon in a dangerous corner of the La Chaya reservation, stumbling over rocks, lightning flashing in the sky. It was like the movie version, vastly exaggerated. But Howie could see that his daughter was impressed.

It was a calm summer night with a sky full of stars, and they were sitting outside on oversized cushions on the small deck of the studio he had built for this visit. A large round candle was burning in a glass lantern, shining a golden light on their faces. Howie had conceived the cushions and the deck and the candle lantern as a background for where he and his daughter would have long conversations getting to know each other. He had never imagined there would be three of them.

Not knowing what to do with himself, feeling unwanted, he stood and went inside the studio to make tea. He wasn't about to offer either of these underage teens anything alcoholic.

As the whistling kettle slowly came to a boil, he considered his options. What he wanted, of course, was to send Rain packing. *You hitched here, and you can damn well hitch yourself out!* But he didn't want to look like a bully in Georgie's eyes. Unfortunately, she seemed to find him fascinating.

By the time the teapot whistled, he had decided what he was going to do.

He poured water into three mugs, each with a bag of chamomile, and put them on a tray along with a jar of honey and a plate of chocolate biscotti. He returned outside and set the tray on a low faux-Japanese coffee table that he bought at Pier One in Santa Fe.

Georgie looked up at her father. "And you dinnae tell me about this! If Rain hadn'a been so quick, you could'a been killed!"

Howie's smile had a bite to it. *If Rain hadn't been there, there wouldn't have been a problem in the first place!*

"Look, here's the situation," he told them. "The cops are going to come looking for Rain and this is going to be the first place they'll look. Breaking out of jail is frowned upon in New Mexico, and when the cops come, they'll be armed. We've got to get him out of here."

"They'll come with *guns*?" Georgie asked. She had vivid notions of American justice.

"Without a doubt," Howie told her. He gave Rain a hard look. "And if Rain has a gun somewhere and shoots back and kills a policeman, he'll be facing the rest of his life in prison. He can spend the night, Georgie, but first thing tomorrow, he has to go. If he's smart, he'll turn himself in."

***

Howie worked out the sleeping arrangements, leaving nothing either to chance or nature.

He put Rain in the cabin at a good distance from his daughter, and he gave Georgie his own bed in the sleeping loft. Howie would sleep on a futon on the pod's floor, not his favorite place to be, but it would be for one night only.

Tomorrow he would resume his visit with Georgie, just the two of them, and all would be well. In the morning, he planned to take her to the Peak and show her around the ski area. He thought they might take the scenic summer chairlift ride up Lift #1 and hike down to the bottom, getting a bit of exercise. It would be a chance for him to recount a few hair-raising ski stories—crashes, caught edges, trees and cliffs narrowly avoided. He was sure she would be fascinated.

They would have a late lunch and afterwards make a tour of the art galleries in town, avoiding those galleries that specialized in paintings of Southwest sunsets and hollyhocks growing up the sides of adobe buildings. Howie saw it as a well-balanced day, sports in the morning, culture in the afternoon, interspersed with gourmet meals from time to time.

Howie's bathroom was barely larger than a telephone booth, but like everything else in the pod, it was cleverly designed. He let Georgie go first. She came out ten minutes later in an old-fashioned cotton nightgown and her bathroom kit in hand.

She sat down across from him at the small kitchen table. Orange jumped up on her lap and made herself comfortable. It was a sign of approval that she allowed Georgie to pet him.

"Does Rain really have to leave?" she asked.

"He does, Georgie. Both for his sake and ours. Like I said, this is the first place the police will look for him and there's no way I'm going to let you get involved in something like that. I promised Ray and Carol I'd keep you safe and get you back to Scotland in one piece. The one hesitation they had allowing you to come on this trip is that my job is occasionally dangerous. I promised them that I would put all work aside during the time you were here."

"But this is different!" she objected. "I mean, it's horrible—a slave camp! You wouldn't think there would be things like that happening today! In America, no less! We've got to do something!"

Howie nodded. He was pleased his daughter had a social conscience. Just not in this particular instance.

"Absolutely," he agreed. "But you see, we've done all we can. We found the camp, we've exposed what's going on down there, and we've passed on everything we learned to the proper authorities. It'll be their job now to make the arrests and rescue those poor trafficked people."

"Yes, but Rain—"

"Georgie, it's a shame that Rain shot those guards. To be honest, that didn't need to happen. In my opinion, we could have gotten into that camp, had a good look around, and gotten away without anyone getting hurt. Rain acted, well . . . intemperately."

Georgie stared at him. "Intemperately?"

Howie had to agree it was a pompous adverb. "Okay, he was a jerk, if you want to know the truth. A total asshole. He went into one of the tents after I told him not to. He woke people up, he made noise, and the guards appeared. He acted like he was some sort of ninja in a video game."

Georgie gave him a look that said more clearly than words that Rain might have been a ninja in a video game, but Howie had turned into a boring adult.

He sighed.

"I'll tell you what. First thing tomorrow morning, I'll phone Inspector Borello—he's the U.S. Marshal we've been dealing with. I'll work out a safe way for Rain to turn himself in. That's the only way this is going to end well. I've already told Borello that what Rain did was in self-defense, but I'll goose it up a little. In a situation like this—a prison camp for trafficked workers—all the sympathy is going to be on our side. If we put what happened in the right light, they're not going to charge him with homicide. The most stupid thing Rain did was escape from custody, and he may have to pay for that. But it'll be pretty minor."

Howie gradually won her over.

He made her a cup of hot chocolate and eventually she climbed up the ladder to the sleeping loft and went to bed.

Howie believed he had the situation under control.

***

But he didn't have the situation under control.

On Saturday morning, Howie was awoken just before dawn by the harsh, metallic voice of a megaphone from the clearing outside the pod.

"This is the police! We have the property surrounded! Come out with your hands clearly visible!"

Howie sat up in his sleeping bag on the floor. He wasn't entirely awake, but his heart was racing. He could hear Georgie stirring in the loft overhead.

The megaphone barked again:

This is the police! We have this property surrounded! Come out with your hands clearly visible!

He had been expecting the cops. But not so quickly.

"Georgie?" he called upward. "Are you awake?"

"What's happening?"

Howie stayed calm. "I mentioned the police last night, remember? Everything's going to be okay, but they're here now. They've come for Rain. I thought we'd have more time to arrange things. Now, here's what we're going to do. Are you listening?"

"Yes!"

"I'm going outside to talk with them, so whatever you do, don't worry. That's Inspector Borello outside, I recognize his voice. He already knows the story, so this won't take long. Meanwhile, I'd like you to get dressed just in case you have to come out, too . . . but it's going to be all right. Okay?"

"I guess."

She didn't sound convinced.

"Can you use a laptop?" he asked tenuously.

" 'Course, I can!"

"A Mac?"

"I have a Mac at home. Claire gave it to me. It was one of her old ones. It's an Airbook."

"Come out now!" repeated the voice on the megaphone. *"Come out with your hands clearly showing!"*

Howie spoke quickly. "Climb down as soon as you're dressed. You'll see my computer nook. Open the laptop. You won't need a password, it's only asleep. Go to Mail, new message, type Office into address blank. That's all you'll need. It'll go to Ruth, my office manager in town. Write her a note and tell her what's happening then hit send. Did you get all that?"

"Sure. I'm getting dressed."

"But don't worry," he said again before he stepped outside. "This is all going to be fine!"

***

The spectacle outside his front door wasn't encouraging.

Four Marshals stood in the clearing between the pod and the new studio, two with shotguns in their arms, the others with nasty looking carbines. The diffuse light of early dawn gave everything the *noir* look of an old movie.

The good news was that Rain had already come out from the studio to give himself up, which avoided a messy confrontation.

Inspector Borello stood in the clearing with his attention on Rain. Along with his cowboy boots, the Inspector was in slacks and a short sleeve polo shirt with a Ralph Lauren pony on it. Rain had a defiant smile on his face as he stood with his arms behind his back to allow one of the Marshals to handcuff him.

"Inspector, I was going to phone you first thing in the morning," Howie said, "to work out a safe easy way for Rain to give himself up."

"Really? You were going to do that, were you?" said Borello turning to Howie.

"Rain showed up here last night, just as my daughter and I got home. You have to understand, Inspector—historically, Indians have had very bad experiences in your White Man's jails, so he had every reason to escape. But I soon convinced him to give himself up. As you know, he only acted in self-defense down in that camp. Once he has a chance to tell his side of the story in court, I don't think any judge in this country will charge him for the deaths of those guards. In fact, he should get a medal."

"Well, that's not for me to decide." Borello looked over Howie's shoulder. "Good morning," he said. "You must be the daughter from Scotland."

Howie glanced behind him and saw that Georgie was standing just outside the front hatch. He hoped she had managed to get a message off to Ruth.

"Georgie, this is Inspector Borello from the U.S. Marshal's department. Why don't you go inside and see if you can get some coffee going. Everything's going to be all right."

"You can forget the coffee," Borello said. "We'll pick up some on the road. Come on, we've got to get going."

"Inspector, Rain has already agreed to go with you," said Howie, "But Georgie and I have other plans for the day."

"No, you don't, Moon Deer. Your calendar is free. I need you all in Farmington to give statements. You, too, Georgie. Now, let's go, please. I have a van waiting at the end of the path. Once I have your statements, you'll be free to leave."

"Then why don't I follow you to Farmington in my car," Howie suggested. "That way we'll have wheels to get home."

"I'll have one of my deputies drive you home. That way I know I can keep you all together."

"I've got a better idea," said Howie. "Let me drop my daughter off at Emma Wilder's. She'll take care of Georgie until I get back. I don't want her sitting around a police station. She has absolutely nothing to do with this case."

"That's too bad, Moon Deer—you should have thought of that when I warned you not to get involved in this. Now let's get going."

"It's okay," Georgie said, taking his arm as she watched Rain being led away in handcuffs. "Think of the stories I'll be able to tell about the Wild West when I get back to Scotland!"

Howie appreciated Georgie's cheerful attitude, though he was aware they could be charged with harboring a fugitive and this could turn out very badly.

Damn you, Rain! he swore savagely to himself as they walked along the path to the police van that would carry them away. *"Damn, damn, damn . . ."*

Chapter Twenty-Three

"We just arrived in Albuquerque," Buzzy said to Emma on his phone. It was Friday morning, and despite the Swedish nymphs cavorting naked in the monastery hot springs, he was relieved to be back in the digital age. "We're at the airport."

"And he's still all right?"

"Emma, Jack's enjoying himself! We spent the week at this Shangri-La like Buddhist monastery in Big Sur and I've never seen him so relaxed. The Abbot was somebody he used to know back when you guys lived in San Francisco. He was Henry the fishmonger who had a store in Chinatown where Jack says you used to shop."

"Henry the fishmonger!" She cried with laughter. "Henry became a Buddhist *monk*?"

"He became the *Abbot*. And before he got so holy, he was also the Grand Dragon of the Red Gecko Tong. That's the guy at the top. The Tongs are a Chinese crime organization."

"I know what Tongs are, Buzzy." Her laughter gradually stopped. It was hard for her to picture Henry the fishmonger in his stained apron as a crime lord who became a Buddhist abbot. She had liked him. He seemed such a modest, sympathetic man. But the older she became, the more she realized how complicated human nature was, and how little you saw of what was going on inside.

"According to Abbot Longwei, Tongs were charitable organizations," Buzzy said. "Giving loans to people who wanted to start a business. Giving protection to the exploited Chinese community."

"That's one side of the picture," Emma admitted. "But don't forget the violence. These are the kings of Chinatown. If you do what they tell you and pay your dues, you'll be all right. But people shouldn't have to live like that, taking orders from gangsters."

That pretty much described the U.S. government, Buzzy thought, but he wasn't about to argue with Emma Wilder. She was nearly as opinionated as Jack, and much better educated. How they got on together, he did not know.

"Anyway, Jack's fine. He's longing to get home. He's hoping to take a long vacation once this case is wrapped-up. We just have one more stop to make—somebody he needs to see—and you'll have him back in San Geronimo in no time."

Emma did a double-take. "Wait a second? What do you mean, one more stop? What's that husband of mine up to?"

"It's a guy in Santa Fe who owns a chain of Chinese restaurants. We need to see him for a second. It's the case we've been working on, I'm sure he'll tell you all about it. Look, Emma, I need to hang up now. Jack's just coming out of the men's room with Katya and he needs help. I'll try to call from Santa Fe . . ."

Buzzy disconnected and shook his head.

"That wasn't easy, Jack. You owe me!"

Jack had not been in the restroom. He had been sitting on the bench next to Buzzy the entire time.

"Okay, thanks." Jack took hold of Katya's harness and rose to his feet. "Now let's get out of this airport! We've got stuff to do!"

***

Jimmy Chou. That was the name Abbot Longwei had given Jack.

Jimmy was a mid-level member of the Hipsong Tong, who were rivals of the Red Gecko Tong, the "society" that the Abbot had once headed in San Francisco. According to the Abbot's information, it was the Hipsong Tong that had set up a hemp operation on the La Chaya reservation in New Mexico worked by trafficked labor.

Jimmy had his headquarters in Santa Fe, but he took his orders from California. On the surface, he was a respectable businessman. He ran a chain of Chinese restaurants in Texas, Arizona, and New Mexico that went by the awful name of Yin/Yang/Yummy, each word separated by a slash. To make the brand easy to remember, all the advertising called the restaurant chain 3Y, hoping it would catch on with the public.

The money for the chain came indirectly from Hong Kong through a number of shell companies that would be difficult to trace. A chain of Chinese restaurants was a respectable investment, entirely legal. Nevertheless, Abbot Longwei believed the government in Beijing was the real boss, the wizard behind the curtain. Unfortunately, there was no proof for any of this. Only the word of an old cop, who had heard the story from an even older Abbot.

"I once went to the Yin/Yang/Yummy in Albuquerque," Buzzy admitted. "I was on a date, Jack, and I didn't have much money. 3Y is upscale compared to fast food, but they're not quite real restaurants either, so they're cheap."

"What did you think?"

"Hey, the food's not awful. It's just generic and looks more like it came from a factory than a kitchen. All the restaurants have full bars and they're big on tall drinks with paper umbrellas, things like Singapore Slings and Mai Tais. Think of Chili's—what Chili's did for Mexican food, that's what Yin/Yang/Yummy is trying to do for Chinese. Everything's geared to gringos with sanitized taste buds. There are big screen TVs in the bars showing all the sports."

According to the Abbot, the La Chaya tribal council had been eager to be corrupted. They had already spent a few years trying to find investors to build a casino on their land, but the respectable financial world turned them down. The market for Indian casinos was already glutted in New Mexico, and the La Chaya reservation was seen as too remote to attract business. Finally, a shady investment company from Texas got interested and the construction began. But the Texas company went bust after a few months leaving behind a half-finished casino. This was when the Chinese underworld came in.

The Hipsong Tong had large amounts of money they needed to launder, and at first, they agreed to give the tribe enough money to finish the construction. But the project was jinxed. They were just getting going again when somebody high up in China pulled the plug. There seemed to be some confusion in the line of command. Several people lost their jobs and were never seen again.

Jimmy Chou was involved from the start, the point man in New Mexico, and he came up with the alternate idea of an industrial hemp farm run by trafficked labor. Hemp had become a profitable business, and if anyone noticed unexpected activity on the reservation, it would be a good cover for what was really going on.

"Guns," said the Abbot. "They're arms dealers. They're smuggling in weapons from China and using the Indian reservation as their distribution center. At least, this is what I've been told, Inspector. All my information is second and third hand, but I believe it's reliable."

Jack liked the Abbot addressing him as Inspector. It almost made him feel young again. And he found the notion of gun running intriguing. Nevertheless, he wasn't convinced. Simply put, there were so many guns in America, legal and otherwise, that he didn't see that there would be much profit in smuggling more of the same into the country from China. There were more guns in Texas than people, and if anything, you'd think the commercial traffic would be going the other direction.

Jack understood that there were advantages in setting up a criminal operation on Indian land. There were sensitive issues concerning sovereign Native rights, and federal agencies were inclined to leave tribes alone. Surveillance from the air would be seen as invading sacred land and would probably lead to a court battle. In short, it would be easier to hide something on Indian land than in other places. But what were they actually hiding?

Jack pondered these questions as Buzzy drove from Albuquerque on I-25 to Santa Fe. Though he had been a detective for most of his life, he hated mysteries. They irritated him. He couldn't stand not knowing what something was about. It was like an itch.

Jack inhaled the desert smell of New Mexico coming in the car window as they drove north. The air was hot and dry, not at all like coastal California, the foggy Pacific with its cold and damp. He realized he'd become a true New Mexican in the years since he had left California. California was a state with a glitzy image of itself, self-important, but Jack found he liked living in a modest outpost of the modern world. Except for a few wealthy neighborhoods in places like Santa Fe and San Geronimo, New Mexico was like being in a Third World country.

Buzzy had already spent time in airport boarding areas on his laptop investigating what there was to know about Jimmy Chou. He had found a single photograph of Jimmy from a restaurant opening in Scottsdale, Arizona. He was a short, round ball of a man in his fifties without much of a neck or waistline. "Think of a Chinese Danny de Vito," Buzzy said.

He got off the freeway at St. Francis Drive and headed into downtown Santa Fe. It was midday Saturday afternoon and the city streets were crowded with traffic. As they approached the Round House, the capital building where the New Mexico legislature convened, the traffic came to a stop and refused to move. Cars honked their horns in frustration, which didn't help.

"What's going on?" asked Jack.

"We're stuck behind a bus that's not moving. It must be because of all the people arriving for the women's march."

"What women's march?"

"Don't you keep up with the news? It's an annual event. Women come from all over to protest pretty much everything. Abortion rights, gender inequality, racism, everything they're angry about. The main speaker is supposed to be some progressive congresswoman from New York."

Jack sighed. "I never would have thought when I was young, even after the Kennedy assassinations, that I would see this country in such a state!"

"The march itself isn't until tomorrow," Buzzy said quickly, to keep Jack from tripping down memory lane. "There's going to be music, speeches, celebrities, tens of thousands of people. This is just the warmup for the party."

"Well, it'll be a party we're going to miss. Now, get us out of here!"

Buzzy did an illegal U-turn in the middle of the block causing more honking from the other cars. In order to make the turn, he had to inch forward and backward several times, coming close to bashing the fender of the Nissan behind him.

Santa Fe's Yin/Yang/Yummy Lounge and Restaurant was on Paseo de Peralta. It was housed in a building that originally had been a Pizza Hut and still had the red roof. In the windows, neon signs sizzled with the names of beer. A free-standing sign facing the parking area advertised a lunch buffet, all you can eat for $9.99, as well as the nightly special, Mandarin Orange Chicken for $7.99.

"You hungry, Jack?"

"Not for bad Chinese, thank you very much! Is the joint crowded?"

"Not really. There's a separate entrance to the lounge at the side of the building, and there are a few more cars there. You want to go inside?"

"No, I don't think that would accomplish anything. Not yet. I'm just trying to get a sense of what we're up against. Let's go to the second address we have, the corporate headquarters."

"You're not tempted by the all-you-can eat buffet?"

"Go, Buzzy!"

Buzzy had found the address of 3Y, LLC, after an extensive search on the Internet. The building was on Manhattan Avenue in a mixed residential street of small businesses and homes a few blocks from the commuter rail station.

"It's coming up on the right, Jack. What do you want me to do?"

"Just park somewhere across the street. I want to feel it out."

"I'll have to park by a fire hydrant."

"Just do it," said Jack. "We're only going to be here a few minutes and we won't get out of the car. Tell me what you see."

"Well . . . there's not much to say about the building. It's a two-story house that could either be a residence or a business. It's half-hidden by a hedge. From what I can see, it's kind of a cross between modern and craftsman style. There's no sign saying 3Y, nothing that indicates what's happening inside."

"Is there a parking area?"

"Just a driveway that comes up from the street. There are two cars near the front door, a BMW SUV and a Toyota Land Cruiser. If you want to hang out here, I'll need to find better parking."

"No, let's just sit a minute."

In fact, Jack didn't have a clear idea of why he had asked Buzzy to bring him here. He was hoping the proximity of Jimmy Chou's headquarters might give him an idea of how to proceed, but it didn't. Meanwhile, he had another problem to ponder. He knew he had important information that he needed to pass on to law enforcement, but he wasn't sure if that would be U.S. Marshal Inspector Borello or his old friend Santo Ruben at the NMSP. Probably it would be Santo, though he was a much lesser gun than a U.S. Marshal. Jack didn't entirely trust the Department of Justice, which was far too political for his taste. But first he had to make sure he truly had something to report. He didn't want to cry wolf and have nobody take him seriously.

Jack was struck suddenly with an alarming thought. What if the Hip-song Tong weren't just smuggling AK-47 knock-offs? What if they were peddling military grade weapons? Explosives, missiles, who could say? This would be profitable enough to justify the energy and expense of using such a remote location.

Jack decided it was time to call Santo, no more pondering. He told his phone to try Santo's personal cell number, which rang three times then went to voice mail.

"Santo, it's Jack. Give me a call as soon as you can. I'm starting to get a bad feeling about the case I'm working."

Next, he tried the San Geronimo State Police switchboard where he reached an officer he knew, Sally Loeb, who told him that Santo was busy at the site of a gas station robbery where a clerk in the convenience store had been shot. He wouldn't be able to return Jack's call for at least an hour. Jack disconnected with the feeling that he was spinning in circles, getting nowhere.

Buzzy, who had been slouching against the car door, sat up with a start.

"Jack, two guys just walked out of the house into the driveway. They're getting into the Land Cruiser in the driveway."

"Describe them."

"Big tough-looking Indian guys. You wouldn't want to mess with them."

"Native Americans?"

"Like I told you. Two Indians."

Jack sighed. "Okay, so they're not from Bombay, I'm guessing."

"Mumbai, Jack. These days the name Bombay is reserved for gin."

"Yeah, yeah. Now tell me what's going on over there."

"They're backing out of the driveway. They're heading toward Cerrillos Road."

"Okay, Buzzy, here's what we're going to do. Just for the hell of it, let's follow them."

"Oh, come on, Jack! You can't be serious—"

"Go, my friend. Let's see how long it takes for them to make you."

***

The Land Cruiser on the road up ahead was light gray, not a distinctive color. Buzzy stayed back a hundred feet and did his best to keep a car between them.

Jack had given him a few lessons in tailing cars and he knew it wasn't possible to do a professional job with one car alone. There were too many variables including the possibility of getting caught in a red light. To do it properly, you needed two cars working in tandem, three would be better still.

"If you lose them, don't worry," Jack told him. "I just won't give you a raise."

"That's swell of you, Jack!"

"And don't break any traffic laws."

In fact, the Land Cruiser wasn't difficult to tail. It took a straightforward route to Cerrillos Road then north on St. Francis Drive. Buzzy was able to keep it in sight while maintaining a buffer of one or two cars between them. The agency Kia that Jack had leased was like a million other cars and it blended into the traffic. He didn't think he'd been spotted.

St. Francis Drive merged into Highway 285 where the Land Cruiser increased its speed to a steady 60 mph. A few miles later it took the exit to the Santa Fe Opera.

"They took the Opera exit? Should I follow?"

"Sure," said Jack. "But be careful you don't get spotted."

The road to the Opera passed under the highway and wound into the hills for half a mile. The theater sat on top of a hill, an architectural wonder with a cantilevered roof that was partially open to the elements, giving the audience spectacular views of the high desert and mountains. In the old days, there was no roof at all which had left the audience exposed to summer monsoon rains. Jack had once sat through a performance of *La Bohême* soaking wet.

Buzzy kept well back. Up ahead, the Land Cruiser disappeared around a bend in the road and then appeared again.

"They don't seem to be showing an opera tonight," Buzzy said. "There's nobody around."

"They don't *show* operas," Jack told him. "They perform them. It's not a movie!"

"Whatever. If it's not rock 'n roll, you won't find *me* there!"

The vast parking area was empty of cars. The sun was high in the sky, burning with midday heat. At first, Buzzy didn't see the Land Cruiser. Then he spotted it on the far-left side of the parking area alongside a stand of piñon trees. It had stopped next to a black Dodge Ram.

"They're meeting somebody in a pickup. There's nobody else in the parking lot, Jack, just them and us. So there's no way they won't notice us."

"Then don't stop. Drive up to the gate and park as close as you can get to the box office. We'll act like we've come to buy tickets."

"It looks like everything's closed, Jack. I doubt if the box office is open."

"Buzzy, this is make-believe," Jack said acidly. "If it's closed, we're clueless opera buffs who got things wrong. Do you think you can play that part?"

"Sure," said Buzzy.

"Your part's easy. You're going to watch what's going on with those two vehicles while I get out with Katya and go to the box office. Take pictures if you can."

Emma was the opera fan in the family, and she had bullied Jack to Santa Fe countless times over the years to see lavish productions of Mozart, Verdi, and company, once even a very strange opera by Philip Glass. Jack wasn't wild about opera, sitting for hours on uncomfortable seats, but he did his best to be an accommodating husband.

It was handy now that he had a spatial memory of the opera grounds. He let Buzzy drop him and Katya off in the handicapped area close to the main gate.

He had been sitting in the car too long and had to unbend to stand up straight. Such were the creaky joys of old age. Katya was glad to be let out of the back and he let her run around and wag her tail before he called her and put her in her harness.

"The box office, girl," he told her. Unfortunately, smart as she was, Katya only understood a few English phrases, and box office wasn't one of them. With a bit of urging, he pointed her in what he believed was the right direction and told her to go. Go was a word she knew. She went as far as the closed iron gate that led to the theater where she stopped to see where Jack wanted to go next. Jack didn't care, as long as he gave Buzzy time to see what was going on with the SUV and pickup truck that were having the rendezvous.

He heard footsteps come his way. "The box office is closed until five o'clock, sir." Jack assumed it was a security guard.

"Closed? Darn! I wanted to buy tickets for *Madame Butterfly!*"

"We're not doing *Madame Butterfly* this season, I'm afraid."

Jack shook his head in disappointment. "I guess I'm getting everything wrong today."

"Would you like help getting back to your car, sir?"

Jack smiled. Apparently, the guard believed he was someone without all his marbles.

"I'll be fine. My dog knows the way."

He pointed Katya back toward where they had come. "The car, girl."

"So, talk," said Jack when he and Katya were back inside the Kia.

"There's nothing to tell. I could see three guys standing between the car and truck talking for a while. But they were too far away to get a real look. I took some photos, zooming out as far as it would go, but I'm not sure how they'll come out."

"Well, okay, we tried. Let's just go home."

"There's a turnaround on the exit road before we get to the highway. I could drive there and wait, then get behind them again," Buzzy offered.

"No, it's too late. They've spotted us now. Anyway, my guess is the guys in the Land Cruiser have done what they came to do, now they'll just return home to Yin and Yippee—"

"Yummy."

"Whatever. We're finished here. But just for the hell of it, drive slowly as you pass them. See if you can get a better look."

Buzzy started up the Kia and turned the wheel toward the exit. The parking area was several football fields long. In past years, Jack and Emma, had joined pre-opera tailgate parties here with some of Emma's fancy friends. Jack had never enjoyed these parties but for Emma's sake, he had always done his best to be civil. Jack knew he was difficult to live with, and he tried to make up for it in small ways.

The road leading to the exit passed along the side of the parking area. It was steep enough so that Buzzy needed to keep his foot slightly on the brake. The two vehicles were halfway down the parking lot against the perimeter fence on Buzzy's right. A helicopter passing by overhead was making enough noise that it was difficult to talk.

"They've started up their engines and they're backing out."

"What?"

"They're backing out," Buzzy said more loudly. "Both the Toyota and the Dodge. Shit! . . . they've stopped! They're blocking the road!"

"Can you get around them?"

"Maybe."

The two vehicles had stopped in a line with the nose of the pickup against the rear of the Land Cruiser. All three men had stepped out onto the pavement and they had guns in their hands. Buzzy could see them better now. Two of the men were the tough-looking Indians they had followed from Santa Fe. The third man, from the pickup, appeared to be Chinese. He waved for Buzzy to stop.

"They want us to stop, Jack! They're armed. The Chinese dude has an assault rifle. I could turn around and make a run for it."

"No, not if they're armed. You'd better do what they say."

As they came to a stop, two of the men pounded on the windows with the butts of their guns from different sides of the car.

"Open up," said the one on Buzzy's side, pointing his pistol at Buzzy's forehead.

"Do it," Jack said quietly, raising his hands. "But don't turn off the engine. Be ready to roll when I say *go*. Let me do the talking."

Buzzy rolled down the electric window.

"Who are you?" the man demanded. "And why are you following us?"

"Excuse me," Jack intervened. "He's only my driver. He goes where I tell him to. So, I'm the person you should be addressing."

"And who the hell are you?"

"Dr. Henry Harrington, retired. I've come to buy tickets for myself and my wife. Now the question is, who are you? Are you some kind of hawker?"

Jack spoke with a tone of disdain, a person of privilege addressing someone from the lower classes.

The Chinese man came around to Jack's side of the car and rapped on the window to ask him to open up. He was huge. He looked almost like a sumo wrestler with his wide Mongolian face.

Jack pressed the switch and the electric motor brought the window down. He faced his adversary with a scornful smile.

"Yes?" he demanded.

"You can stop the bullshit now. You were parked outside our office building. We saw you. We got you on our security cameras. And you followed us here."

"Why in the world should we follow you?" Jack said as though he were addressing a bug. "We stopped on some side street in order to make a phone call. Then we came here to buy tickets. I don't have the foggiest idea what you're talking about."

Buzzy could see it wasn't working. Jack could sense it too. These men were dangerous. Jack was about to tell Buzzy to floor the gas pedal when something remarkable happened.

Two dark green cars came roaring into the parking lot from the direction of the highway with red and blue lights flashing from their front windows. They separated in the parking lot, one to the right, the other to the left, with the clear intention of encircling them in a pincher move.

The two Indians and the Chinese man didn't wait to see who the newcomers were. They were already in motion, running back to their vehicles. They had left their engines running. They jumped into their cars and sped away toward the exit road through the gap the green cars had made as they had separated. The newcomers didn't chase after them, but came up hard and stopped on either side of Jack and Buzzy's Kia.

All this happened faster than Buzzy could narrate. A man stepped out from one of the green cars and walked their way. He also had a gun in his hand. He bent forward and leaned in Buzzy's open window. It was the man with the red/blond hair he had last seen in California.

Buzzy managed a nervous smile.

"Mr. Hurston, please come with me," said the man with the red/blond hair. "Mr. Wilder, you will need to remain in the car with Katya. I understand your wife is expecting you home, so we won't detain you for long."

"Jack, you gotta help me!" Buzzy exploded. "This is crazy! It's the guy who was tailing us in San Francisco!"

"Better go with him, Buzzy," Jack said.

Alone in the car with Katya, it took Jack a few minutes to figure out what had just happened. At first, he was confused that it was Buzzy they were after, not himself. Then he got it. It was the fact that the man not only knew Katya's name, but also knew that Emma was waiting for him in San Geronimo. To have this much information, excluded all but a few possibilities.

It was a serious situation, but Jack laughed.

"Katya," he said to the back seat, "I think our cyber genius has come to the attention of a very select crowd!"

Clearly, they'd had Buzzy under close observation for some time as a person of intense interest. Whether they had come to arrest him or enlist his services was an open question.

Chapter Twenty-Four

It wasn't a good moment for Howie on Saturday morning in the parking area by his land as he, Rain, and Georgie were stripped of their cell phones, checked for weapons, then put into the back of one of the ubiquitous white vans.

He wasn't even given a chance to use his brand-new iPhone (nearly a thousand dollars) to call Ocean and Sage and ask them to feed Orange while he was gone. Fortunately, it was summer, she had the cat door to go in and out, and she was a good hunter. She wouldn't starve.

"We're going to take you to Santa Fe to get your statements," Inspector Borello said to Howie, pulling him aside before they left. "We'll hold Rain, of course. But once you tell us how you got that kid out of jail, I'll let you and your daughter go."

"Hold on! I did *not* get Rain out of jail. I had nothing to do with that! That was *him*! He pushed a guard and ran!"

"Sure," said the Inspector. He turned away as Howie was accompanied into the back of the van by two strong marshals who meant business. The door was closed securely, a door with no handles on the inside. They were squeezed together, Howie on the right, Rain the left, and Georgie in the middle. They were on a bench seat behind a metal security mesh that protected the driver and the guard in front. Rain's handcuffs had been removed for the long drive.

For the first few miles, Howie was so depressed he barely noticed where they were going. He had promised Ray and Carol he would absolutely keep Georgie safe in the wilds of America, no matter what. He could hardly bear to think about the disaster he had made of her visit! What kind of father invites his daughter for a vacation in New Mexico only to have her carted away by the cops?

This was all Rain's fault! *Damn, damn, damn that kid!* he said to himself again and again.

"Everything's going to be okay," he said hopefully to Georgie, who was sitting shoulder to shoulder with him. She gave him a brief flicker of a smile then turned her attention back to Rain on the other side. She and Rain were discussing international politics, climate change, and the sad state of the planet. Howie was glad that Georgie hadn't yet registered the trouble they were in. So far, she appeared to regard this as an interesting adventure. She and Rain were in agreement that the older generation—Howie's generation—had made of mess of everything.

"Quiet back there! You're not allowed to talk!" said the guard in the front passenger seat.

A shiver went through Howie as he peered through the metal mesh and saw who the guard was. It was one of the La Chaya tribal cops. Howie recognized him from the confrontation by the dead woman on his shortcut from hell. The driver was a cop he recognized as well.

Howie began paying more attention to where they were going. The van had no windows in back, but he was able to get an idea of where they were through the front windshield, which he could see imperfectly through the metal mesh. They definitely weren't heading south to Santa Fe. They were driving west on Highway 64, a lonely two-lane highway that headed across the high desert toward Farmington.

Howie couldn't breathe for a few seconds as he absorbed the implications of this.

They were at the mercy of corrupt, brutal La Chaya tribal cops. They were heading back to the reservation where Rain had shot two guards. It was hard to imagine how their situation could be any worse.

Howie closed his eyes as something deep and primal rose up inside of him. He knew he would kill, he would die first before he would allow any harm to come to his daughter.

He had just become a dangerous man.

***

As the hours passed, driving through the empty land of mountains and mesas near the Colorado border, Georgie and Rain appeared to fall asleep.

Howie was glad to have them out of the way. It made it easier to think. The problem with thinking, unfortunately, was the more he thought, the more he worried.

Rain slept with his head leaning against the side of the van. Georgie drifted toward him until her head, following the laws of gravity, settled on Rain's shoulder. Howie didn't like this, but there wasn't anything he could do.

After a while, Georgie sat up half-awake, surprised to find herself leaning against Rain. Now she slumbered in the other direction and her head fell over onto Howie's shoulder. *Much better!* said Howie to himself.

Just as he was getting used to the weight of her head, she whispered into his ear.

"Rain says we're in deep shite. He said to tell you the fellas in front are La Chaya coppers. He said you'd know what he was talking about."

"Tell him, I've already figured that out," Howie whispered back with irritation. "Now listen, Georgie, because this is important. Tell him he's absolutely not to do anything on his own. He's to wait for my signal. Is that clear?"

"Yes."

"That kid's done enough damage! So make sure he knows I'm in charge from now on. He needs to keep his eye on me for what to do. We're going to get out of this, I promise you. But we need to be patient."

Georgie went from one shoulder to another for a while. It proved to be a way for Rain and Howie to communicate without the two cops in

212

front hearing. Not that communication did much good. Rain's final message summed up the situation.

"You wait for your moment, Moon Deer. I'll wait for mine."

***

It was midafternoon when the van turned south on a dirt road that seemed familiar to Howie. He couldn't be sure, but he suspected they were back on the shortcut from hell where his misadventures had begun.

It was the hottest part of the day, and though the air conditioning was on loudly in front, little of that air made its way to the back.

Howie banged on the iron mesh. "Hey, we need a stop for water and a bathroom break!"

The two men in front didn't answer. They didn't even bother to shake their heads. Without a word, they kept going south for another hour through a dry land of red desert that could have been Mars.

The slant of sun was lengthening when at last they descended on a steep switchback road into a canyon that had a shallow river running through it. There were narrow strips of green vegetation on both banks, cottonwood trees and weedy marshes, but otherwise the land was bare. Howie had been through here before. Up ahead on the road he could see the half-finished casino and hotel.

"Tell Rain to wake up. We're here," Howie whispered to Georgie, whose head was on his shoulder.

She sat up sleepily and slumped over to Rain. If the tribal cops in front had been paying attention, this leaning back and forth might have seemed suspicious.

"He's awake," Georgie told him, returning to his shoulder.

The van passed the main entrance to the shuttered casino and turned into the gas station/convenience store. Everything looked deserted, skeletons of a glorious future that had not arrived.

The van stopped and the two tribal cops got out of the front and came around to the sliding doors on each side.

Howie was ready. This was probably their last chance.

The door on Howie's side pulled open, revealing a sleepy-looking cop. He was large but sluggish. As soon as the door was open, Howie launched himself into a flying tackle, using the edge of the door as a springboard. The cop didn't have a chance to go for his gun. Howie landed with a grunt, pulling the man with him to the ground. He was about to lash out with his fists and fight for his life when he saw that the cop's head had hit the cement by the gas pumps and he wasn't moving.

Howie rose to his feet gasping for breath. His left knee throbbed with pain from where he had hit the ground. Georgie was still in the van with the door open, staring at him in astonishment. He couldn't see Rain, but he heard grunts and thuds coming from the far side of the van. There was no one else in sight.

"I'm here," Rain said, appearing from around the van. He was holding a black semi-automatic that he had taken off the tribal cop. "That mother isn't going anywhere soon!"

"Let's go!" Howie told them. "Quickly!"

"Get his gun!" Rain said, nodding toward the cop Howie had brought down with his flying tackle.

There was barely time. Two tribal cop cars had just appeared from the switchback road and were racing toward the gas station. The man on the ground was just beginning to stir. Howie reached down and grabbed the gun from his holster. It was a heavy revolver.

"That way!" Rain called, pointing toward the unfinished hotel.

They took off running. Both Rain and Georgie were faster than Howie, but he wasn't far behind. They ran along a path with construction debris that passed the swimming pool and the outdoor area with tables and umbrellas. The pool was still surprisingly full of water. Howie wondered if it would be best to keep going past the hotel into the desert where they might lose themselves. But he heard the slamming of car doors and knew the tribal cops weren't far behind. To climb the hill behind the hotel and escape into the desert would leave them exposed from below until they were over the top.

Rain, in the lead, was already running around the back of the hotel and Howie decided this was probably the best of their bad choices. Rain came to a stop by the frame of a doorless door. Georgie and Howie came up behind him.

"We can hide in the hotel," Rain told them. "And get away when it's dark."

Howie wasn't sure about this. He peered inside the empty frame and saw only dank and darkness. He could see a cement mixer and a jumble of construction material that had been left behind. The interior of the building looked like the sort of place where there might be rats the size of chihuahuas.

"We could get trapped in there," he objected. But he knew Rain was right. "Okay, there's no other choice."

"I'll lead!" Rain said stoutly.

For once, Howie was glad to let Rain go first. He was strong and fast and young, while Howie was still winded from his scuffle with the tribal cop, feeling every second of his age. He had been lucky so far, but he had always been a bookish person, never a brawler.

He watched as Rain disappeared into the darkness of the building and held out his hand for Georgie to follow. Soon they were both swallowed up in the shadows and chaos of the interior.

Howie followed.

Chapter Twenty-Five

Saturday afternoon, Emma Wilder arrived home at close to 5:30 from a stressful day at the San Geronimo Public Library to find Jack and Lieutenant Santo Ruben gathered around the kitchen table talking about the case.

"It was the CIA! Can you believe it?" she heard Jack say to Santo as she stood in the hallway putting her sun hat and umbrella on the pegs by the front door. Summer in San Geronimo, you never knew which of these two you might need.

"The CIA! Those were the guys who were following us around the Bay Area! Spooks!" Jack seemed to find this hilarious. "And it was Buzzy they were interested in, not me. This had nothing to do with the case."

"This could be a nice break for Buzzy," Santo said

"If they don't throw him in prison first! They've been vetting Buzzy to come work for them in Washington, that's why they're giving him a hard look. They like outlaw cyber geniuses, as long they can be controlled. When they saw he was in a jam, they pulled off that rescue at the Opera. They sure moved fast. Apparently, a kid like Buzzy needs to be protected. If he works out for them, he'll be worth more than a battalion of tanks."

"Cyber security's huge these days," Santo agreed. "The Russians, the Chinese, interference in elections, ransom attacks . . . a kid like Buzzy would be ideal for them. There are times when it takes an outlaw to catch an outlaw. But do you think he'll take the job?"

"Well, that's the funny thing. He's an anarchist, you know. He wants to tear down the government not join it. But I think the money will tempt him. I was only allowed to see him for a moment before one of their guys drove me and Katya home. I gather they're taking Buzzy to some hotel in Santa Fe to have a serious conversation about his future."

"You're laughing, but I hope Buzzy takes it. Something like this would give his life focus."

Emma came through the hallway into the kitchen. "You're home!" she said gruffly to her husband.

Jack smiled sheepishly. He stood to give her a hug, which she accepted in silence. She was angry. He had gone off gallivanting to California when he should have been resting. How could he be so idiotic? Did he *want* to die? But with Santo present, she left it alone. She was from a generation that believed in keeping marital disputes private.

Jack's color was better than when she had seen him last, she had to admit that. He'd always done best when he was working, hot on the trail of something. It was sitting around that sapped his energy.

"So how are things?" he asked. Stupidly, she thought.

"Well, I'm glad you asked. Besides worrying about you, I spent the day dealing with a group of idiots who don't want books in the library that aren't their idea of patriotic. They want to erase any mention of slavery. You think it's easy being a librarian today? I've already been through hell and back with the Christians who want to ban Harry Potter, and now it's politics! But how about you, Jack? How was California? Did you have fun?"

Santo kept his eyes lowered to the kitchen table, sensing marital discord.

"Well, it was interesting revisiting old places," said Jack cautiously. "Henry Liu sends his regards, by the way. Do you remember Henry? The fishmonger?"

"From the seafood market in Chinatown? Sure, I remember Henry. Buzzy told me you met him again at the monastery in Big Sur. Buzzy phoned a few times when you were gone to let me know you were alive. It was good of him."

Jack sighed. "I'm sorry, Emma, I really am. But I had to go through with this. I've just been telling Santo about how Henry was the Grand Dragon of the Red Gecko Tong, the honcho of the whole thing. I guess he felt he owed me after I helped him out that time during a holdup. He was able to give me some information I was after—the name of the guy in New Mexico, Jimmy Chou, who's running a hemp operation on Indian land with trafficked labor. Only that's just the front. What they're really doing is dealing illegal arms. This is a big deal, Emma. You wouldn't want me to turn my back on something this important, would you?"

"Jack, it's only a guess that they're running guns on the reservation," Santo interjected from the table. "You don't know that for certain."

"Santo, I know it. It's what the Abbot told me and I feel it in my bones!"

Santo laughed. "Right, because a holy man wouldn't lie? Gimme a break, Jack! You of all people shouldn't fall for nonsense like this. You're a cynic!"

"Exactly. Which is why you should trust me on this. I'm not the sort of person who falls for nonsense."

Santo turned to Emma for support. "Your husband wants me to launch a full-scale State Police operation to raid that compound! All on the word of your old fishmonger. Now, here's what I'm thinking," he said, turning back to Jack. "I want to put Jimmy Chou and his chain of restaurants under the microscope for a week or so. Investigate the hell out of him. Then, if we find something solid to go on, that's when we bust the camp."

"Santo, I don't think there's time for that," Jack objected. "We need to go in now."

Santo shook his head. Among other things, he was thinking of the trouble he would be in if a raid on an Indian reservation turned up nothing. There were problems here that Jack wasn't considering.

"You should go to the U.S. Marshals with this, Jack. If there's human trafficking involved, this should be a DOJ operation."

"I don't trust Inspector Borello," Jack told him. "In fact, I'm not sure I entirely trust the Department of Justice."

"Oh, come on, Jack! Why not?"

"It's just a feeling I have," Jack answered vaguely.

Santo looked disgusted.

Emma didn't ordinarily join in discussing cases, but in this instance she couldn't stay quiet.

"Santo, Jack is right. You can't leave those poor trafficked people another day longer in that terrible place. Not another hour, if you can help it. Howie hiked down into the canyon where the camp is located. It's very remote, apparently, but he had a Navajo as his guide."

"Howie actually went down there?" Santo asked.

"You've spoken to Howie?" Jack demanded at the same time before she could answer. "I've been trying to get him for days!"

"Yes, yes," Emma said to both of them. "Howie broke his phone in Shiprock and he couldn't be reached for a few days. He got a new phone when he got back to San Geronimo, so I don't know why he's not answering now. Unless he turned it off. His daughter from Scotland is here. And he's determined to focus entirely on her, no work at all. By the way, Ruth has been trying to reach you. It seems she got an email from Georgina."

"Emma, Emma! Let's back up!" Jack demanded. "When did you talk to Howie? I need to know everything."

Before she could answer, Santo looked at his watch and jumped up from the kitchen table.

"Christ, it's nearly seven!" he said. "Emma, I'll catch this story later. I gotta go! I'm taking Crystal to dinner! Man, if I'm late for our first date, I'll never get anywhere with her!"

"Santo, forget your date—this is more important," Jack told him.

"No, it isn't, Jack," Emma interrupted. "I'm sorry, but Santo gets to have a life!"

"Honestly, Santo, Crystal who? I've never even heard you talk about this girl?"

"She's not a girl, she's a woman, Jack." Emma turned to Santo. "At least, I hope she is."

"It's Crystal Rodriguez," Santo said in frustration. "She's forty-six years old, for chrissake."

"Crystal Rodriguez? Why is that name familiar?" Jack knew that he knew the name. But his memory was slipping recently, especially when names were concerned.

"Of course, the name's familiar!" Santo said as he rushed toward the door. "You know her. She runs the county jail!"

Jack opened his mouth in astonishment.

"Don't say a word, Jack," Emma told him. "Not a word!"

***

Jack was in bed before nine o'clock. Emma had insisted on it because he was visibly exhausted.

He was frustrated because Santo, despite their friendship, had refused to commit himself as to what he would do. Before Emma had arrived, while they were talking among themselves, he had promised to "look into the matter." He would speak to his boss in Santa Fe, the head of Public Safety, and also to an FBI Special Agent he knew in Albuquerque. The FBI would be essential to any raid on the La Chaya reservation, since they alone had the authority to investigate felony crimes on Indian land. If the NMSP were to be involved, they would need to go in under the auspices of the Feds.

For Jack, this was the usual tangle of various law enforcement agencies interacting with one another. It was disheartening. You would think justice could be achieved more easily. But of course, true justice was never easy.

Meanwhile, he was worried. He had tried Howie's cell phone number several times over the course of the evening without any luck. Each time, Howie's phone rang only a single time then went immediately to a message telling him the voice mail was full.

How could his voice mail be full? Wasn't this the new digital age of wonders? Jack fumed.

And why wasn't Howie answering? Yes, his daughter was here—and Jack was looking forward to meeting her. But for chrissake, Howie could still answer his damn phone!

Emma came into his room and sat in the rocking chair by the bed just as he was getting under the covers.

"Well, how are you holding up?" she asked.

"Tired," he admitted. "And not entirely happy. Santo wants me and Howie to bow out, let the Feds take over. Blah blah blah!"

"It's not blah, blah, blah, Jack. It makes sense. The way Howie described this place, it's going to take an army to raid that canyon. Helicopters, too, I imagine. There's something I haven't mentioned yet, something Howie told me."

"Yes?" Jack encouraged when she hesitated.

"The Navajo guide I mentioned. His name is Rain Walker and he's the 19-year-old son of Sun Walker, the flute player. Have you heard of him?"

"Sun Walker? Of course."

"Well, he's dead now, killed by the La Chaya cops. At least, that's what the son says and he's on the warpath for revenge. A real hothead, as Howie put it. More brawn than brains. Rain shot and killed two tribal guards after they were discovered in one of the tents where the trafficked victims slept. Howie says this didn't need to have happened. He and Rain high-tailed it out of that canyon to where Howie had left his car. They would have gotten away except federal officers had a blockade across the road out. They held the 19-year-old Navajo, apparently, but let Howie go."

"Federal officers" Jack asked. "Did Howie give you a name?"

"He did, but I'm not sure I remember."

"Borello? U.S. Inspector Elliot Borello?"

"Yes, I think that's it. I remember it made me think of the Italian pasta brand."

"Good memory trick, Emma." Jack didn't want to let on how alarmed he was. "The pasta is Barilla. I was telling Buzzy about your *spaghetti alla vongole*. We should have it again one of these nights."

"New Mexico doesn't have clams, Jack. They have to be so fresh their little foot is still wiggling."

"But you used to hate that," he reminded her. "Dumping the clams into the boiling water when they were still alive. Now, you said something about Ruth trying to get me?"

"Right. She said she got an odd email from Howie's daughter this morning. But she didn't say what it was about. You'll have to talk with her."

She leaned over and gave him a long hug that turned into an embrace. Jack held her and felt every part of himself open and relaxed. Then she kissed his cheek and was gone. They'd had separate bedrooms for six or seven years now, due to his chronic insomnia and his habit of pacing the floor deep in thought at odd hours of the night.

There was nothing more Jack could do until morning. He told his computer, Nancy, to play something relaxing. Brahms, he decided. The Fourth. Soon soft music flowed into the bedroom, and Jack, exhausted, drifted away into its river of sound.

He was nearly asleep at two in the morning when his phone rang.

It was Howie, phoning in at last. But the news wasn't good.

Chapter Twenty-Six

U.S. Marshal Inspector Elliot Borello kept a furnished apartment in Santa Fe in a block of modern buildings off Cerrillos Road. It was a convenient base for a busy man with secrets, two blocks from a large shopping center, ten minutes from downtown.

The apartment was more like a hotel than a home. There was nothing of himself in it. He rented by the month which cost more but he didn't know how long he would be staying. Due to security concerns, he hadn't rented under his own name, but as Harvey Lee, under which he had both credit cards and a driver's license.

Borello loved his job as a U.S. Marshal. It was exciting, a life of action and possibilities. He also enjoyed the power that came with it. The only problem was it didn't pay very much. Which was why he had taken on a few side jobs that brought in extra cash. Everybody did it, you'd be a fool not to. You met useful people in his line of work. You came upon useful opportunities.

Unfortunately, the work Elliot did on the side was proving to be stressful. It was frustrating because he had come up with the perfect deal that was going to allow him to retire in style. But it meant being middleman between the Chinese on one hand, and the La Chaya tribal leaders on the other, which was about as easy as herding cats. He had introduced them to each other and told them how profitable arrangements could be made, money for all sides, but it wasn't long before there were problems.

Borello hated the Chinese. Chinks, he called them. But at least they were good at business. It was the Indians who were driving him nuts. The La Chaya tribal clique who ran things were a greedy bunch, but stupid. As a result, everything was behind schedule, one delay after another. His perfect money-making deal was in danger of falling apart.

Then there was the Lakota detective, Howard Moon Deer. Borello hadn't taken Moon Deer seriously enough at their first meeting, which is why he had let him go. Moon Deer had seemed like a harmless academic type, but he had proved unexpectedly persistent. He was like the bunny in the battery commercial, he kept going and going . . . until he had become a problem that Borello had been forced to take care of. Howard Moon Deer would not be bothering him again, but making people disappear permanently had its own dangers, such as getting caught. The Inspector had hoped to flow in and out of this situation without leaving a trace. He didn't want to come to anyone's attention just now.

He had a meeting set with Jimmy Chou, the head chink, on Saturday night in which hopefully matters would be resolved. He didn't like Jimmy, and he was going to make it clear that either they made the delivery tomorrow morning, or he and his money were history.

At ten o'clock, Borello put on his jogging shoes and shorts, and with a small fanny pack on his waist headed out for a run along the maze of back streets toward the downtown railyard where a commuter train ran daily to Albuquerque. The neighborhoods he passed through were a mix of small houses and businesses.

Borello got into a rhythm as he ran, counting out his paces, one, two, three, four, feeling almost like a dancer. The night was dark and only occasionally lit by streetlamps. As he approached the railyard, he passed expensive little restaurants with candles in their windows that were just finishing up with their last customers.

Slowing slightly, he jogged toward a black Cadillac SUV that was parked at a meter near Tomasita's, one of the oldest restaurants in the area. The Inspector stopped, looked in both directions, then quickly opened the front passenger door and slipped inside.

An overweight Chinese man in his late forties sat behind the wheel. Jimmy Chou was a gruff, brutal man and the meeting went badly from the start.

"That was fucked today," Jimmy said in greeting. "I want to know why those guys showed up!"

"Which guys are those?" Borello asked politely.

"A private detective. A guy from San Geronimo called Jack Wilder. And I had to use my own contacts to find out about this guy, when you should have been the one to warn me. One of my people was having a meeting with some Indian guys in the parking lot at the Opera when this detective shows up. I want to know what you know about that, Borello!"

"I don't know anything about that," the Inspector said truthfully.

"Oh, yeah? You'd better think twice about double-crossing me, asshole!"

Borello managed a smile, but it was frayed. He smelled whiskey on Jimmy's breath. The man was a thug, a real nothing. Borello assumed he had important family connections because on his intellect alone, he would be flipping burgers not running an operation like this.

"Look, Jimmy, we're all going to do well out of this. But we need to keep our cool. We need to be patient."

"That's what you say!

"So, let's just proceed like we planned. You go with your people, pay the council their one mil, pick up the device, then deliver it here by dawn. Can you still do that?"

"Did you bring my money?"

"Jimmy, Jimmy! The agreement! You get paid when I see the merchandise. And if I don't see it by tomorrow morning, you can forget the whole deal. It's off."

So, here's what I want to know." Jimmy gave Borello a hard look. "Just what are you planning to do with that device?"

"That's not a question you need to ask, Jimmy. You should know that. The fact is, I don't know either. I didn't ask. This is a third-party deal, I sell the item, they do with it what they will."

"If they're planning something big, something that's going to be in the headlines, that affects me, you see. It adds to my risk."

"You'll be getting a lot of money to take that risk."

"Sure, but not for what they're going to do. Not for the investigation that's going to come afterwards. You're going to need to give me more money. For what I'm risking, I want another mil."

"You're fucking crazy if you think I'll give you another million bucks!"

"They're going to blow up the capital, aren't they? For that you got to pay more. And if you don't like it, tough."

Borello took a long breath. He was angry. He didn't appreciate deals where one side changed things in the middle.

"Listen, I'm only the middleman here. I'm not blowing up anything. And I don't like being held up at the last minute by a cheap chink bastard. We had a deal!"

"You call me a chink, wop? Did I hear you correctly? Well, I tell you what—we're making ourselves a new deal. I want three mil now."

"You want three million dollars?" Borello asked deadpan.

"That's what I said, grease ball. Or you can go fuck yourself!"

"Jimmy, let's be clear about this. You're getting paid one million dollars period. That's what we agreed on. And remember, next time you deal with me, it won't be as a client—it'll be as a cop."

Jimmy leaned closer. His breath was foul. He said softly, "There's not going to be a next time, asshole!"

The situation exploded, like a switch had been pulled. The Inspector saw Jimmy's right hand coming out from inside his sports jacket with a gun. Borello didn't have time to go for his own gun in his fanny pack, but his right hand brushed against his jogging shorts, and, like magic, there was a knife in his hand.

With no hesitation, his hand jutted forward knife first into Jimmy's throat.

It was a gruesome death, unpleasant to watch. There was a great deal of blood as Jimmy gurgled and died. Borello hadn't meant for this to happen. He sat for a moment in shock breathing hard. It had happened too fast, spinning out of control.

And now what was he going to do?

"Fuck!" he said in a meditative way.

Fortunately, he had always been calm in situations like this.

First things first, he needed to get away. He opened the passenger side window and looked up and down the sidewalk. There was nobody around. Santa Fe at night was quiet and deserted, everyone inside— unless you were within a few blocks of the downtown Plaza.

Borello used his shirt as a rag and tried to wipe the surfaces he had touched. But there was too much blood, too much mess inside the Cadillac, and he didn't have time to erase his presence completely. He would just have to improvise if things went south.

He stepped out of the car and in a single motion resumed his evening run. In Santa Fe, runners were common at all hours and he hoped this would give him near invisibility.

As he ran, his thoughts spun with different options. Jimmy's death was going to be a problem for him. It was going to be necessary to return to the reservation, a place he had hoped never to see again.

But there was something he needed to take care of first.

Chapter Twenty-Seven

The interior of the unfinished casino/hotel on the La Chaya reservation was full of surprises.

Some of the rooms were nearly finished and, except for the lack of furniture, appeared almost ready for a guest to arrive. Other rooms were bare shells with dangling electric wire and no glass in the windows. Howie, Georgie, and Rain moved cautiously along the ground floor hallway because the light was fading and there were obstacles. They passed a room that had a mattress on the floor and a dozen empty beer cans. Someone had been partying here. Further along, they came to a stretch of the hallway where there was no floor, only steel beams that spanned a dangerous hole underneath. They were able to cross on a wood plank one at a time.

They came to a flight of concrete stairs that wrapped around an unfinished elevator shaft. The stairs appeared to climb to the second and third floors, but it was impossible to say anything for certain.

"Let's go upstairs," Rain urged. "It's good to have the higher ground."

"I'm not sure that's true in this case," Howie cautioned. "We could get trapped like cats in a tree. And if these stairs give out, we'll be in trouble."

"They have to be finished, otherwise the workers wouldn't have had any way to get up and down."

"That's only a guess, Rain. Remember that break in the floor we had to cross. Nothing here is the way it's supposed to be."

Howie turned to his daughter. As always, she was surprisingly calm and self-contained. Throughout this entire ordeal, she hadn't panicked once, nor had she complained. He was deeply moved by her bravery, inordinately proud.

"Georgie, I'm so sorry to put you through this! I hadn't meant for any of this to happen!"

"It's not your fault, Howie," she told him. "You were trying to do something good."

As far as Howie was concerned, trying to do something good wasn't good enough, not when you failed. But Georgie was right, it wasn't his fault. It was Rain's fault! If Rain hadn't broken out of jail and showed up on his land, they would have been getting ready for dinner at the Blue Mesa Café about now, which had been on the original schedule for today. But he left that unsaid. They were in enough trouble without getting into a blame game. It was vital now to stick together.

"So, what's your vote? Do we climb to higher ground or stay low?" he asked her. She was a smart seventeen and had as much right as any of them to decide what they were going to do.

Georgie shook her head. "I dunnae. Stuff like this dunna happen in Glasgow."

"You're safe as long as I'm here!" Rain said stoutly. Howie wanted to slug him. "I say we go up. We'll find a place to hide, and when it's dark we'll get away."

Not if they bring in reinforcements and have the hotel surrounded, Howie was about to say. But just then, they heard a door open and footsteps down the hallway where they had just come from. Another door opened in a different part of the hotel and there were more footsteps.

"We know you're in there!" someone shouted. "Come on out!"

Howie tried to appear optimistic for the sake of his daughter. "I guess it's up we go!" he whispered with a strained smile. "There should be plenty of good hiding places in this fun house."

***

Hoping to make less noise, they climbed with their shoes in hand two flights to the third floor. The concrete stairs were crude and there was no railing, but they were usable.

The third floor was like the first, a long corridor with unfinished rooms on either side. None of the rooms had doors or glass in the windows. Howie was reminded of images he had seen of bombed-out cities in Syria. The rooms were little more than urban caves.

They rejected several possible hiding places until they came to a room halfway down the hall that was empty except for a metal grille leaning against the wall. Concealed behind the grille, there was a rectangular opening to a dark space beyond. Rain poked his head inside and felt around with his hands.

"It's maybe three feet deep, five feet wide," he said after moment. "I have no idea what it's for. It's dusty but it seems to be clean. We could climb inside, pull the grille closed, and they'll never find us."

"Are you sure the floor's solid?" Howie asked. "It could be some kind of dumbwaiter with a chute going down to the ground floor."

"No, it's okay, I've scoped it out. Look, there are only a few guys searching the building and they're not going to be able to look everywhere. This is the best place we're going to find. And if they find us, we're armed. They pull the grille open, they'll get a surprise!"

Howie wasn't eager for a gun fight. But the voices and footsteps of the people who were searching for them were moving closer. It wouldn't be long before they arrived on the third floor.

"Okay," he said reluctantly. "Let's give it a go."

***

One by one, they squeezed into the hole. Rain was the last one inside and he managed to pull the metal grille more or less closed behind him. It was only leaning over the opening, but unless the tribal cops were extraordinarily thorough, there was a decent chance they wouldn't be discovered.

They sat in total darkness, squeezed together so tightly Howie was worried Georgie wouldn't be able to breathe. Their hiding place was as claustrophobic as a tomb.

"I will sure have a tale to tell when I am back in Scotland!" Georgie whispered. "The Wild West is definitely a wee bit wilder than I imagined!"

Howie took her hand in the darkness and gave her a reassuring squeeze. He was so overwhelmed with a fierce surge of love and worry that he didn't dare speak. In his free hand, he clutched the revolver he had taken from the tribal cop and knew there was nothing he wouldn't do to keep her safe. He wished he had taken the time to see how many bullets were in the chambers. There should be at least five rounds with the hammer on an empty chamber, but that wasn't a certainty. Rain had the more serious weapon, a semi-automatic, which was appropriate. Howie knew very little about guns and didn't like them very much. Point and pull the trigger was the extent of his expertise.

Rain and Georgie whispered between themselves for a short while but gradually they fell silent. They could hear the search as it continued below. From the voices, there seemed to be only four men. They spent nearly an hour on the ground floor going through every small nook and cranny, but quite a bit less time on the second floor. That was the good news. These La Chaya cops were far from professional, and Howie hoped they would be getting increasingly sloppy by the time they reached the top floor.

"I have to pee!" Georgie whispered.

Howie had been afraid of this. In fact, he had to pee too.

"Hold on as long as you can," he whispered back. "And, well, if you have to, just let it go."

"Howie, that's awful!"

"It's okay, Georgie. We can't stand on ceremony in a situation like this."

It seemed like hours before the four searchers arrived on the third floor, but probably it wasn't as long as that. Their voices were louder now.

"We're wasting our time," he heard one of them say. "They didn't come this way. They must be out in the desert somewhere."

"Maybe," said a second cop. "But we gotta make sure."

The four searchers had split up into two groups. Two pairs of footsteps came closer until they arrived at the bedroom where Howie, Rain, and Georgie were hiding. Howie prayed that none of them would sneeze or cough. Through the grille, he could see the beam of a flashlight playing around the room. The beam stopped on the grille where it lingered for a long moment before moving on.

"Nothing here," said the cop. "Let's go. I want to get this over with."

Howie listened as the two pairs of footsteps returned to the hallway and continued searching the rooms that were further along. Neither Howie, Rain, nor Georgie made a sound until the voices and footsteps had moved off into the distance.

"Let's stay put a while longer," Howie suggested. "How's your bladder, Georgie?"

"I'm okay," she said. "As long as I don't move."

They waited until they could hear all four pairs of footsteps on one of the lower floors. After nearly another hour, there were no sounds at all in the unfinished hotel. Rain pushed the grille out of the way and they climbed out into the room one by one. Howie had to shake his left leg which had fallen asleep. Outside the glassless window, he saw that it was night.

Howie and Rain went out into the corridor to allow Georgie to use a corner of the room as her bathroom, and when she was finished, Howie found a different corner and did the same. Rain was the only one who didn't need to relieve himself. As an Indian warrior of old, he probably had perfect control of his perfect body.

Once these preliminaries were finished, they settled in a room further down the corridor to consider how they were going to escape.

***

Very cautiously, Howie looked out the open window to the ground below. The room faced the front of the hotel and he could see two tribal police cars in the parking area near the gas station. The cops themselves were nowhere in sight.

"Let's try the other side of the hotel," he suggested.

They crossed the hall to a room on the opposite side and crouched by one of the open windows. From here, they could see only open desert and mesas. Moonlight lit the landscape with a silvery glow but the moon itself was hidden. From this view, there was no sign of the police. But their view was limited.

Howie tried to visualize the layout of the hotel from what he had seen of it from the outside.

"There must be at least two stairways on either side of the building," he said. "That would be the usual set up. We came up the stairway on the right. I think that's our best bet. It'll take us down to the rear of the building where we came in. If we go out that way, we can get away into the desert."

"But then what?" Georgie asked. "There's nothing out there."

"We'll help ourselves to one of the cop cars," Rain said. "I can hot wire it. We're going to need wheels to get away. Anybody tries stopping us, they're toast."

Howie sighed. Rain seriously annoyed him. He glanced at his daughter, wondering what she thought of him. They were kneeling on the floor by the window, Georgie in the middle. Georgie had a thoughtful look on her face as she stared out into the desert, but as usual, she gave nothing away.

"Let's get out of here without anybody spotting us, Rain," Howie said. "I've told you this before and it ended badly because you didn't listen. We're not looking for a Gunfight at the O.K. Corral."

"Okay, okay, Moon Deer. You don't need to be sarcastic."

"I'm not being sarcastic. I'm being serious. You may have grown up on video games, landing on an alien planet and blasting everyone in sight. But I didn't. And we're not going there."

"I grew up on an Indian reservation, bro!" Rain said tensely. "And I know what it means to fight!"

Georgie glanced first at Howie, then Rain, then she returned her eyes to the desert.

"Good," said Howie. "Both Georgie and I can use a fighter about now. But it's the last resort, that's all I'm saying. It would be better to make ourselves invisible. Can you do that?"

"Sure, I can!" said Rain. "Any Indian can do that. You would know that if they hadn't shipped you off to those colleges and made a White Man out of you!"

Howie took a breath. "I am not a White Man, Rain. I am a human without borders. I'm proud of my Lakota heritage, but I don't define myself by it. Brown, white, red, purple—I don't care about skin color. All that's done is to cause lots of problems. As a species, we need to outgrow our differences or we'll end up like the dinosaurs."

"Hey, I get it! But until that rosy future arrives, we've got to fight like hell!"

Georgie was definitely paying attention now, turning right then left, looking from Howie to Rain.

"Maybe we can discuss this later," Howie said, deliberately turning down the heat. "First, we need to get out of here, one step at time. So, let's go downstairs and see what we see."

It was completely dark now inside of the building and their phones, with their flashlight apps, had been taken away. Rain claimed he could see in the dark, and Howie was glad to let him lead the way down the hall to the stairs. Howie stuck the revolver into his belt in the front of his pants. It wasn't comfortable but it left his two hands free. He hoped the gun didn't go off and end any love life that might—*might!*—be in his future.

They stayed close to the right wall, feeling along the concrete to guide them. They kept their shoes on, even if that meant making more noise. Now that it was night, there was no way they could walk blind in stocking feet in a construction zone.

Rain's eyesight was good, Howie had to give him that. They made their way to the stairs, Georgie's left hand on Rain's shoulder, Howie's hand on Georgie—three blind mice. They hugged the wall as they went downstairs, cautiously, one slow step after another.

Down they went, round and round. Descending the two floors in the dark seemed to take forever. One by one, they came down onto the ground floor, Howie in the rear. Rain was unfailing with his helpfulness. He gave Georgie a hand to steady her as she stepped onto the bottom landing. He gave Howie a hand as well, and Howie was grateful. In the darkness it was hard to know what was up and what was down.

"Can you find the door where we came in?" he asked.

"I got it."

The door creaked open loudly and moonlight flooded inside. Howie could now see the silhouette of Georgie in front of him, and Rain kneeling by the open door. He slid past Georgie and joined Rain at the door. As far as they could see, the path alongside the back of the hotel was clear. There was nobody around.

It was good to be outside again, free of the hotel. There was a canopy of stars and planets overhead in the black New Mexico night, dazzling in their brilliance. As always, Rain walked ahead on the path, slightly crouched, moving (in Howie's opinion) more like a kung fu imitation than an Indian warrior. He sensed Rain had watched too many Bruce Lee movies.

They came to the end of the building. From here they could look to the left and see the gas station and parking area where they had made their escape. At the far end of their view, they could see the edge of the swimming pool, whose waters were dark and silent. There were no people in sight and no cars. The van that had brought them here had been driven away. The concrete plaza was empty.

To the right, the desert hills rose a short way then leveled off into the distance. There was no one to be seen in that direction either.

As Howie, Georgie, and Rain gathered to discuss their next move, the swimming pool suddenly lit up with underwater lights that sent aquamarine patterns into the trees overhead. The light spilled to where they stood at the edge of the building, and they were forced to move back into the shadows.

A voice began speaking in Chinese from the pool area. At first, Howie assumed there must be two people having a conversation, but from the pauses he quickly realized it was a man speaking on a telephone.

Howie couldn't understand the Chinese, but it sounded like Mandarin, the northern dialect. Soon he heard English words and phrases mixed with the Chinese. Chinglish. *No problem*, he heard several times. Then came a few sentences in English.

"Okay, we had a delay, I'm sorry about that. Look, I'm only on the tech side, I don't know about the other stuff. All I can tell you is it didn't happen on our end. The device is ready. He just has to come pick it up. I don't care if Borello is angry. Now, listen to me . . ."

The English turned back to Chinese, leaving Howie curious. He certainly knew the name Borello. As for "device," that was a word with several meanings, but he feared the worst.

Above all, what got Howie's attention was that somebody was talking on a telephone.

A telephone! Howie would give his kingdom, if he had one, for a telephone. Just one call to Jack and help would be on its way. Ever since Inspector Borello had stripped them of their cell phones, that was the one device Howie most longed to have.

"Wait here," he whispered to Georgie and Rain. "I'm going to creep around the corner and try to see who's talking."

"Better let me do that, Moon Deer," Rain whispered back.

"No, this is something I need to do. What I need from you, Rain, is to stay close to Georgie and keep her safe. I won't be long . . ."

Without further discussion, Howie sank onto his hands and knees and crept around the corner toward the swimming pool. He had to crawl almost to the front of the hotel before the speaker came into view. Howie flattened himself on the path.

The Chinese man was dressed in tan pants and a white short sleeve shirt. Howie could see him in profile holding a telephone receiver up to his ear. He was in his forties, he judged, thin and slightly stooped. He looked like someone who spent most of his time in an office bent over a computer screen. He was standing on the far side of the pool alongside a counter that appeared to be part of a future poolside café.

"Yes, yes, of course," the man said, hanging up the receiver. A moment later, the pool lights went dark and he heard footsteps as the man walked away.

It took Howie a moment to understand the importance of what he had seen. The base of the phone had a cord that disappeared over the counter. It was a historical relic, a landline. Rain had told him there was no cell service on the reservation, but this was a phone that worked. He just needed to get to it.

Howie resumed crawling toward the pool. He moved slowly, cautiously, stopping every few feet to listen for danger. It took him nearly ten minutes to reach the gate into the pool area. He stopped again, listened, and was almost certain he was alone.

The darkness was welcome. He stood the last few feet and walked quickly to the phone.

It was a Princess phone, touch tone. He hadn't seen one in years. He picked up the receiver and heard a dial tone.

He dialed.

"Jack!" he said, before Jack could even say hello. "Thank God!"

Chapter Twenty-Eight

Jack was relieved to hear from Howie. At last. Though Howie had been hard to understand on the phone. He had spoken very quickly in a harsh whisper, with his lips too close to the receiver. Jack wasn't certain he had understood everything, and before he had a chance to ask a single question, Howie said abruptly, "Gotta go! Don't call back on this line!" Then hung up.

Jack sat for a few minutes digesting the call. "What time is it?" he asked Nancy.

"10:12 PM, Mountain Daylight."

It had been a very worrying call, particularly the news that Howie and his daughter were currently in danger at an unfinished hotel on Indian land hiding from people who were trying to kill them.

If Jack understood correctly, a Chinese gang was running a large operation on the reservation and a device of some kind was about to be picked up. Picked up by who, Howie couldn't say. For toppers, he said Inspector Elliot Borello was bent as overcooked spaghetti. This was an old joke between them, an allusion to one of Jack's disastrous dinners, cooking blind with everything ending up on the floor.

Jack knew or suspected most of Howie's news already, except for the fact that he and his daughter were in serious trouble. Normally, this would be the time to call in the Feds, but if Borello was bent, it was impossible to know who he could trust at the Justice Department. In Jack's experience, big money bought little men.

Santo was off on a dinner date with Crystal Rodriguez, the hard-nose woman who ran the county jail. Jack had found this funny at the time, but it was no joke now. Jack had to reach him. He told Nancy to ring Santo's personal cell, which answered with a recorded message that he was unavailable but leave a voicemail. Next, he tried Santo's landline only to get the same message. Jack left his own message twice. "Santo, it's me. I've just spoken with Howie, and I need to talk to you right away, no matter what time it is."

He leaned back into the pillows and groaned.

"Nancy, get me the station!"

Nancy knew which station he meant.

"New Mexico State Police," said a voice that Jack recognized.

"Sergeant, good evening—this is Jack Wilder. I've been trying to get Santo on his cell but he doesn't answer. He told me earlier he had a dinner date tonight. I need the name of the restaurant he's at—I have to reach him."

"Mr. Wilder, I'm sorry but I can't do that. He's off-duty and he left instructions not to be disturbed unless it's a police emergency."

"This is an emergency! I tell you what, give Santo a call and tell him we need to speak. He can call me at home."

"I'm sorry, I just can't, Mr. Wilder. He'd have my head on a platter!"

They went back and forth several times, but the sergeant wouldn't budge. Jack disconnected feeling even more frustration than before. However, he was a detective and there weren't that many restaurants in San Geronimo where Santo and Crystal could be.

Jack started with the Blue Mesa Café, currently the most expensive restaurant in town where everybody went on special occasions. He knew the owner who told him no, Santo hadn't been in tonight.

Next, he tried Ernesto's, an Italian place that was popular, but Santo wasn't there either. From here, he went down the list of local restaurants, from gourmet to ordinary. Both Santo and Crystal were public figures, so perhaps they had gone someplace where they wouldn't run into people they knew. Jack tried the Purple Sage, the Pink Palace, the Toad in the Hole, reaching down the culinary ladder, but Santo wasn't at any of these places.

There was the possibility that Crystal had invited him to her house for dinner. Were they in bed by now? Santo was an attractive middle-aged man and there were always women in his life, one after another. None of them ever lasted more than a few months. There had been something jagged about Santo ever since his divorce, and he drank too much. A few years ago, Santo's wife of 18 years, Darlene, had left him for another man and the wound still had a long way to go before it healed.

"Damn, damn, damn!" Jack said to the room. He needed help and since Santo wasn't available, he considered other possibilities.

"Back in the old days, Nancy, I could have picked up a phone and got an army rolling to raid that compound! One phone call! But now everybody is either dead or retired! . . . or in bed with a floozie!"

"I'm sure Crystal Rodriguez isn't a floozie, Jack," Nancy told him. "According to the information I have, she's an attractive woman."

"Okay, let me think a second. Who do I know in Washington?"

"Someone who is still alive?"

"That would be helpful," said Jack.

"There's Ronald Cheeves, that nice assistant to the Assistant Deputy Secretary at Homeland Security."

"Nancy, I don't want the assistant to the assistant of anybody. I need to move a whole lot faster than that. Is there anybody at the Justice Department I still know? . . . no, wait! I got it!" he said before she could answer. "Who was that woman who hired Howie to look into all this? I forget her name."

"Lydia Cordell-Smith, Jack."

"Yes, yes, that's her. The do-gooder. Her brother-in-law is the Attorney General. Get her for me, Nancy."

"It's two hours later on the East Coast, Jack—"
"Nancy, get me Lydia Cordell-Smith! Right now!"

***

Inspector Elliot Borello jogged back to his apartment where he remained just long enough to change clothes, put on his ankle and shoulder holsters, and make certain his two guns were loaded and ready: a standard issue 9mm Glock and a small Colt .22 semi-automatic that was easy to conceal.

There was also the spring knife with which he had just killed Jimmy Chou. Borello reflected on this death for a moment, but he didn't feel anything about it one way or the other. He really didn't. What bothered him was the fact that he would need to change his plans. Jimmy Chou had been a fat slob, and his death was merely an inconvenience.

He needed to get rid of the knife as soon as possible, bury it in the desert. There would be traces of blood on the blade that a forensic lab would find, no matter how thoroughly he cleaned it. However, the knife wasn't the problem. The problem was the chance that someone had seen him at the railyard, a reliable witness.

But Elliot couldn't worry about that now. He was in emergency mode and there was nothing to do but move forward. He needed to finish the current op, get his money, and vanish.

It took him less than half an hour to pack his personal belongings in three suitcases and leave no trace of himself in the leased apartment. Very little in the apartment was actually his. The furniture had been leased, as well as the TV and stereo. His own belongings consisted of a few clothes, his bathroom kit, pills, papers, money, and guns.

When he was ready, he loaded the suitcases into the back of his leased Ford Explorer and drove north from Santa Fe to Tesuque. From here, he followed a two-lane highway into the piñon covered hills until he arrived at a ranch house surrounded by a high wooden fence. The night was dark and overcast, unusually warm. There were menacing signs by the front gate. PRIVATE PROPERTY! NO TRESPASSING! BEWARE OF DOG!

Elliot despised these people. One day, when his ship came in, he planned to buy a villa in Italy, from where his ancestors had emigrated, and surround himself with fine art and culture.

Borello rang the buzzer.

"Who's there?" came an angry challenge over a small speaker.

"Borello."

"You're late!"

"Yeah, sure. Can we discuss this inside?"

The gate opened with a buzz. Borello walked along a gravel path toward the house, an old Territorial style building that sagged with age. The house was most likely over a hundred years old and it looked like it was sinking slowly back into the earth.

The front yard was bathed in bright lights that were mounted on metal towers, each fitted with four spotlights. There were three flags raised on poles near the front gate: an American flag, Confederate flag, and a white flag with the raised fist of The White Sons of Texas, of which this house outside of Santa Fe was considered their New Mexican "embassy."

Borello thought these people were nuts, but that was neither here nor there. They were the buyer and they had money.

The front door opened before he reached it, revealing a thin, shirtless man with an assault rifle slung across his bare chest. Borello knew him. He called himself Stick.

"Do you have it?" Stick demanded.

"Let me in. I need to talk to the Colonel."

Stick used the barrel of his rifle to gesture Borello inside.

The inside was tidy for a communal house. There were several women in the living room watching late night television, and two young children who were still awake, running around making a good deal of noise. The women looked anaemic and hollow.

Borello passed a kitchen where half a dozen White Sons were lounging around a formica table eating Domino's pizza from two cardboard boxes. The men were of various ages, slim to fat, late teens into late middle age. A few of them turned to give Borello a passing look. Several rifles leaned against the far wall near the refrigerator.

Stick led the way down a hall. He stopped and knocked on a door.

"Yeah?" called a voice from inside.

"It's the cop," said Stick.

"Ah-ha! Our man from the Department of Justice, at last! Do come in!"

The Colonel, as he called himself, thought of himself as a wit and an intellectual. He always spoke elaborately, though he never said what he was a colonel of. He was an overweight man in his forties with a big belly and a babyish face. The room was a kind of study with several computers and a desk. The Colonel was seated in a huge leather armchair with a bottle of beer in his hand. He gestured for Borello to sit opposite him on a straight-back wooden chair with wobbly legs.

"Well, Inspector, we've been waiting patiently. You were supposed to be here two hours ago. I trust you have it."

"I have it," Borello lied, "but not with me now."

"Not with you now? But that's not what you promised. That's not what we paid you for!"

"It can't be helped. The thing's dangerous to transport. It's a large device, Colonel, as you requested, and at the last moment my people decided to make a kind of cushioned bed to bring it here in a van. You'll be glad we're taking the extra precautions."

"Will I be glad? That remains to be seen. Where is the device now?"

"That's not something you need to know. That's not our deal. The less we know about each other's business the better. The only thing you need to know is that I'll deliver it to you here by noon tomorrow."

"But you assured me I would have it today! So how can I have confidence that you'll have it for me tomorrow? How do I know you're not merely stringing me along? Do I dare say it? How do I know this isn't a sting?"

Borello knew he was in a dangerous situation. With his baby face, the Colonel didn't look like someone you needed to take seriously, but that was a mistake.

"Look, Colonel, I'm only the middleman here. I get a commission, that's all. After working in law enforcement for decades, I decided I was tired of being poor. You know my record. I've done this before for other groups like yours. I'm the guy who's going to help you launch your second civil war. But I'm in it for the money, that's all. So be patient for another few hours and I'll have the device for you here by noon tomorrow. I'm throwing in the van for free, by the way, and that's nearly $20,000. The engine number has been filed off and it has stolen plates, so you don't need to worry about it ever being identified. What I need to know is that you'll have the rest of the cash ready."

The Colonel nodded. "Okay, I'll wait until noon tomorrow. But not a second longer, you understand? And you don't have to worry about the money. You give me the van with the device, I'll give you the *dinero*."

"It wouldn't pay to double-cross me," said Borello. "I have a whole lot of fire power at my disposal. After all, I have the law on my side."

They had a laugh over that and parted almost as pals. Borello was glad to get away in one piece.

Stick accompanied him out of the house to his vehicle. As soon as he was alone, the Inspector searched through the glove compartment for a plastic vial of pills. He had a long night ahead of him and he needed something to help him stay awake.

Chapter Twenty-Nine

Howie put the retro Princess phone back onto its cradle with a sense of relief. He had gotten through to Jack, help was coming. Now he needed to get back to where he had left Georgie and Rain.

The pool area was dark and silent except for the restless night breeze. Howie listened intently. He stood in the moon shadow of the unfinished café and became aware that he wasn't alone.

A shadow appeared on the path outside the pool area. It was the silhouette of a tall man walking swiftly from the parking area toward the casino where a single light was showing on the ground floor. Howie stayed low and didn't move until the man had walked around the corner and disappeared. Howie remained still. He had recognized the silhouette. It was the meanest of the mean tribal cops, the one who had punched him in the stomach while he was on his shortcut from hell. The one he had named Buzzcut because his hair was cut into a square, which made the brutality of his face even scarier.

Buzzcut was the last person Howie wanted to encounter.

He forced himself to be patient and stand very still. He had the revolver stuck down into the front of his pants, so he wasn't completely helpless, though he knew he would be quickly outgunned. He wanted to make sure Buzzcut was safely inside the casino before he made his way back to where he had left Georgie and Rain.

Howie made his way slowly from the pool area, crawling on his hands and knees. It was only when he reached the path at the side of the hotel that he rose to his feet and moved quickly.

He reached the end of the building where the path turned toward the backside, and quickly saw that neither Georgie nor Rain were there where he had told them to stay. He stopped and tried not to panic.

Howie turned in a circle, searching first along the path that went along the rear of the hotel, and then toward the hills. He hoped to see some sign of them. He turned to the slice of the parking lot that he could see from his vantage point, then all the way back to where he had begun. Georgie and Rain had disappeared.

The blood pounded in his ears, his heart was racing. He took a deep breath. Something must have convinced them to move. Had they run into Buzzcut . . .

Where were they?

It wasn't until he looked down at the ground that he saw the sign Rain had left for him. It was an Indian sign, he presumed, though he didn't know it. The sign was subtle but unmistakable once you knew what you were seeing: the feather of a small bird with two pebbles near the base. The tip of the feather pointed toward the parking area, around the bend of the corner of the hotel. The feather was very slightly angled to point to the side of the gas station more than a hundred yards away.

Moonlight lit the side of the garage. As Howie looked, he saw a figure, a man waving his arms at him across the distance. It was Rain, standing by the garage wall. Howie waved his arms back to show he'd seen him, and Rain receded into the night shadows behind the gas station. Howie wished he had seen Georgie.

He looked out across the concrete expanse of the parking lot which separated him from the garage. There were future electric light fixtures on stanchions with dangling wires, but they were a long way from ever working. The only light was the crescent moon, but it was enough so that he would be exposed—if only as a silhouette—while making the crossing.

Howie froze. He had been about to attempt the crossing when he saw Buzzcut with two tribal cops. They were walking together from the direction of the casino across the pavement toward the garage.

Had they seen Rain and Georgie? It seemed likely from the deter-mined way they were walking. If Rain and Georgie were behind the garage, they would be caught. Howie couldn't let that happen.

He could think of only one thing to do, create a diversion with him-self as the bait.

He pulled the revolver from his belt, raised it in the air, and fired.

The explosion was shockingly loud in the quiet of the night.

Buzzcut and his henchmen cops stopped abruptly. They paused only briefly to figure out where the shot had come from. Then they came at a run, their guns drawn, to where Howie was hiding.

***

Santo Ruben's face was serious and drawn as he rode in the front passenger seat in a six-person State Police helicopter heading west from Santa Fe. Four heavily armed troopers were in the two rows of seats behind him. No one spoke a word.

The first hint of dawn was behind them in the east, but the western sky ahead was black as pitch. They were in a convoy of four helicopters flying over mountain ridges and canyons that were barely visible in the dawn. The huge blade overhead beat on.

Santo had gotten Jack's voicemail at 9:43 PM as he was waiting in bed for Crystal, who was in the bathroom preparing herself for love making. She was an athlete, a marathon runner and mountain climber, and her body was hard and perfect. She was a sexy woman and Santo was looking forward to sex with her. This would be their first time, and that always had a certain thrill. But while she was in the bathroom, he couldn't help picking up his phone from the bedside table to check if he'd had any important calls. It was an old habit from years of police work. There were always emergencies, always people trying to get you.

Santo was listening to Jack's voicemail just as Crystal emerged from the bathroom in a transparent negligée.

"Damn it, I can't stay, Crystal!" he told her, rising naked from the bed. "There's a very bad situation I have to deal with."

"But, Santo—"

"I'm so sorry, Crystal. People's lives are at stake. I really got to go."

The come-hither look on her face turned to stone. When he couldn't find his left shoe, she threw it at him.

From that moment, everything happened fast. Someone very high up in the government was involved, pushing events forward. Human trafficking had suddenly become a priority. Phone calls were made back and forth from Washington and Santa Fe. A joint operation of the FBI and the New Mexico State Police was put together in a matter of hours.

Santo drove to Santa Fe with his lights flashing, talking on his speaker phone most of the way. At a few minutes past four in the morning, after a sleepless night, the convoy of helicopters rose into the sky from a far corner of the Santa Fe Airport and began their journey to the La Chaya reservation. By air, the flight would take less than an hour.

As the helicopters droned onward, Santo watched the sky lighten to a fragile blue. Planet Earth was so wondrously beautiful from the air, it was hard to comprehend how ugly it was so often on the ground.

***

Elliot Borello found himself deep in thought as he drove through the night. He became increasingly anxious the closer he came to the reservation.

He had come to hate the land itself, the harsh craggy desert. But his main worry was the tribal cops, the small clique who had taken power over the peaceful majority of Indians, most of them simple shepherds who were both good-hearted and easily shorn. They were too busy being content with their lives to fight back. Not until it was too late. Which was why Elliot was happy not to be a good person himself.

In Borello's opinion, the world was divided between smart crooks and stupid crooks. The smart crooks became presidents and billionaires. The dumb ones ended up in jail. As for the La Chaya tribal cops, they were about as dumb as crooks ever were. In the past, they had always feared his authority, a U.S. Marshal Inspector from Washington, D.C. But now . . . he didn't know.

Then there were the Chinese, the San Francisco Tong members who had dreamed up this scheme. He had killed the head of their New Mexico operation, Jimmy Chou. It hadn't been planned, he hadn't wanted it to happen, and now the Tong was going to want revenge. They were going to come after him.

And as if that weren't bad enough, the White Sons of Texas were not going to be pleased if he didn't deliver the explosive device he had promised and for which they had already paid three million dollars . . . an additional two million due on delivery. That's what it was going to cost them to start their war, five million dollars, cheap at the price.

Jimmy had come from California to be the local Tong chief in charge. Jimmy's main business was transporting trafficked labor from China to San Francisco, and when this proved so successful, he expanded into smuggling weapons and explosives on the same ships. Why not? He didn't do nuclear because that would get him caught. But other than that, you could hide anything in a huge container ship, if you had control of a small, secret area far below the waterline.

The weapons, manufactured in China, were to be sold to the militias who were hoping to provoke a second American Civil War, groups like the White Sons of Texas who were willing to pay millions for what they wanted. Ground-to-air missiles, explosives, rocket launchers, everything was available as long as you had the cash. Elliot believed Beijing was behind all of this, allowing the export of military hardware in order to destabilize America. The country was falling apart and there was big money to be made by those in China, Russia, and the Middle East who wanted to help things along. Providentially, ultra-right wing American billionaires with unlimited cash were also, for their own reasons, planning chaos.

As Elliot liked to say, he was only the middleman, but his cut would be substantial . . . as long as the damn Indians let him have the device!

The problem was multidimensional due to the number of players involved. Chinese technicians had brought the explosives to New Mexico and put the bomb together. The Indians hadn't done a thing except allow the Tong to use their land, but they were expecting a million dollars for this service.

Jimmy had been the one who was supposed to give the Indians their final payment, pick up the bomb, and give it to Borello in Santa Fe, who in return would give it to the White Sons of Texas and receive their final payment of two million dollars.

That would be Borello's cut. He would keep the two million and theoretically the deal was complete. Except Jimmy had become greedy and crazy and drunk which had changed everything. Now that Jimmy was dead, Elliot didn't have the cash to pay the tribal cops. It was Jimmy who was supposed to pay that money, but Jimmy got angry and everything fell apart.

Borello pondered his options as he made the long drive through the emptiness of New Mexico. Around four in the morning, he stopped at a small-town all-night convenience store to fill up with gas. He had a hot dog and a 32-ounce coke, hoping it would calm his stomach. It didn't.

"I can do this!" Elliot said to himself. "There's not anyone who can stop me!"

Borello was no softie. So he didn't know why he felt such a sense of dread that everything was going wrong.

Chapter Thirty

When he fired the revolver, Howie had no idea what he was going to do next.

At that point, all he could think about was creating a distraction so Georgie and Rain could make their escape. But now he heard people coming his way from the parking lot, three pairs of footsteps, and he knew he was in danger. The thought of Buzzcut made his blood shiver.

He couldn't see the men yet; they were still around the corner. Howie found himself instinctively stepping backward along the path to the door that led inside. He didn't want to go back there, but he couldn't think of anywhere else to hide.

His right hand brushed against a cinder block wall that was about six feet high, an unfinished retaining wall to keep the hill behind the hotel from encroaching forward. Howie had worked on a wall like this once, earning money after high school to go to college, and he knew what had to be on the other side: a ditch, a gully of some kind so that the ground was level and builders could put down plumb lines and such.

Without thinking any more about it, Howie grabbed the top of the wall with both hands, and then in one move used his feet and knees and arms to pull himself up and over. He tumbled hard onto his back in a rough gulley on the other side. He couldn't help a short cry of pain.

Uuuumphh!

There was a rock sticking into his left shoulder but he didn't want to move. The three men were less than twenty feet away and they were coming closer on the path. With luck, and if he didn't make a sound, the retaining wall might hide him. As he lay in the gully trying to breathe quietly, he worried about Georgie, hoping Rain had managed to get her somewhere safe. He knew Rain would do his best. The kid had some brain cells missing, but he was strong and had heroic aspirations. Chivalry might not be a bad thing at the moment. In fact, Rain was probably a better choice to be Georgie's bodyguard just now than he was. Meanwhile, help was coming, Howie had set that part in motion. Now they only had to hide and stay safe for an hour or two until it arrived.

He heard voices as the three men stopped on the path to consult.

"We've got to get these assholes, do you understand?" one of the men said. His voice was low in the throat, more a growl than speech. It was a voice Howie recognized. Buzzcut.

"We're on it, Chief. There's nowhere they can go from here."

"I'm calling for help," said a second man.

"I got enough to worry about now!" said Buzzcut. "You guys don't fuck up on me, you hear?"

There was more rough talk. Every other phrase was *fuck you* and *fuck you* back. It was what Howie would call a low conversation. From his hiding spot, he could hear every word. He had to concentrate on breathing slowly, softly.

Two of the men continued along the path to the door that opened to the inside. The door opened with a screech and he heard their footsteps disappearing into the innards of the hotel as they searched for the source of the gun shot.

Buzzcut stayed behind. Howie could hear him pacing up and down on the path, just inches from where he was hiding.

Howie heard a Zippo lighter flip open and he smelled tobacco. It smelled good. For the first time in years, he thought how good it would be to smoke a cigarette. He deliberately nipped that thought in the bud, as well as any thoughts of the feather and the two rocks on the ground, the sign Rain had left for him. *Don't look down!* he willed. He tried to think nothing, though that was the hardest thought of all.

As Howie listened, he heard a car pulling up into the parking lot. A door slammed.

"Fuck!" Buzzcut said aloud. "Borello's here!"

***

Elliot Borello drove into the casino parking lot at nearly five that morning. He wasn't well. His stomach churned and he felt nauseous after the long drive. The time was long gone when he could stay up all night without ill effects.

He slammed the car door and began walking toward the casino. Raven Fontana, the man Howie called Buzzcut, had set up his headquarters in one of the finished areas on the ground floor. In fact, Raven and his tribal police department did very little on the reservation. The real security here was handled by the Chinese, but they were based up at the hemp camp and factory several miles away. Borello would be happy never to see this piss-poor patch of Indian land ever again. If everything went well, this would be his last visit here.

He was nearly at the casino entrance when he noticed the police chief coming his way from around the corner of the hotel. Borello changed course to meet him halfway across the parking lot.

"Where the fuck is Jimmy?" Raven demanded. "He was supposed to be here last night!"

"Chou couldn't make it," Borello replied mildly. "So he sent me instead to pick up the goods."

"What do you mean, he sent you instead? That's not how this was supposed to work!"

"Things change, Raven. Sometimes you need to go with the flow. Anyway, what does it matter? I'll make the delivery and the job will be done. We'll all get paid and live happily ever after."

"Yeah? I don't think so. Those three people you sent me, the two Indians and the girl, they got away."

"You're joking, I hope! You let them escape? How the hell did that happen?"

"It was a fuck up, that's all. Somehow they got the jump on Pete and Stu as they were getting out of the van. But it's okay. They didn't get far. They're hiding out in the hotel and I have two of my guys right now flushing them out. We'll have them any second now."

"For chrissake, what do you mean, you have two guys looking for them? You should have your whole crew searching that damn hotel! Don't you get it? Moon Deer knows too much. If he gets away, we've had it. How stupid can you be?"

"Hey, Borello, shut your face! Nobody talks to me like that! Nobody! Anyway, I don't have no more guys. Donnie's inside on dispatch. Pete and Stu were here all night, but they're hurt so I sent 'em home. Dwayne won't be here until ten, and Shawn and Chris are in the hotel. That's all I got right now. I guess I could call the chinks up at the camp, but I don't want to do that 'cause I got the situation under control. I mean, where the hell are they going to go? I got 'em, man. Moon Deer and those two others—they're rabbits in a trap."

"Sure," Borello said wearily. He was three steps ahead thinking how he was going to use the passport he had under the name of Frank Scully to disappear into Argentina where he had a stash of money.

"Okay, Raven, whatever—just make sure they don't get away," he told the cop. "Now, give me the key to the truck and I'll be on my way. I've got to get my ass to Santa Fe before our clients get nervous."

Raven smiled. "Sure, Borello. I don't care one way or the other. Gimme the money and I'll give you the key."

Borello smiled back. "Chou has your money; you don't have to worry about it. Tell you what I'll do. I'll bring your cash when I come back to pick up my car tomorrow."

Raven's pretend smile vanished. His eyes were deadly. "Fuck, you will! That's not the deal and you know it. Jimmy was supposed to be here with the cash, the second payment. He gives me the money, I give him the van. That's the deal!"

"I know that's the deal. But like I said, Jimmy got tied up. You can call him if you like, but I don't think you'll get him until tomorrow. He had to fly to San Francisco for some reason."

"You think I'm stupid, don't you? The van's ready to go. But you're not going anywhere with it until I get what's owed me!"

"Raven, unless I get that van to Santa Fe, none of us are going to get anything that's owed us. Now, look—there's nothing to worry about. Jimmy is going to be doing business with us for a long time to come, so you need to relax. He's not going to double cross us."

"What's that?" Raven asked, suddenly looking up at the sky. The eastern horizon had turned gray with the coming dawn. "I thought I heard something."

"There's nothing there. Now give me the key."

"No, I heard it."

As Raven stood with his back to Borello peering up at the sky, four helicopters came into view flying over the top of a mesa toward the casino.

"Jesus, fuck!" cried Raven.

Borello was shocked as well. But he had the advantage of having a clear idea of what the appearance of four choppers might mean.

As Raven was looking up at the sky, Elliot Borello slipped his Glock from his shoulder holster and shot the tribal police chief in the back of the head.

Feeling weary, hating the necessity of these things, he knelt on the pavement and took the keys from the dead man's pocket.

***

Howie listened to the helicopters arriving from his hiding spot behind the retaining wall. He heard a gun shot, then the sound of two men running out from the inside of the hotel along the path toward the parking lot. He presumed these were the cops who had been searching for him. A moment later there was more gunfire, four shots in quick succession.

Howie didn't know what was happening, but it sounded like all hell was breaking loose. He took a deep breath, worked himself into a standing position, and hoisted himself back over the top of the wall onto the path. Somehow while he was climbing over the wall, the revolver came loose from where he had stuck it into the front of his pants. He heard it land with a clunk back in the ditch where he had been hiding. There was no time to find it.

He hurried to the corner of the hotel and peered out onto the parking lot. There were two bodies sprawled on the pavement, tribal cops. Meanwhile, helicopters were landing and the noise was overwhelming. It sounded like a military assault. Help had arrived but the situation was dangerous.

Howie turned his eyes to the garage on the far side of the pavement but he couldn't see any sign of Georgie or Rain. He hoped they were long gone, hiding in the desert. As far as he could see, there wasn't anyone alive in the parking area, only the two bodies on the ground. He decided this was the best chance he was going to get to make a dash to the garage. He didn't bother to duck. He ran with all his might the hundred yards across no-man's land to where he had last seen Rain.

Happily, no one took a shot at him. The tribal cops probably had their hands full with the helicopters.

Howie tried to catch his breath and consider his next move. His concern, of course, was Georgie. He made his way around the rear of the garage to see if there was any sign of her. The garage backed onto the empty desert where there was a faint path leading up into the hills. The ground was loose and dusty, so it was hard to be sure, but it seemed to him that there were several shoe prints where two people had been running. He hoped this was where Rain and Georgie had gone.

Howie was so amped up he could barely breathe. He wasn't sure whether to follow them or go for help. Once again, he decided to put his faith in Rain, that he had gotten her to safety. He retraced his steps to the south side of the garage to see if he could make contact with the helicopters. The casino was blocked from his line of sight, hidden by the hotel, but he heard sporadic gunfire coming from that direction. He could see two helicopters resting on the pavement close to the road, their rotor blades slowly turning. They were too far away for him to call for help.

Howie moved cautiously toward the front of the garage, staying close to the side of the building, hoping to get a better view of what was happening. From this new position, he could see a third helicopter parked further up the road, quite a long distance from where he was standing, but he still couldn't see where the gunfire was coming from.

The garage was the usual sort of repair shop attached to a gas station where tires could be fixed and oil changed, but not much more. Through the closed glass doors, Howie saw there were three work bays inside. Two of the bays had pneumatic lifts that could raise vehicles so they could be worked on from underneath, but the third bay was simply an open space at the side of the building where a flatbed tow truck was parked. A Volkswagen van rested on the rear of the flatbed attached with cables. It appeared to be the camper he had seen alongside the mysterious metal building near the tent city where the trafficked workers slept. The body of the van was a faded green. He had only seen it from a distance, so he couldn't be sure, but how many faded green VW vans could there be on this reservation? An emblem on the door of the flatbed truck said High Desert Towing.

Everything about this unfinished hotel/casino complex in the middle of nowhere was odd, but this old hippie van resting piggyback on a tow truck struck Howie as the strangest of all. Had some eco-tourist broken down on La Chaya land? Howie didn't think so.

Before he got any further, he heard footsteps, someone coming his way from the direction of the unfinished convenience store. He stepped back around the side of the building where he wouldn't be seen.

Howie was slowly backing away along the side of the garage, when his hand felt a metal door. He tried the knob and to his surprise the door opened. The footsteps were coming closer and he knew he had to hide himself without delay. He stepped into the garage and closed the door behind him. The interior of the garage was lit with daylight coming through the glass door, but dark in the oily shadows of the far end.

Somebody was fiddling with the lock of one of the glass doors at the front of the garage. Howie tried not to panic.

The door began to open upward into the ceiling. The whirr of the electric motor made enough noise to cover his movements as he hoisted himself up onto the flatbed, opened the side door of the van, and slipped inside onto the floor. It was the only place he could think to hide. The rear of the van had a miniature sink, a fridge, and two-burner stove with a bench along the length of one side that would turn into a bed. Howie hid himself as well as he could under the bench.

The boots came closer, stepping across the concrete floor. Cowboy boots, Howie decided, from the hard click of their soles. Boots such as

U.S. Inspector Elliot Borello wore. The van rocked slightly as the man climbed up into the driver's seat of the tow truck and started the engine.

"No!" thought Howie.

This was a possibility he hadn't considered. The truck with the van on the back grumbled out of the garage, changing gears as it accelerated onto the highway.

Trapped in the back, an unwilling passenger, Howie had no idea where they were going.

Chapter Thirty-One

Santo saw the tow truck from the helicopter. With the VW van on the back, it made a curious sight from the air as it snaked its way through the arroyo canyons. He resisted the temptation to tell the pilot to give the vehicle a closer look. Everything was about to break and there was no time for a detour.

There were three other helicopters in the air nearby. Four State Police choppers would attack the casino complex, while simultaneously five FBI helicopters would assault the camp a few miles north where the trafficked victims were kept. That was the plan.

Santo's chopper landed on the highway several hundred yards from the unfinished casino. He could see at least seven heavily armed cops in body armor running toward the casino.

There were a few bursts of gun fire, but the resistance was sporadic. The attack from the air must have seemed overwhelming and the tribal cops were quick to surrender. The prisoners were searched and cuffed with plastic ties that were cleverly designed for mass arrests of this sort. Santo kept hoping to see Howie and his daughter, but so far there was no sight of them.

After a quick search of the casino, he returned outside and headed toward the gas station. The garage door was open and Santo walked inside to investigate. He stopped in the third bay where there was only empty concrete and crouched down to examine an oil stain that looked recent.

The walkie talkie on Santo's belt gave an electronic burp.

"Lieutenant, we found two people in the sagebrush a couple of hundred yards off the highway. A young man and young woman. She says she's Howie's daughter. They'd like to speak to you."

"Bring them here," said Santo.

This was good news. Rain and Georgie appeared a few minutes later and they were both unharmed.

The girl was clearly exhausted. She looked up at Santo with troubled eyes.

"Where's Howie?" she asked. "Where is he?"

Santo could only shake his head because he didn't know.

***

"They haven't found him!" Jack said to Emma, his telephone still in his lap. They were sitting in their shaded garden patio in San Geronimo finishing breakfast. Santo had taken a few minutes to make a quick call to let him know how matters stood. It was shortly after 8 o'clock.

"Damn that kid!" Jack added. "Why does he always end up causing me worry?"

"This isn't Howie's fault! Maybe he shouldn't have taken the trafficking case. But it was a very good cause. He gave that Cordell-Smith woman a few days of his time, that was all, then he made it clear he was off the case—"

"Emma! There's no off-the-case when it comes to human trafficking. You stick your nose in, you're there for the duration. Like it or not."

"Then why didn't you tell Howie that from the start?"

"I was sick, remember?" Jack knew this was unfair. At the time, he hadn't been paying attention. He hadn't realized what they'd be in for.

"Being sick didn't stop you from flying off to San Francisco!" Emma fired back. She had never let Jack bamboozle her.

"All right, but I had to. You can't not do anything in a case like this."

Being a librarian, Emma considered the double negative. "You can't not do anything?"

"Not in a case like this. Come on, Emma, we're talking about the dark side of hell! Human trafficking! When you come across something really evil like that, you have to do what you can."

Emma sat over the remains of her meatless version of a breakfast burrito and studied her husband of many years. She didn't quite believe in the quasi-religious word *evil*. Emma was more prone to look at the human narrative and societal factors. She and Jack had argued this subject in the past, but she wasn't going to argue now.

"So, they're finally raiding that reservation?" she asked.

"It's a joint operation, the State Police and the FBI. They raided the tent city and took all the trafficked workers into protective custody. There were more than two hundred of them. Jesus! To think a thing like this was happening in New Mexico! They found a warehouse where they believe weapons and explosives were stored. It was empty."

"That's good," said Emma.

"No, it isn't," said Jack. "Not if those weapons and explosives are on the move somewhere."

"But where's Howie?"

"I don't know, Emma. They found Howie's daughter, I'm glad to say. She was hiding in the desert with a young Navajo man. But they didn't find Howie. They've been looking everywhere."

"If he's . . ." Emma didn't dare finish her question.

"If he's dead, they'll find him," Jack said brutally. "Damn! Damn! Damn! They haven't found a bomb either! The whole thing's a disaster!"

Emma stood from the patio table and began clearing dishes. Neither of them had eaten more than a few bites of breakfast.

"Anyway, Jack, Denise is picking me up at 9:30 so I have to hurry. You're going to be on your own today. We're driving down to Santa Fe."

"Fine, fine," Jack said distractedly. His mind was on a bomb course he once took in San Francisco. "Santa Fe, huh?"

"I'm going to the Women's March with Denise and a few of the girls," she told him. Denise was Emma's assistant at the library. "I didn't go to the march last year. I was feeling burned out, frankly. I couldn't take any more. But this year, I feel I really need to attend. This is bigger than women's rights. This is about standing up for democracy."

There was a certain soapbox tone in Emma's voice as she spoke to imaginary masses. Jack didn't want to appear to be the sort of guy who didn't believe in democracy, so he remained silent.

Suddenly he sat up straight in his chair. "The Women's March? Today in Santa Fe?"

"I probably won't be home until eight or nine. If you're hungry, you'll need to—"

"Wait a second!" Jack interrupted. "How many people are they expecting at this protest?"

"It's a *march*, Jack. Protests are *against* something. Marches are *for* something."

Emma was revved up. Jack was glad that Emma was concerned with the state of the planet. He liked being married to someone who was a better person than he was. Personally, Jack had given up on the planet a long time ago.

"Okay, a march," Jack agreed. "How many people are expected at this shindig?"

"Tens of thousands, Jack. Maybe more. There are going to be two congresswomen from the progressive caucus. Along with Senator Laurie Lopez, who's part of the Squad."

What squad? Jack wanted to ask. But Emma, caught up in her cause, rode over him.

"There are going to be marches all over the country today," she told him. "Women are fighting back. Millions and millions of women are standing together and saying no!"

"God help us!" Jack muttered.

"You know about the Lysistrata Movement, don't you? That's what's sweeping the Women's Movement right now."

"The, uh—"

"The Lysistrata Movement. It's from the Greek play by Aristophanes where all the women of the city go on strike and refuse to have sex until the men ended the Peloponnesian War."

"My God, and these women today—"

"They've sworn off sex until men adopt the net zero greenhouse gas emission policy that Senator Lopez has proposed. She's from California, you know. The Bay Area."

"I can imagine," said Jack.

Jack had to admit, when it came to sex and gender roles, he was grateful to be an old man, no longer on the playing field. He had enjoyed San Francisco when he and Emma were young, which all seemed long ago yet strangely present. But he was glad he wasn't young today. And he didn't really like the idea of Emma going off on her own into a crowd like that.

"There are going to be thousands of men there as well," Emma was saying. "Men who support women."

"Good for them," he said. "I support women. I support you . . . wait, a second! My God!"

"What, Jack?"

A shiver ran up Jack's spine as a terrible suspicion came over him. How he didn't see this earlier, he didn't know.

He stood abruptly from the table. "Emma, I'm coming with you!"

Emma studied him. Jack had never volunteered for this sort of thing before.

"You might have to wear a Pink Pussy Hat," she warned him.

"Emma, we're not waiting for Denise, we'll go in your car. We need to hurry!"

Chapter Thirty-Two

The wind buffeted the faded green VW camper riding on the flatbed of the tow truck. The van rocked back and forth as though it were being pummeled by ocean waves. Howie was starting to feel a little seasick. They were going at least 70 mph on Interstate 40 heading east toward Albuquerque.

Inspector Borello was in the cab driving. Howie had gotten a good look at him before they were on the freeway, when he stopped by the side of the road to pee. It was a very quick pee. Before Howie could decide whether to risk escaping miles from anywhere, Borello was back in the cab gunning the engine. Whatever he was up to, he was in a hurry.

And that was what worried Howie.

With a fire fight in progress and law enforcement helicopters making an assault on the casino, why would Borello take the trouble to drive off with a broken down 1960s van? What was so important about this old camper? There was obviously something very wrong here

Howie had most of the pieces of the puzzle. He knew that growing hemp was only a cover for what was really going on at the La Chaya reservation. Human trafficking was awful, but there was something even worse in progress. From the beginning, Howie had wondered what was happening in the big metal building by the tent encampment. According to Rain, his father, Sun Walker, had been investigating this question when he was murdered. Whatever Borello and his cronies were doing, it was worth killing for.

Chinese gangsters, trafficked labor, corrupt tribal cops, and now a vintage hippie van on the back of a flatbed tow truck. Howie didn't believe peace, love, and flowers had anything to do with this scenario. Clearly, the van was carrying something valuable.

Drugs? That was possible, he supposed. But he didn't think so.

Uranium was another possibility. Uranium mining had been a contentious issue on the nearby Navajo reservation. Historically, the White Man had given indigenous tribes only the most barren land that they had no use for. In the 19th century, whenever valuable resources were discovered on Indian land—gold, silver, copper—the White Man simply broke the treaties he had made and forcibly removed the tribes to land that was even more useless.

Today, the theft continued but it was more subtle. There were laws in place that protected Native American reservations, but this didn't stop predators who thought of Indians as easy prey, too poor and stupid to put up a fight, and if there was enough money involved, there were always some Indians—not all, by any means—who were eager to be corrupted.

As the tow truck drove east on the freeway, Howie had time to search the inside of the van from one end to the other hoping to discover what made it so valuable. He looked everywhere. He took the bed apart, he pulled up the carpet, he went through the refrigerator, he made a thorough examination of the stove, the cabinets, the area beneath the small sink. He climbed over the seats into the front and searched the glove compartment and under the dashboard. He looked under the seats, he pulled up the floor mats by the gas pedal and brakes. He looked and looked and found nothing suspicious. As far as he could see, the van was nothing more than what it seemed: a well-restored relic that would probably fetch a good price.

Of course, traveling at 70 mph on a freeway, Howie could only examine the interior. There was a good chance that what he was looking for was concealed in the engine area at the rear or underneath the chassis. There were hundreds of hiding places he couldn't get to while they were in motion.

The hours passed as Howie pondered and searched and worried about Georgie. The morning turned into a warm summer day. Just before Albuquerque, Borello took the exit that led north on I-25 toward Santa Fe. Howie sat behind the wheel in the front seat of the van and did his best to fight off the exhaustion that threatened to overwhelm him. He had gone without sleep for over twenty-four hours and the stress and adrenalin of danger was taking a toll on his body. As they approached Santa Fe, he knew he had to stay alert. At some point, when Borello slowed down, he would need get out of the van and jump off the side of the truck. It would be important to find the right moment.

Borello continued past the first two Santa Fe exits without stopping and Howie worried they might be heading up into Colorado, perhaps even Wyoming. He was relieved when Borello moved into the right lane and took the St. Francis exit that led into downtown Santa Fe. At some point soon, they would hit traffic lights where Howie would be able to hop down and make his escape

As they turned into the sun, a beam of morning light caught Howie directly in his eyes. Exhausted from lack of sleep, the light was unbearable. Without thinking, he pulled down the sun visor and saw that there was something taped to the inside. The sun visor was probably the only place inside the van that he had neglected to search.

He wasn't certain at first what he was seeing. It was flat and rectangular, almost like a candy bar.

Howie carefully pulled off the two strips of silver tape that held the object to the back of the sun visor.

It wasn't a candy bar. It was a phone.

A cell phone!

Howie was so tired, he nearly dropped the phone as he freed it from the tape. He held it in astonishment, uncertain why anyone should hide a cell phone at the back of a sun visor.

It was an iPhone. He pressed the power button and watched the screen come to life. The phone hadn't been turned off; it was only sleeping.

The screen lit up with the timer on the Clock app. It was an app Howie often used to listen to music while he was falling asleep, setting the timer to turn off after twenty minutes. But he didn't want the Clock app now, he wanted the phone.

He slid his left index finger upward from the bottom to bring up the home screen. But the timer didn't disappear as it was supposed it. The digits were set at 0 hours, 5 minutes, 0 seconds and as soon as he touched the screen, it began moving, counting down relentlessly to 04:59, then 04:58, 04:57, second by second as it continued its journey to zero.

Howie kept trying to swipe the screen so that he could go to the phone app, but the timer refused to be turned off. He had never seen a phone act like this. He tried to power the phone off, but that didn't work either. The seconds kept ticking down.

At 03:43, Howie finally got it. He should have gotten it sooner, but his brain was mush.

He was sitting in a ticking time bomb.

***

The Women's March in Santa Fe was set to begin at noon, but people had been gathering in Railyard Park since early morning.

The marchers carried signs supporting a variety of causes, including abortion rights, climate change, racial justice, and more. These were people, some innocent, others dogmatic, who wanted a fairer, more peaceful, greener world. Many wore colorful costumes and pink hats with cat ears. The causes were serious but the mood of the crowd was more like a big outdoor party.

The planned route would take them from Railyard Park down Cerrillos Road to Guadalupe Street, through the Santa Fe Plaza, then back on Don Gaspar Avenue to the New Mexico State Capitol. The SFPD would later calculate the crowd as ten thousand people, though the organizers declared this a vast underestimate. Many in their group believed there must have been at least fifty thousand marchers in Santa Fe that Sunday: men, women, children, dogs, even the occasional horse and lama.

Jack, Emma, and Katya joined the march near West Alameda Street. Emma carried a sign that said, PROTECT YOUR RIGHT TO READ! NO BANNING BOOKS!

This was Emma's current outrage—her fight against the far-right's attempt to ban over 850 books from libraries. She could often be seen these days carrying her copy of *Fahrenheit 451*.

Jack walked with one hand on Emma's arm, the other on Katya's harness. He refused to carry a sign, saying he needed both hands free, but he wore a knitted pink cap with ears. He was too old, he said, to care what he looked like.

"Is there anything unusual happening?" he asked Emma, sniffing the air and listening intently.

"Unusual? Well, now that you mention it, Jack, there are about a hundred thousand people marching to the Capitol. That doesn't happen every day."

Emma was exaggerating the numbers. But that's what the crowd felt like to her.

"Do you see cops?"

"Only at intersections stopping cars. But otherwise, they're keeping a low profile."

"Water canon?"

"Not that either. Jack, this is Santa Fe!"

Without warning, there came a tremendous explosion. The shock wave nearly knocked Jack off his feet. Emma gave a cry of surprise. Katya barked. There was excitement all around them, angry voices and cries of dismay.

"A bomb!" Emma cried.

"Where?" said Jack

"I can't tell. But there's a big plume of smoke coming up from a few blocks away. South of the Plaza, I guess. The area that's half-residential."

"Emma, let's go," Jack commanded, taking her arm. "Take us to where you see the smoke."

"*Toward* where the bomb went off? Are you nuts?"

"Let's go . . . quickly! There's no time to lose!"

Jack's tone was so compelling that Emma did as he said. Several helicopters had appeared overhead and the noise was temporarily so deafening it would have been useless to argue.

All the human traffic, thousands of marchers, were moving in the opposite direction to where Jack wanted to go. Some of the people in the crowd were close to panic. They wanted to get away. The wave of people moving against them made it slow going. If it hadn't been for Katya, they might not have gotten anywhere at all. Katya could be very intimidating when she wanted to be. She barked, she snarled, she made a path through the people.

They managed to get two blocks into the residential district before they arrived at a new obstacle: two black State Police cruisers that had the road closed off.

"Santo!" Emma cried. "Jack, Santo's here! He must have just come in one of the helicopters.

"I called him," Jack said. "I told him to get here."

"You *knew* there was going to be a bomb today?"

"I did. I suspected."

"And you didn't say anything? Jack!"

"I told you, I called Santo as soon as I figured it out."

"But you didn't warn the marchers! Jack, you let all these people be in danger!"

"Emma!" He could only shake his head. "I did everything I could. But no one listens to me anymore, that's the problem. At least I got Santo's attention."

Emma was about to say something when Santo spotted them and stepped over.

"Jack, you're the last person I would have expected at a women's march!"

"I *like* women," Jack said crisply. "Now, what the hell is going on?"

"It was a bomb. It was a large device and we haven't begun to assess the damage."

"But where's Howie?"

"I don't know, Jack. I wish I did. We didn't find him at the casino. I left a whole team of people looking for him. But we have his daughter, thank God. She's here. I arrested the kid she's with, a Navajo boy. But I have her waiting in a squad car a block from here."

"What did the kid do?"

"Jack, he's broken all sorts of laws. I couldn't just let him go."

"Okay, Santo. Take us to where the explosion happened. I want to sniff around."

"Sorry, I can't, not until it's safe. We don't know yet if there's a second or third device. But if you want, we can get maybe a block or two closer."

"Emma, why don't you stay here?"

"I'm coming with you," she said with determination, taking his arm so he couldn't get away.

A grey cloud of smoke hung over the neighborhood. There was a burnt smell in the air. Santo led the way past the police barricade down the residential street. As they were walking, a young woman came running up behind them. Somehow she had gotten past the police barricade. There was a uniformed cop running close behind her.

"Lieutenant, I couldn't stop her!" the cop shouted.

"It's all right," said Santo. "Let her come. It's Georgie, Howie's daughter.

"Where's Howie?" she cried. "Is he here?"

"I am!" whispered a raspy voice from deep in the smoke.

"We don't know where he is," Santo told her solemnly.

"Georgie," said Emma, taking the girl's hand. "I'm Emma and Howie is my special friend. We need to wait just a while longer!"

"But I'm here!" the raspy voice said again.

Howie emerged from the smoke coughing profusely. His face was blackened. His shirt was torn up one side. He looked like he was a figure made of ash. But he was alive.

Emma stepped forward to give him a hug, but Georgie got to him first.

"Oh, Howie!" she cried. "You're alive!"

Chapter Thirty-Three

Howie finally got his visit with his daughter, two weeks without either murder, mayhem, or a 19-year-old Navajo kid who belonged on the cover of a romance novel.

He took Georgie camping for three nights in Monument Valley, with gourmet meals each night cooked on a two-burner Coleman stove. He took her to a production of *Tosca* at the Santa Fe Opera. He took her on a culinary tour of the best burrito carts of San Geronimo.

In the evenings they often sat outside around a fire pit he had built in the clearing near his vegetable garden, watching the sparks fly into the New Mexico night. They talked about life, music, the state of the planet, whether they believed in God, and Brexit (an important topic in Scotland).

When it came to music, Georgie was currently in a 1960s phase. She claimed that rock and roll that came after the 60s was "commercial" and "corrupt." Georgie was voluble on these points, but it was a great deal more difficult to get her to talk about herself. Howie adored his daughter. He was constantly amazed by her. But he wasn't sure he knew her. Her broad Scottish accent was a constant reminder of the culture and the lost years that separated them.

To his surprise, she didn't want to sleep in the studio he had built especially for her visit. Georgie wanted to sleep in the tepee his hippie neighbors had set up on the wooden platform overlooking the creek. She wanted to live like an Indian.

During the two weeks that remained of her visit, Rain stayed in FBI custody at a holding facility in Albuquerque. The Feds were undecided whether to charge him in the deaths of the two guards at the tent camp, or let it go as self-defense. Georgie spoke with Rain twice by telephone and she encouraged Howie to speak on his half. Howie was glad to do this, as long as the Bureau continued to hold the kid for exactly two more weeks. Selfishly, he wanted his daughter to himself.

"Rain saved me," Georgie told him. "When that cop appeared, the really nasty one—"

"Buzzcut."

"Is that his name?"

"That was my name for him," Howie told her, changing tenses from present to past. He was glad Georgie didn't ask for details.

"Anyway, after you left to use the telephone, Rain saw that man coming our way. He thought fast and got us over the retaining wall where there was a kind of ditch on the other side where we were able to hide. Wasn't it genius of him to think of that?"

"Genius," Howie agreed.

"When we heard the footsteps go, we ran across the parking lot to the garage. We waited there a bit, but then Rain found a path into the desert and said we would be safer there. I hope you didn't think we'd abandoned you."

"Not at all, Georgie. All I could think about was wanting you to be safe."

"And what about that other copper? The one who picked us up on your land?"

"Inspector Borello." Howie shook his head. "He didn't make it, I'm afraid."

"He was bent, was he?"

"Bent as a rusty nail," he agreed.

Borello had died in the explosion. There had been so little left of him, that he could only be identified by his DNA. Remarkably, there had only been three deaths and twelve people injured, none of them critically. Four houses had been destroyed in the blast, but luckily none of the inhabitants had been home. The bomb would have done considerably more damage if it had exploded near the State Capital, its intended target. As for Buzzy, it was looking as though he was about to make a big career change and join the CIA's elite cyber team at a starting salary of $150,000 per year. That was one of the good things that had happened. As long as Buzzy didn't blow it.

The other good thing, of course, was Georgie.

Howie often brought up Cambridge where she would be starting school in September. He extolled the serene joys of academia, and how wonderful it was that she was going to such a fine university.

"But you left academia," she reminded him. "You became a private eye. You wanted something more adventurous."

"Yes, but I'm a well-educated private eye," he answered. "That makes all the difference."

"Does it help you catch crooks?"

"Maybe not," he admitted. "But at least I catch crooks with all sorts of clever thoughts running through my head."

She laughed at this. Georgie had a sense of humor. She found her father eccentric and funny. Harmless, too, most likely.

"Look, Georgie, education shouldn't be *for* anything. Whatever you end up doing, whether you're a plumber or a movie star, knowledge is what makes your life deep and rich and meaningful."

Howie was eager to promote Cambridge because he had a nagging feeling that the Native American life was calling to her in the form of Rain Walker. He was afraid the adventures she'd had in the Wild West would make university life seem boring by comparison. Howie knew this syndrome well, since it had happened to him.

Georgie asked many questions about the Rosebud reservation in South Dakota where he had grown up and Howie decided to take her there to see for herself. They would need to fly since the distances were too great to drive in so short a time. Three days before the end of her visit, they boarded a small commuter plane and flew from Santa Fe to Sioux City where he rented a car and drove south to Rosebud.

Georgie was subdued but observant during her visit to Rosebud. The poverty obviously disturbed her. Rosebud wasn't the romantic Indian life she had imagined. There were more trailers than tepees. Howie often caught her squinting at the people and the land with a look of intense concentration as though she were trying to make sense of it.

Howie's mother had died two years ago, but his father was alive, living in the residential part of the government funded Indian Health Center. He had dementia and it broke Howie's heart to see him this way. In Howie's youth, his father had been a slim, hopeful, energetic man.

"This is my daughter, Dad!" Howie said too loudly, as though volume would help his father understand. "Your granddaughter!" he added brightly.

Georgie looked at the wrinkled Indian face of her grandfather with wonderment, but once again, Howie couldn't make out what she was thinking. It seemed to him that there was kindness in her gaze, but she didn't comment. His father returned Georgie's look of amazement with wonderment of his own, as though he had never seen such a beautiful young Lakota girl. But he didn't say anything either.

Howie took her to the three-room schoolhouse where he had gone as a child and told her about the two do-gooder women from New England who came to teach on the reservation and who had set him on the path to Dartmouth.

Howie had meant to introduce Georgie to his cousin, Lawrence, but the postmaster at the reservation post office told him that Lawrence had died six months ago from an overdose of fentanyl.

The high point of the visit was a few hours at the home of Tom Field Lark, his childhood best friend. Tom had been in an Indian rock band for a decade and had been badly into drugs. But now he was clean, married, and working as a contractor building tract houses in Sioux City. There was a new Ford pickup in the driveway, and he was obviously doing well.

Tom invited them to stay the night but Howie had made reservations at a motel outside of the reservation. He was glad for Georgie to see the Lakota side of her complicated heritage, but he wasn't sure how much more authentic Indian life she could take in a single visit.

All in all, Howie believed his daughter to be the most wonderful person who had ever walked on the planet. He loved her inordinately, and he began to think of how he would go about telling her this. He knew he needed to find the right moment.

He didn't want to be soppy.

He didn't want to embarrass her.

Make it short, he told himself. *Better understatement than overkill.*

He decided to save this important talk for the last moment when they were in the airport before she left.

On the morning of her overnight flight to Glasgow, they flew from Sioux City to Denver where they arrived at the airport with four hours to kill.

They had a long lunch at T.G.I. Fridays.

Don't get soppy too early! Howie told himself.

Instead, he spoke about the practicalities of getting her a U.S. passport. He would gather all the documents to prove that he was her biological father. It would be a lengthy process, but he thought it would be an advantage for her to have dual nationality.

"It'll give you freedom to go back and forth from Scotland to America whenever you like," he told her optimistically.

At last, they walked down the concourse through the International Terminal toward the security area. Georgie had her pack on her back,

Howie pulled her suitcase on wheels. Now that the moment was near, he wasn't at all sure what he was going to say.

Maybe I should just give her a hug!

No, she needed to know his love was unconditional. She needed to know she had a father who loved her.

"Georgie, I want you to know how much this visit has meant to me," he began.

But the words were barely out of his mouth when they heard the sound of somebody running.

"Georgie! Wait! Don't go!"

Howie turned and his mouth fell open. It was Rain. He was running their way down the concourse, dodging travelers with suitcases.

"Georgie!" he cried again. "The Feds let me go!"

He continued speaking in short bursts because he was out of breath. "They decided not to charge me. I took the bus from Albuquerque. I had to get here before you left. Remember, you told me the time and date of your flight!"

"Rain—"

"No, let me finish. I love you, Georgie and I want you to stay with me. Don't go back to Scotland. We'll move into a hogan on Diné land where I was born. We'll live the Old Ways. We'll be together!"

"Rain, I can't," she told him gently. "I only have a tourist visa."

Howie was glad to hear his daughter give such a practical response. Meanwhile, neither Rain nor Georgie were paying the slightest attention to him.

"Don't worry about your visa," Rain told her. "We can lose ourselves on the rez. They don't keep track of us, we're only Indians, we don't matter. We'll get married! You'll be an Indigenous Person!"

As proposals of marriage went, Indigenous Person didn't appear to meet Georgie's standards of romance.

"Rain, I'm going to university this fall, to Cambridge then medical school. Perhaps when I've finished school I'll come back and see if you've waited for me."

"Georgie, stay! We'll herd sheep together! It'll be a wonderful life!"

"Baaa!" Howie said softly. Fortunately, neither of them heard him.

"I can't," Georgie told him. To Howie's relief, she gave Rain a peck on the cheek and said the fatal phrase of her generation: "We'll text."

She turned to Howie and gave him a longer hug.

"I love you, Dad!" she whispered in his ear.

And then she was gone.

Howie watched Georgie enter a line and disappear. He was stunned. She had called him Dad. She had said she loved him. But had he told her he loved her in return? He hadn't! Would she leave thinking her father didn't care?

When she was gone, Howie turned to Rain. The kid was in worse shock than Howie. Probably he had never been turned down before. He couldn't understand why Georgie should choose Cambridge University rather than life with him in a hogan in the desert herding sheep.

Rain looked at Howie in despair. "I thought she loved me!"

"Women are a mystery," Howie told him. "They keep us on our toes."

Rain sighed and shook his head a few times more. "I guess so," he said vaguely. Then he swept back the hair from his eyes with a swipe of his hand, his signature move, and gave Howie the hint of a smile.

"Look, Moon Deer, I don't have wheels. You think you can give me a lift back to New Mexico?"

About the Author

Robert Westbrook is the author of two critically-acclaimed mystery series, including *Ancient Enemy,* nominated for a Shamus Award as the Best P.I. Novel of 2002, and *Intimate Lies,* a memoir detailing the relationship between his mother, Hollywood columnist Sheilah Graham and the author F. Scott Fitzgerald, published by HarperCollins in 1995. His first novel, *The Magic Garden of Stanley Sweetheart,* was made into an MGM movie. Robert lives with his wife, Gail, in northern New Mexico. Visit his website: www.robertwestbrook.com

Coming Soon!

EAGLE FALLS
A Howard Moon Deer Mystery
Book 9
by
ROBERT WESTBROOK

Howie has been hired by Ryan Marlowe, an ex-governor of New Mexico, to discover why his 17-year-old granddaughter, Zia, committed suicide. Governor Marlowe, long retired from politics, is a friend and Howie is glad to be of help in what appears to be a straight-forward investigation. But when there is a second suicide, it's starting to look like murder, and Howie must discover what it was Zia knew that got her killed.

EAGLE FALLS is a tale of ambition and ego that takes Jack, Howie, and his daughter Georgie—now twenty-one—into the high-tech world of New Mexico's private space industry run by billionaires who, having won the treasures of the Earth, are now vying with one other to get to the stars.

For more information
visit: www.SpeakingVolumes.us

Coming Soon!

MONTEZUMA'S FIRE
A Sheriff Lansing Mystery
Book 11
by
MICAH S. HACKLER

The establishment of a Native American Reform Church in San Phillipe County draws immediate controversy. A former Wildlands Firefighter searches to find a new purpose for his life. State and national elections campaigns are underway.

Sheriff Cliff Lansing finds his hands full with a series of bizarre murders on is hands.

For more information
visit: www.SpeakingVolumes.us

On Sale Now!

ROBERT WESTBROOK'S
Howard Moon Deer Mysteries
Books 1 – 7

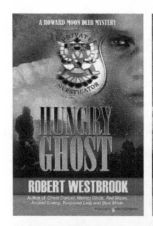

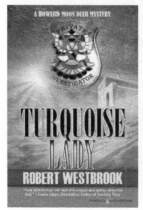
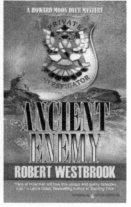

On Sale Now!

MICAH S. HACKLER'S
Sheriff Lansing Mysteries
Books 1 – 10

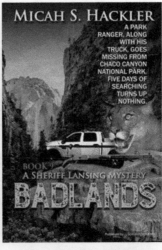

For more information
visit: www.SpeakingVolumes.us

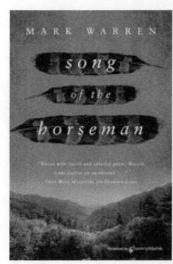 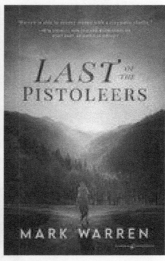

Coming Soon!

CHILD OF EARTH AND SKY—
WOMAN OF WIND AND FIRE

SHE WAS CALLED GRAY EYES

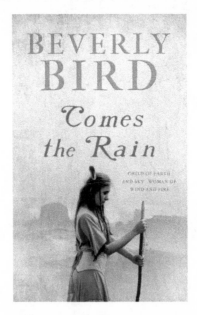

**For more information
visit:** www.SpeakingVolumes.us

CPSIA information can be obtained
at www.ICGtesting.com
Printed in the USA
LVHW041918020123
736291LV00001B/49